A Conve
by

"Am I making

Shallie closed her eyes, all of her certainty dissolving into a misty panic.

"For making love to me?" Mac asked.

"For thinking…for wanting…" She hesitated.

"For wanting something more for yourself?" he finished for her.

When she nodded, he cupped her jaw, gently turned her head so she had to look at him.

"Where's the harm, Shallie? We're both unattached, healthy adults who care deeply about each other. I trust you. You trust me. What could possibly be wrong with making each other feel good?"

"Nothing," she whispered. "Nothing at all."

"So we won't be sorry in the morning?"

"I've been sorry for a lot of things in my life. I can't imagine that spending a night with you would be one of them…"

A Splendid Obsession
by Cathleen Galitz

ᓂᕐᑲᕐᕋ

"I can't believe how good you are to me," she whispered into his ear.

Smelling like heaven, Kayanne leaned in even closer to make sure Dave heard that ridiculous assertion. With the evidence of his arousal pressed hot against her, he dared not allow her to pull away for fear that everyone else in the room would be aware of his lack of self-control as well. Holding her against him, he swore softly in response to her assessment of his character. The way Kayanne was looking at him as though he were some kind of knight in shining armour made him feel a sham.

How could he possibly tell her that his armour was tarnished by the fact that he'd agreed to escort her tonight for the sake of getting into her head? When she laid her head trustingly against his shoulder Dave resolved to keep her safe from all men – himself included.

Available in August 2008
from Mills & Boon® Desire™

In Bed with the Devil
by Susan Mallery
&
High-Society Mistress
by Katherine Garbera

A Convenient Proposition
by Cindy Gerard
&
A Splendid Obsession
by Cathleen Galitz

Playboy's Ruthless Payback
by Laura Wright
&
Like Lightning
by Charlene Sands

A Convenient Proposition
CINDY GERARD

A Splendid Obsession
CATHLEEN GALITZ

MILLS & BOON®
Pure reading pleasure™

*First published in Great Britain 2008
by Harlequin Mills & Boon Limited,
Eton House, 18-24 Paradise Road, Richmond, Surrey TW9 1SR*

The publisher acknowledges the copyright holders of the
individual works as follows:

A Convenient Proposition © Cindy Gerard 2006
A Splendid Obsession © Cathleen Galitz 2006

ISBN: 978 0 263 85910 2

51-0808

*Printed and bound in Spain
by Litografia Rosés S.A., Barcelona*

A CONVENIENT PROPOSITION

by
Cindy Gerard

CINDY GERARD

Since her first release in 1991 hit a bestseller list, Cindy Gerard has also won numerous industry awards to her credit – among them the Romance Writers of America's RITA® Award.

As one book reviewer put it, "Cindy Gerard provides everything romance readers want in a love story – passion, gut-wrenching emotion, intriguing characters and a captivating plot. This storyteller extraordinaire delivers all of this and more!"

Cindy and her husband, Tom, live in the Midwest on a mini-farm with horses, cats and two very spoiled dogs. When she's not writing, she enjoys reading, travelling and spending time at their cabin in northern Minnesota, unwinding with family and friends. Cindy loves to hear from her readers and invites you to visit her website at www.cindygerard.com.

This book is dedicated to readers everywhere.
As a writer, I am so grateful for your passion and
enthusiasm and support of what I do.

One

A winter sky hung heavy over the Shadow range, spitting dime-size snowflakes like a white blanket shedding lint. As the rattletrap of a pickup slowly approached Sundown, Montana, Shallie Malone stared through the passenger side windshield, wishing she could shake the notion that maybe this snowstorm was an omen. Maybe coming back to Sundown was a huge mistake.

Imagine that. Her making another mistake. So what else was new?

She expelled a weary sigh as the old truck bounced along the snow-packed road. She'd made a lot of mistakes in her twenty-seven years. She hadn't wanted her return to Sundown to be one of them, though. She'd wanted it to be—well, she'd wanted it to feel like home again, not like another misstep on the very rocky road of life.

Face it, she thought, as a jagged line of mountain peaks disappeared behind a heavy clot of clouds; mistake or not, it wasn't like she'd really had many other choices.

She focused on the forest beyond the windshield as the wipers shoved wet flakes off the glass. The pine boughs bent like old shoulders under the weight of winter. She, too, felt very old today. And weighted down. Mr. Coleman, the elderly rancher who she vaguely remembered had been kind enough to give her a lift from the bus station in Bozeman. He had the heater going full blast. Even so, Shallie shivered beneath her lightweight jacket. And tried to ignore the queasy feeling in the pit of her stomach—the feeling that suggested the old adage might be true: You can't go home again.

A name on a mailbox at the end of what she knew was a long curving lane leading deep into the forest and halfway up the mountain caught her eye as they drove by.

She cranked her head around to catch another glimpse of black lettering partly covered with snow. "Did that say Brett McDonald?"

"Hum? Oh, yeah." Concentrating on keeping the truck from slipping off the slick road, Bob Coleman squinted through his bifocals after a cursory glance at his rearview mirror. "The boy bought the old Fremont place about the same time he bought the Dusk to Dawn."

Whoa. Mac? Her childhood buddy, Brett "Mac" McDonald, now owned the Fremont cabin? And she couldn't believe what else Bob Coleman had just said. "The Haskins sold the Dusk to Dawn?"

"Beats all, don't it?" Bob grimaced beneath the brim of a worn gray Stetson. "Never thought I'd see the day when Nadine and Chet would hang it up, but I guess they got a hankering to do some traveling and Mac had the cash to make it happen."

The Dusk to Dawn was Sundown, Montana's, local watering hole for the community and the ranchers surrounding town. It was bar, restaurant, coffee shop and minimart all wrapped up in one well-used, well-loved establishment. If someone got married, the reception was held at the Dusk to Dawn. If someone died, it was where the family had the wake. Birthday parties, graduations and regular Saturday-night party-hardy crowds had gathered under the green tin roof for as long as Sundown had been Sundown. And for as long as Shallie had known Sundown, the Haskins had run the Dusk to Dawn.

Finding out that they were no longer there—a major change to something so stable—made her a little sad. She'd been a long time coming home. She hadn't wanted to see changes. She'd wanted everything to be the same as when she'd left. There was security in the status quo, and that's what she needed most right now.

Foolish, yeah. But it had been comforting to think that in a world in constant evolution, Sundown with its slow pace and plain, honest folk would always remain pretty much what it had been.

"Seems Mac made quite a business for himself in Bozeman," Bob added, oblivious to Shallie's melancholy thoughts. "Got himself a fancy I-*tal*-ian restaurant folks flock to from all over. I've even taken the missus there a time or two when we could get a reservation. Word is he decided he'd just as well branch out a bit and bring some business back home."

Mac was a hometown boy. Thinking of him running, as Bob Coleman put it, a fancy Italian restaurant made Shallie grin.

Wild. Lord, had that boy been wild. Not mean wild. Devilish, fun-loving wild. Whatever mischief he and John Tyler couldn't think of to stir up when they were kids wasn't worth talking about. More often than not, she'd been in on making some of that trouble with them.

Shallie sobered. *Trouble.* Imagine that. Didn't take long to come back around to the point that she was in trouble again.

She placed a hand protectively over her flat tummy and the budding new life sleeping there. Assured herself that coming back was a good thing. The right thing. And when the truck rounded the ridge and the tiny hamlet of Sundown came into view, the little shiver of unease shifted to anticipation and told her, yes. Yes, this *was* right.

How many times had she driven this road and seen Sundown from this vantage point, nestled in the valley like a multicolored and well-worn skirt at the base of the Shadow range? That skirt was now blanketed in white. Chimney smoke spiraled up in wispy drifts, like steam rising from a bubbling kettle. How many times had she taken this simple beauty for granted?

Way too many.

Well, she wouldn't make that particular mistake again.

She was almost home. At least she was as close to home as she'd ever been. She might be coming back with her head held low in shame, but she wouldn't let her decision to return turn into another mistake. More to the point, she wasn't going to make the same mistakes her own mother had made.

Okay, she amended, absently touching her tummy again. She wasn't going to make *all* of the same mistakes. Joyce Malone had let down everyone who'd ever counted on her—including, Shallie figured, herself.

They'd no sooner rounded a switchback on a steep downhill grade when a sleek black pickup came roaring up the road and snapped her out of her thoughts. The club cab fishtailed on the slick skiff of new snow glazing the road's surface and headed straight toward them.

"Tarnation," Bob muttered.

He jerked the steering wheel hard right to avoid getting clipped by the big truck. "Hang on," he said, his jaw tight, his hands white on the wheel as he slammed on the brakes.

When Shallie saw the size of the tree directly ahead of them, she braced a hand against the dash and clamped her jaw together to keep from screaming.

Not that it worked. The sound that came out of her mouth was just this side of ear splitting. And the pain that knifed through her wrist when the truck crashed to a stop in a drift made her physically ill.

Swearing under his breath, Brett McDonald brought his truck to a skidding stop on the shoulder of the road. Damn. He hadn't seen that patch of ice. But he had seen Bob Coleman's pickup—and just in the nick of time. He'd risked rolling his truck to miss it. Thank God he *had* missed it—just barely.

Jamming the gearshift into park, he set the emergency brake and shoved open the door. Heart hammering like a piston, he jumped to the ground. Engine exhaust rose in white clouds as he sprinted toward Bob's truck, scared to death the old man had gotten hurt when he'd swerved to miss him.

The good news: the old Ford had stopped in a snowbank just short of a head-on with a huge white pine. Not a scratch on it. The bad news: the truck was sitting sideways on the narrow road; the front bumper buried deep into the drift the plow had left along the shoulder.

"You okay, Bob?" Mac yelled through the rancher's closed window.

"Yeah, I believe I'm of a piece." Bob turned his head toward the passenger seat. "What about you, Shallie? You okay over there?"

Shallie? Mac had only ever known one Shallie—but this couldn't be *his* Shallie.

He ducked his head so he could see across the cab. My God. His heart hit him a couple of good ones as old memories and old feelings tussled with the shock of seeing her.

Shallie. His Shallie Malone. He hadn't seen her since high school, when she'd lit out of Sundown like her tail was on fire. But he'd recognize those big brown eyes and that tangle of short brown curls anywhere.

And he'd recognize the mad scramble of his heartbeat and the catch in his breath as the reaction he'd always had around this woman. Okay. She'd been a girl last time he'd seen her. That hadn't made his feelings for her any less real. She didn't know it—he'd been too proud to ever spill his guts about how he felt about her—but Shallie Malone had been the one. The one that got away.

He scrambled around to the passenger side, waded through the knee-deep snow and jerked the door open with a grin on his face. Shallie was back—and unless she was married, engaged or otherwise taken, she wasn't getting away this time.

"Shallie! Darlin'. If you aren't a sight for sore eyes."

She'd been one fine-looking girl. She was beyond fine as a woman. His grin faded, though, when he searched her face and saw the unmistakable strain of pain in her eyes.

"Oh, damn." His heart sank as concern tangled with self-disgust. "You're hurt."

She shot him a valiant smile. "Leave it to you, McDonald. I travel almost two thousand miles without a scratch, then I'm one mile from home and you manage to break my wrist."

TWO

"Okay, worrywart, you can wipe that death-door look off your face," Shallie assured Mac as she walked out of the emergency room three hours later. "I'm fine. It's hardly more than a sprain."

Mac's breath of relief when he finally saw her was tinged with the antiseptic scent of hospital. He rose from the hard, waiting-room chair and hurried toward her. Her brown eyes looked up at him from a face that was pale and weary. Dark smudges of fatigue painted violet bruises beneath her eyes.

Her left arm was supported by a sling. Inside the sling he could see what looked like a cast. *Sonofabitch.* He'd done this to her. "If it's just a sprain, why did they put it in a cast?"

She shrugged, as if the cast was of little importance.

"Okay," she finally conceded when he gave her a hard look. "So maybe it's a hairline fracture."

"Then it's *broken,*" he pointed out with a sinking sensation in his gut as she tried, again, to minimize the damage. *Damn.* He'd broken her wrist.

Though pain pinched tight lines around the corners of her mouth, she still worked up a smile for him. "Well, if you're going to do something, just as well do it right."

"Damn, darlin'." He slung an arm over her shoulders when what he wanted to do was fold her into his arms and absorb all of her pain. Instead, feeling protective and responsible, and like a first-class ass, he pressed a kiss to the top of her head. "I am *so* sorry."

"Stop." She gave him a squeeze with her good arm, then pushed away from him. "I'm fine. Quit beating yourself up."

He needed more than a beating. He needed to be drawn and quartered for putting her in this fix. Once he'd bundled her into his truck, then made certain Bob Coleman and his pickup were okay and back on the road, he'd headed straight for Bozeman and the hospital.

She'd sputtered and tried to minimize the damage all the way. "I just *came* from Bozeman. And I don't need to see a doctor. I was joking about it being broken, for Pete's sake. It's just banged up a little."

It was just banged up a *lot.* Mac had suspected as much from the way she so very carefully cradled it against her ribs. He'd have given anything not to be right.

"They give you anything for the pain?" He snagged her jacket from the chair where he'd been holding on to it for her.

"I'll do fine with some Tylenol."

"You need something a helluva lot stronger than that," he insisted, helping her slip her good arm into the right sleeve. Carefully settling the jacket over her shoulders, he fought the urge to leave his hands there and pull her back against him. "What's the matter with that doctor?"

"I said no to a prescription, okay?" She glanced at him over her shoulder, then looked away, like there was more she had been about to tell him but changed her mind at the last second.

She'd said no to a lot of things since he'd found her in Bob's truck, Mac suddenly realized. Like medical care for starters. Mac had finally figured out why when they'd checked in at the E.R. desk. She didn't have health insurance.

The lightbulb finally went on. Which was probably why she'd refused the pain medication, Einstein. Maybe she can't afford it.

"Look, short-stack," Mac turned away to snag his own jacket, reverting to his old nickname for her because of her love for pancakes, "I already told you, I'm picking up the tab for this. It's my fault. That makes it my bill. Besides, my vehicle insurance will cover it, so it's nothing out of my pocket. Now…let's reconsider that prescription, okay?"

But she was already heading out the door.

On an exasperated breath, Mac stomped after her.

"Same ol' hardhead," he muttered. That was one of the things he'd loved about her. She was stubborn and strong and a survivor, in spite of what she'd had to endure growing up. She'd been a damn stubborn girl. Stood to reason that she'd grown into a damn stubborn woman. A damn beautiful woman. A woman who had set the bar for all others, none of whom had measured up.

"Okay," he conceded, catching up with her as he cleared the revolving door. "We do it your way—for now. But if I hear so much as a whimper of pain or see that you're suffering, we're going to have us a little talk."

"Let's talk anyway," she suggested as they walked side by side toward his truck. "How the heck are you, McDonald?"

Mac cupped the elbow of her right arm—telling himself it was to steady her and not because he couldn't resist touching her—as they picked their way carefully across the snow-covered parking lot.

"Hungry, that's how I am," he said hoping she wouldn't notice how aware he was of her.

The snow had started falling like it was going to get serious again by the time they reached his truck. With his hand still on her elbow, he punched the keyless remote and opened the passenger door. "How about we talk over a nice hot meal?"

That was one way to keep her with him a little longer.

"Works for me," she said as he helped her step up onto the running board then ease into the seat. "As long as it's not Italian."

His face must have fallen because she laughed and, making a gun with the thumb and forefinger of her right hand, fired at him. "Gotcha."

He grinned as he buckled her in then walked around and slid behind the wheel. "Har, har. It would be nice to think that news of my restaurant has spread far and wide." Just like it would be nice to think that maybe she'd kept track of him during the past several years and that's why she knew about his restaurant. But that amounted to ego and wishful thinking drawing the conclusions.

"If it makes you feel good, then you go right ahead and think it."

What would make him feel good was if she was pressed up against him on this cold winter night, but that was just crazy. So he grinned his good-ol'-boy grin instead of suggesting she slide on over close. "What I'm thinking is that Bob Coleman, as usual, must have done a lot of talking."

"No one would argue with you on that one," she said with a smile that looked like it zapped all of her energy.

She was dead beat, Mac realized as he cranked up the heat and headed out of the lot. And still beautiful and still turning him on like a strobe light.

Shallie. He still couldn't believe it. What stroke of luck had prompted her to return to Sundown after— what? Nine? Ten years?

He'd find out soon enough. In the meantime he didn't really care what had brought her back into his life. Or why she'd left and he'd never heard from her again. He was just damn glad she was here. He'd never stopped thinking about her—which was just plain dumb since he'd probably only crossed her mind in passing now and again in the past several years.

But still, despite the fact that he was responsible for breaking her wrist, he was happy as hell that he'd *almost* run into her today.

* * *

"I have to stop." Shallie reluctantly pushed away her plate of tortellini carbonara. She was too full to eat another bite. "I don't want to, but I have to. Good Lord, Mac, this food is amazing."

"That would be *good* amazing, right?"

Mac's lively blue eyes danced in his familiar, handsome face that still bore shades of a summer tan. She'd forgotten how blue his eyes were. Montana-sky blue. Still smiling. Still teasing. Still the eyes of a friend.

It was so good to see him. Not that Shallie was willing to simply come out and say so. That wasn't the way things had ever worked between them. She'd known. Even as a girl she'd known that, with a little encouragement, Mac would have taken their relationship past friendship into something more.

And it had been tempting. But tempting as it had been—as tempting as it might be now—she hadn't needed a boyfriend back then. She'd needed a friend. Just like she needed one now. Bottom line, she could not afford to screw things up between them. She'd never forgive herself if she did.

Besides, it would have been easy to fall in love with Mac. Looking at him now, it would still be easy. Too easy. She didn't trust easy. *Easy* wasn't a word that had ever been a part of her life experience. Especially where men were concerned. And when it had started to look easier to let her teenage emotions take over and fall that little bit of distance in love with Brett McDonald, she'd left Sundown. Running scared away from her emotions. It would have ended badly, and bad was something she couldn't bear when it came to Mac. That's why she hadn't kept in touch. She'd had to make the break clean. Final.

"Yeah. That would be good amazing," she said in response to his fishing expedition, then fell back into the safe pattern of gentle ribbing they'd established as kids. "Some things never change, I see. You're still trolling for compliments."

"What can I say? I've got a big ego. It needs lots of stroking."

That was so not true. He *should* have an ego; it was amazing that he didn't. Mac had always been the cutest, the most athletic, the smartest, the most macho, most sought after guy in school. Not by her, of course, because she *had* been very careful to always treat him like a brother. But he'd never taken himself—or his looks—seriously.

Speaking of serious, aside from the circumstances that had prompted her return to Sundown, and aside from her broken wrist, it had finally started to feel like she *had* done the right thing in coming home again. And sitting here with Mac smiling at her across the table in a quiet corner in his restaurant, Spaghetti Western, was reason enough to have come back.

Mac was her friend. She was mature enough now to keep him in that niche. One of the best she'd ever had. He'd been one of the few constants, the few comforts in a childhood where she'd lived a far cry from Mr. Rogers's neighborhood. In this moment he felt as comfortable as a warm blanket on this cold, end-of-December night. And comfortable was the extent of the feelings she could afford to let herself have for him.

"Damn it's good to see you," Mac said, shaking his head as if he couldn't believe she was really here. "So what brings you back to Montana, doll face?"

Logical question. The double trip of her heart was not, however, a logical response. Good friend or not, she wasn't quite ready to come clean with that little tidbit of information. Equal measures of guilt and shame kept her from telling him about the baby. At least for now.

"Just had a yearning to see the mountains again in the winter," she said evasively.

She glanced away when his eyes said they didn't quite buy her explanation. He'd always known her a little too well. But he didn't press, and for that she was grateful.

"And to see *you,* of course," she added, realizing how true it was. She really had missed him. Missed her friend, and she felt real bad, suddenly, that she'd allowed them to lose contact over the years.

"I'm sorry I haven't been much for staying in touch."

He lifted a shoulder in a throwaway shrug but she sensed, more than saw, the hurt behind his reaction. "Goes both ways. I'm just as guilty. It's a guy thing," he added with a grin.

"So catch me up," she prompted, smiling across a table draped in a charming red-and-white-checkered cloth. A white tapered candle burned between them, the flame flickering, making shadows dance across a masculine face that had matured with amazing grace. "How are your folks? Are they still in Sundown?"

"Dad is." He hesitated then added, "Mom's in L.A. They divorced several years ago."

If he had said they'd moved to the moon, she couldn't

have been more shocked. Tom and Carol McDonald had seemed like the perfect couple. Loving, caring, fun. They'd been the perfect family. Perfect parents. The ones she'd always wished she'd had. "Oh, Mac. I'm sorry."

"Yeah." His jaw hardened. "Me, too."

She wanted to ask what had happened. But she saw an uncharacteristic bleakness in Mac's eyes and understood that he didn't want to talk about it. That it was very painful for him.

"So what's happened to the old gang in the last nine years?" she asked brightly, determined not to put a damper on the evening. "Where's J.T.? And Peg and the rest of the crew?"

She listened with interest as he ran down the list. Many of the kids they used to pal around with, it seemed, had left the little pond for bigger ones.

"Peg's still in Sundown, though," Mac said as he toyed absently with the stem of his wineglass.

Candlelight glinted off his dark hair, cast his hard jaw in shadow. Handsome, she thought as she watched his mobile mouth. Devastatingly handsome.

"Married with two kids. Settled in raising bucking stock with Cutter Reno and Lee and Ellie Savage."

Shallie blinked, shocked out of an unexpected fantasy of the press of his beautiful mouth to hers. *What was wrong with her?* "Reno? Peg married that outlaw? He was chasing silver belt buckles and women on the PRCA rodeo circuit last I knew."

"Yeah, well, he's about as far from an outlaw as Preacher Davis now. I'm told a good woman can do that for a bad man. Same goes for J.T."

"J.T.? John Tyler is married?" They had been the three musketeers—Shallie and J.T. and Mac.

Times do change. And don't think about his mouth. Or the thickness of his biceps beneath his shirt. Or the breadth of his hands, the length of his fingers…

"Yep. Just this fall," Mac continued, his smile returning while she forced herself to take a sip of water. "He did a stint in the military after college. Ended up in Afghanistan. Messed him up a little—not that anyone but me knew it. Anyway, he took a liking to the new vet, and the feeling was mutual."

She chanced a look at his face, then surprised them both by laughing when she realized what she saw in his expression. "And the idea that J.T. tied the knot makes you nervous as heck, doesn't it?"

J.T. and Mac had sworn they'd never get married. There may have even been a blood oath involved. Of course, they'd been eleven years old at the time. The three of them had been big on blood oaths back then.

"Me? Nah."

"Liar, liar," she teased in a sing-song voice.

He ignored her taunting. "J.T. can't help it if he went soft in the head. I'm made of sterner stuff. You won't catch me settled in with a ring in my nose—I mean, on my finger."

She shook her head. "You're awful."

His eyes twinkled. "Just calling it like I see it."

"Hmm. Or did word about that sour disposition of yours finally get out and any woman with half a brain knows enough to stay away from you?"

"Hey—" He affected a wounded look. "Some of my

favorite dates only have half a brain, so don't go bad-mouthing my taste."

Shallie rolled her eyes and hoped her curiosity about the women he dated didn't show.

"What about you, Shallie Mae? Where've you been? Whatcha been doing?"

Yeah, well, she'd known they'd get around to this sooner or later. She laid her napkin on the table by her plate. "Not much of a story there."

"Somehow I find that hard to believe."

"Believe it," she assured him, feeling more than self-conscious about her lackluster career. "School and work pretty much tell the tale. It took me eight years to get my degree."

That was because she'd had to work to pay her way through college, and sometimes she'd have to drop classes altogether to stay on top of the frills like food and rent and electricity.

"But now I are a teacher," she said, adapting a goofy grin to go with her goofy grammar. Both made him smile.

He leaned back in his chair, considered her, then nodded. "A teacher. That's cool, Shall. Really cool."

"Yeah," she said reacting to his warm smile with one of her own, remembering why he had always been so special to her. He was proud of her. He always had been. Even when she hadn't been able to muster up a shred of self-pride. "It is cool. Kindergarten."

"So, you're on winter break?"

She *would* have been on winter break if she hadn't been asked to let go of her contract when the school board in the small town in southeast Georgia had found out about her pregnancy. Unwed kindergarten teachers, it seemed, did not make the popularity list in small town, rural South. She knew she could have fought it and won. The truth was, she hadn't had any fight left in her. And she'd wanted to get away from the mess she'd made.

"Yeah," she said, instead of leveling with him. "I'm on break."

Silence settled and with it another layer of guilt. Shallie had the feeling Mac saw right through her lie. If he did, he didn't quiz her on it, thankfully. He wouldn't be so proud of her now if he knew the whole truth.

"You sure you don't want some wine?" he asked instead. "I've got a nice red in the cooler."

She shook her head. "None for me. You go ahead, though."

He gave her another one of those considering looks, but let it drop. "That's okay. I've had enough. Besides, you have to be beat. And don't lie, I know your wrist has to hurt like hell."

She *was* tired. And her wrist *did* hurt. "It *has* been a long day," she admitted without acknowledging the pain. "I thought I'd be holed up in the Sundown Hotel tonight, but it's a little too late to head back now. So, kind sir, if you'll point me to a decent motel here in Bozeman, I'm ready to call it a day."

He snorted. "Yeah, like that's going to happen. You're not staying in any motel," he informed her as if that was the most ridiculous idea he'd ever heard. "You're staying at my place here in Bozeman."

She shook her head. "Mac—"

"No," he insisted, cutting her off. "I've got an extra bedroom, extra bath. Cripes, Shallie, it's the least I can do after banging up your wrist. And before you wind up for a fight, save what energy you've got left. This is not open for debate. You're staying with me. End of story."

She knew from experience that she was dealing with one stubborn Irishman. She should fight it a little harder, but the thought of not having to hassle with checking into a cold, generic motel room was just too appealing.

"And what will the woman in your life think about another woman staying over?" She hadn't planned on asking about his women. She hadn't planned on being this curious, either. And until he answered, she hadn't realized how relieved she would be with his response.

"There's no woman. So there's no problem."

Now there was a tidbit of information that she could happily dwell on if she let herself. She didn't let herself.

"Okay. Fine. I'll stay. Add *bully* to *insufferable*," she groused through a smile that acknowledged she knew she'd met up with a brick wall and was actually grateful.

"Don't forget *incredible cook*."

"And then some." Shallie stood when Mac did. "I'm not going to be able to eat for a week."

"So I shouldn't have the kitchen box up some tiramisu for a late night snack?"

"Tiramisu?" Oh my God. Tiramisu. Sweet. Chocolate. Heaven help her.

But she couldn't. Then her stomach growled.

He chuckled. "Thought that might perk you up. Still

got the same ol' sweet tooth, huh? Be right back." With a nod toward the front door, he pointed her to a waiting area and headed for the kitchen.

Shallie strolled over to the welcoming bench and sat, aware that she was smiling. Interesting. Despite her throbbing wrist, despite the fact that she had no idea what she was going to do for money now that she'd been given doctor's orders not to work for several weeks, she was smiling.

She shook her head at her own lack of concern about the direness of her circumstances. Then she cut herself a little slack. There'd be time enough to worry about money tomorrow. Tonight she was in the company of a special man, a good friend; she was warm, and her tummy was full.

And then there was the prospect of the tiramisu.

Just the tiramisu, she reminded herself when the delicious sight of Mac strolling toward her set a few hormones zinging in a very dangerous direction.

"Whoa," Shallie said as Mac rounded the last turn on a street on the outskirts of Bozeman and she got a look at his house. "The restaurant business must be *very* good."

Mac grinned as he punched the remote on his garage door opener, pulled into his drive and eased his new truck inside the triple-car garage. Yeah. The restaurant business was damn good. He'd just moved into the house he'd had built to his own specifications last month.

"Who knew that a love of spaghetti, a beer major and

a business minor could translate into the American dream."

He killed the motor, jumped down out of the truck and pocketed his keys, thinking it was a damn good thing he finally had a chance to put a little distance between them. Riding in the dark truck with soft music playing on his CD changer and nothing but dim dash lights and streetlights illuminating the night had made it a little too intimate. He'd clamped both hands on the wheel, finding himself resisting the urge to reach out and cover her hand with his a little too often.

What would she think if he had, he wondered. What would she think if he'd just covered her slim thigh with his hand, squeezed gently and said, "I've missed you, Shall. I've missed you, and this time I'm not letting you go."

She'd have slapped him up alongside the head, that's what she'd have done, he thought as he walked around to the other side of the truck. And he'd have deserved it.

She was tired. She was hurting. And if he knew his Shallie, there was something else working behind those intelligent eyes of hers. Something big. Something that bothered. Something—other than him—that had brought her back to Sundown.

All in good time, McDonald, he thought as he opened her passenger door. She'd tell him what was bothering her all in good time.

"It's stuck," she said, trying to work the seat belt latch one-handed under the stark, bright light in his three-car garage.

"Here. I'll get you out of there." He reached across her

lap and gave the buckle a try. And met with resistance. Not to mention the solid heat of woman beneath her thin jacket.

This could be trouble.

And it was.

"Damn. It *is* stuck. Hold on."

He climbed up on the running board and leaned across her so he could get a better angle—and ended up pressed against more of her with more of him. And the front seat of his big club-cab truck suddenly shrank to roughly the size of a soup bowl.

"Ah…" He fumbled with the latch and made it worse. "Oh. Here's the problem. It's your jacket. It's caught in the latch."

And he was caught up in lust. She was so soft and full against his arm. Her skin so pale and flawless.

Because she's exhausted, jackass. For God's sake, get a grip.

"Just get me a blanket and a pillow," she said dropping her head back against the leather seat and closing her eyes. "I'll be fine right here for the night."

She looked so tired right then that Mac figured she was halfway serious. And he had to do something to jar himself out of his sexual haze.

"Okay. Have a little faith, will ya? I'm not the sharpest tack in the drawer but I'm smarter than this seat belt and I don't care how many people say otherwise."

That pried a weary smile out of her. She'd always had such a pretty smile. Sure hadn't changed. Pretty smile. Pretty eyes—cinnamon brown shot through with gold. And she smelled good, too.

His head was merely inches from hers. Their bodies

bumped as he worked to free the seat belt latch. Strike that. Her breast, *specifically,* brushed against his arm, *specifically,* while he worked away at the jammed buckle.

She felt soft and full against him. But this was Shallie, he reminded himself. The woman who had never wanted to be anything more than his friend.

A memory flashed. He'd been thirteen and in the process of discovering what all the fuss was about over the opposite sex. He'd tried to kiss her one night and cop a feel, randy little brat that he'd been then. Not that she'd let him get by with it. His tongue had been sore for a week where she'd bitten it. His thumb had been swollen for much longer after she'd bent it back to his wrist and beyond.

But he'd never gotten over the thrill of that first, tentative contact. That wild, gut-knotting kick he'd experienced when he'd touched her breast through her sweater.

"Don't you ever pull that crap with me again, McDonald," she'd warned and, trying not to whimper in pain, he'd promised that her mouth had seen the last of his tongue.

And that should have ended any "awareness" of Shallie Malone as a sex object.

It should have, but it hadn't. And he'd never felt the same thrill in a kiss since.

"Any luck?"

He'd been so wrapped up in getting a handle on his physical awareness that her question startled him. So did a sudden realization. If he moved his head, turned toward her just so, their mouths would be in perfect alignment. He'd be able to experience firsthand the scent and taste of the chocolate mint she'd tucked in her mouth after dinner. And to find out up close and personal if those lush, full lips were as soft as they looked. If they still tasted the same. Like wild sex and young love and the sweetest heat this side of the equator.

The urge to find out—the strength of it—blindsided him.

"Nope," he said, jerking his attention back to the latch and putting all he had in resisting that urge. "Not yet. But if I don't have you out by morning, we may be looking at a lifelong commitment."

He hoped his little joke came out *sounding* like a joke instead of the desperate bid to break the unsettling sexual tension that had suddenly shrunk the inside of the truck yet again—this time to the size of a soup *spoon*. Man. Between running SW and working on the Dusk to Dawn, he'd pretty much been out of circulation. All work and no play and all that, made Mac a horny boy.

If only. The truth was, it was her. Just her that put him in this state.

"Got it," he said when the buckle finally gave. He backed out of the truck, feeling way too much regret that the warmth of her breast no longer heated his arm and way too little relief that his sojourn into lust was suddenly over.

But it *was* over. Over. Done. Never happened.

This was Shallie. Short-stack. The woman who only wanted to be his buddy. She'd kick his sorry butt clear across Montana if she knew what he'd been thinking. At least she would tonight. It was too soon. And it was too much for now. With a little time, though. A little time and a little patient persuasion, maybe, just maybe all these years of waiting will have been worth it.

And as he helped her down out of the cab, though, and retrieved the box of tiramisu and her one piece of luggage, all of a sudden it didn't seem like such a bright idea to have her sleeping across the hall from his bedroom. What if he couldn't control himself?

"Now you're just being stupid," he muttered under his breath as he unlocked the door to the house and let them into the kitchen.

He held the door open for her and stepped back so she could go inside ahead of him. "Being stupid about what?"

Once he flicked on a light, he didn't have to figure out a plausible answer. She got sidetracked when she saw his kitchen.

"You have *got* to be kidding."

Her eyes were wide with surprise and admiration as she took in his state-of-the-art kitchen with its gleaming stainless steel restaurant-grade appliances, black granite countertop and large, multipaned skylight that was currently laden with snow.

Mac tossed his keys on the counter and shrugged out of his jacket. "It's not much, but it's home," he said then added on a proud grin that he just couldn't dampen, "and damn spectacular, huh?"

"In a *word*." She continued to inspect and admire as he helped her carefully out of her jacket. "Little Brett McDonald. My. My. You've come a long way."

"Got lucky," he said, shrugging off the compliment. "Come on. I'll give you the fifty-cent tour, but let me warn you right now, I just moved in a few weeks ago. I don't even know where all the light switches are yet. I think there might even be a room or two that I haven't found."

Turning on lights as he went, he led her down three marble-tiled steps to the great room. A flip of another switch and the fire flickered to life in the native stone fireplace dominating the south wall from the floor to the ceiling that was two stories high.

Beside the fireplace stood a holdover from the season. A very dry and ready-to-pitch fifteen-foot Christmas tree was losing needles like a white dog shedding hair on a black sweater.

"If I know you—and I think I do," she said, "that poor tree has probably been up since the first of the month."

What could he say. He'd always been like a kid about Christmas.

Brittle needles had fallen on a yellow pine floor that gleamed under the soft light. A multicolored area rug in muted tones of greens and blues and tan was soft underfoot in the seating area.

"Oh, Mac. This is all so lovely."

"Well that's a kick in the butt. It's *supposed* to be masculine," he pointed out, making a show of sounding insulted as she crossed the room to run her fingers across a polished mantel cut from a single slab of rose-beige granite.

"Lovely and *masculine,*" she amended. "It's also you."

It was the nicest compliment she could have paid him. Yeah, he'd hired a decorator to help him but he'd dictated the colors—rich jade greens, slate blues and taupe. At least, that's what the decorator called it. He called it sand.

He'd chosen the textures, too—native stone for the fireplace, warm wood for the floor and supple leathers for the furniture. And the artwork reflected his feelings for the Bozeman area.

He'd purchased all the pieces from locals artists—colorful, vibrant oil paintings of the mountains on the walls, metal and stone sculptures on the tables and floor blended with gas-fired pottery pieces on the mantel and hearth.

"Oh, sweetie, I'm sorry," he said when he realized she was about to topple over from fatigue, "I was having one of those God-I-love-this-place moments. They tell me it will wear off when I get my first tax bill."

He held out a hand. "Come on. Let's get you settled in. We can catch up some more in the morning. Unless you've got to be someplace. Man—I didn't even think of that. Do you? Have to be someplace?"

She shook her head and besides the exhaustion and pain, he swore he saw a brief but palpable sadness fill her eyes before she looked away. "Nope. No place to be. Nothing specific to do. I'm sure you've got plenty on your plate, though, so don't think you have to enter-tain me tomorrow."

His heart did a dance at the news she was free for a while. "Entertain you? Honey, this is Bozeman. In the winter. You'll be entertaining me."

He met her halfway across the room and folded her carefully into his arms again. He couldn't help it. For all she knew, it was simply a fraternal hug. He was hugging his friend who he was simply glad to see after so many years and whose presence brought back memories of good times and cheap thrills—that unfortunately had jump-started his hormones into thinking they should be perking right up after an unseasonably long hiatus.

Well. There you go, he thought. There was part of the explanation for reacting to her so strongly. Seeing her made him feel like a kid again—and he'd always been a randy kid.

"Remember the time we—you and J.T. and I—took Jacque, the foreign-exchange student out cow tipping?" he asked, reining things back into perspective.

She wrapped her good arm around his waist as he walked her toward the guest bedroom. "We were so bad."

She was grinning when she glanced up at him and for more reasons he didn't want to analyze, he was happy to see her smiling. "To the bone," he agreed, and all felt right with his world again.

Three

The next morning Shallie lay flat on her back in Mac's big guest room bed and wondered if she dared to get up. It had been a week since she'd had a bout of morning sickness, but that didn't mean it was over.

To be on the safe side, she'd just lie here for a little while longer. Plus, it was as good an excuse as any to wallow in this huge bed with the smooth, expensive sheets and soft, down mattress topper.

Heaven. Mac's house was absolute heaven. This bed was cloud-nine quality. She'd been afraid that her wrist would keep her awake. Or that she'd be too wired to sleep when he'd shown her to the spacious guest bedroom done in rich earth colors with brick-red accents. She'd been wrong on both counts.

Even with thoughts of the big carry-out container of

tiramisu tucked neatly in his spotless refrigerator waiting for her, she hadn't been able to make herself leave the comfort and warmth of this bed for a little midnight snack. Once she'd given it an experimental pat to test its firmness and discovered the down mattress beneath a plush native print comforter, she'd taken care of her bathroom ritual, slathered on some lotion, tugged on her favorite sleep shirt and had sunk into decadent luxury. She'd propped her throbbing arm on an extra pillow, closed her eyes and that was all she wrote.

Now it was morning. And she really should get a move on. She glanced down at her arm. Lifted it experimentally—and gasped. Every raw nerve in her body seemed to congregate in her wrist and remind her that broken bones—even hairline fractures—hurt like the devil.

"So, Malone…now what?" she wondered aloud as the pain dulled to a throbbing ache. She had virtually no use of her arm, so what was she going to do to support herself? Teaching was out of the question for the moment. Even though she hadn't anticipated finding a vacancy midterm, she'd hoped to find some substitute teaching work in the area. Maybe supplement her income waiting tables somewhere until she found a full-time position. She'd done plenty of waitressing when she'd worked her way through college. Sure, she had a little savings to tide her over and she had one more paycheck coming. Neither would last long, not with student loan payments and basic living expenses to cover.

Thankfully, a soft tap on the door diverted her attention from her financial dilemma.

"Hey, short-stack. You awake in there?"

Mac.

How could she not smile?

"Awake. But barely." She scooted up a little, flinching when her wrist protested.

"Are you decent?"

She propped one of the extra pillows behind her back. "I have *always* been decent. *Your* respectability, on the other hand, has always been questionable."

The door cracked open, and Mac, with a gorgeous smile, popped into the room. He was dressed in a plaid flannel shirt and tight, worn jeans, and if he'd been any man but Mac, she'd have thought, wow, I could get used to starting my mornings this way. He was gorgeous.

"Not nice to tick off the cook—especially when he's bearing breakfast in bed."

"Oh, my gosh. You shouldn't have done that. I'm already imposing. I don't want you cooking for me."

"Hel-lo. Cooking is what I do, remember?" He walked over to the bed carrying a tray laden with juice and coffee and pancakes that smelled like heaven—for about five seconds.

Oh, Lord.

Shallie threw back the covers, jumped out of bed and ran for the bathroom. Where she promptly got sick as a dog.

"Was it something I cooked?" Mac asked in a really feeble attempt at humor, hoping to undercut his concern.

"Oh, please. Go away. This is gross. I don't want you to have to deal with this."

And what are you dealing with, sweet friend of mine, Mac wondered, but didn't ask.

"Comes with the deluxe package at McDonald Inn." He wet a washcloth for her. "Clean sheets. Breakfast in bed. Nursing skills. It's printed on the door along with the rates. You must have missed it."

Poor baby. She looked so miserable. He squatted down on his haunches beside his little short-stack, a comforting hand gently rubbing her back as she hunched over the toilet bowl.

He would like to ignore the conclusions he'd started to draw. He'd like to think she was dealing was a case of nerves or the flu. If he was right about what he suspected, however, he wondered how long it was going to take her to come clean.

Hell. Maybe he was jumping recklessly to conclusions. He hoped so. He hoped to hell he was wrong about what he was thinking. Because if he was right, there was a serious chance that he was going to get good and pissed off before this day was over. An even better chance that all those romantic thoughts he'd been thinking when he'd prepared her breakfast had all just gone up in smoke.

Her hand shook when she accepted the cool wet washcloth he offered her. "I'm figuring checkout time just got bumped up an hour or two."

"Don't be a goof." Thoughts grim, he watched with concern as she wiped her mouth. "So. What's up, kid?"

She started to shake her head, then thought better of it. "Don't know. I suppose I...could have picked up a flu bug on the bus."

Okay. Logical explanation, but somehow Mac didn't think they were dealing with a case of the flu.

But if she wanted to play that game, fine. He'd give her time to decide to level with him.

"You came here by bus? From where? Never mind." What was he thinking? She was dog sick. Now was not the time for twenty questions. "We can talk later when you're feeling better. Think you're tummy's settled some?"

She closed her eyes. Considered. "I think so."

"Then let's get you back into bed."

"I cannot tell you how sorry I am about this," she said as he helped her to her feet and walked her back to the bedroom.

"Like you never held my head when I tossed *my* cookies?"

They had not been angels during their teens. They'd never done drugs and had rarely drunk before they'd become legal. There had been occasions, however, when they'd experimented with some homemade wine or tapped the keg a little too often at any number of parties that always cropped up in the spring around graduation time. Mac and J.T. had always gotten sick. She never had.

"In you go." He covered her up and helped her to lie back on the pillows.

And that's when he saw how hard she was working to hold back tears. His Shallie, who used to come to him all quiet and sad eyes and sometimes have bruises on her face and tell him she was fine. That nothing had happened. That she'd fallen out of bed. Or run into a door in the dark.

He'd known damn well, even as a kid, he'd known, that what she'd run into was her mother's fist, or a backhand from one of Joyce Malone's transient boyfriends.

"Honey, what's wrong?"

"Don't…be so nice to me. I…I don't deserve to ha-have you b-be so nice to me."

"Hey, hey. What kind of talk is that?" He eased a hip onto the bed beside her, brushed the hair back from her forehead as a huge tear leaked from the corner of her eye. "You're my buddy. I love you. There's nothing you could do to ever change that."

He tugged a tissue from the table by the bed and handed it to her. "You ready to tell me what's going on?"

She closed her eyes, looked away from him to the far side of the room, and he could see that a huge measure of pride was in play for her.

For him it was pure disappointment.

"Maybe later," he suggested, knowing she'd tell him when she was ready.

Still not looking at him, she nodded.

He squeezed her arm. "See if you can get some more rest. Snow pretty much shut things down during the night, so I'm not going anywhere for a while—at least not until the city crew finds its way to this end of town."

Then he pressed a kiss on her forehead and left her.

Puzzled. Concerned. Afraid that he knew what her problem was—dejected by what that meant to the future he'd plotted out for the two of them in the wee hours of the morning when he'd lain alone in his bed and let himself think about the prospect of a future with Shallie Malone.

When she came looking for him later, Mac was sitting on the sofa by the fire with his laptop, where he'd spent the past hour glaring at his screen and reading about various stages of pregnancy.

"You took down the tree," Shallie said inanely. Somehow, it made her a little sad. There was something about a Christmas tree—even one that had shed most of its needles—that lit a warm little glow inside her.

Odd, since she didn't remember many merry Christmases in her childhood, or even her adulthood, for that matter.

And she was just plain pathetic to be thinking about that now.

"I think that tree was violating about fifty fire codes," Mac said, watching her carefully. "It was way past its prime. That's what I get for putting it up the day after Thanksgiving."

"Some things never change," she said, working up a smile as she walked to an oversize leather chair that faced the sofa and was close to the fire. She sank down into it. "You're still the little boy who loves Christmas."

"So," he said after a long, very silent moment, "how are you feeling?"

There was no avoiding this conversation. "Foolish."

She curled her stocking feet up under her, tugged her sloppy red sweater down over the knees of her jeans and propped her injured wrist on the arm of the chair. And damn, if she didn't feel tears well up again.

She was not a weeper. Never had been. Pregnancy-induced hormones had become the bane of her existence. She hated this constant surge of emotion that seemed to lie just below the surface.

How had she gotten herself in this fix? By being stupid. That's how. Damn Jared Morgan. She'd loved him. At least, she'd thought she had…just as she'd thought he loved her. Until he'd started losing his temper over nothing. At first he'd just shove her a little. Then it had been a slap. Then it had gotten to be a whole lot more. Even if she hadn't caught him with another woman—the last straw—she'd been going to leave him.

Oldest, saddest story in the book. She'd fallen for an abuser and a cheat—just like her mother had. It was a pattern as old as time. Grow up and move away from an abusive situation and land in another one.

Well, she'd gotten out of it. But then she'd made things worse. Still feeling low and undesirable and angry and hurt a month after she'd ended things between them, she'd let her friends talk her into going out with them one night to a singles bar.

Just to get back among the living again.

Just to remember what it felt like to have a man look at her and not want to hit her.

It had been a little Band-Aid for her ravaged pride when the first man who had smiled at her made her feel like a woman again.

She'd needed his lies so badly. To ease the hurt. To fill the void. To salvage her self-esteem.

One night. One stupid, stupid night. When she'd awakened the next morning and had to face what she'd done, it was the lowest point in her life.

And then it had gotten even lower.

Brad Bailey of the charming smile and winning ways was just another cheater. Only, he'd been cheating on his wife.

Which had made Shallie feel like the biggest slug on the face of the earth.

The apple didn't fall so far from the tree after all, did it, Mom? she thought now, as she'd thought many, many times since that night.

And just like her mother, who Shallie had vowed she'd never become, now she was pregnant by a man she abhorred—not only for lying to her, but for what he'd done to his wife and family.

Like Shallie, the baby growing inside her may not have been conceived under ideal circumstances, but Shallie was determined to do the right thing by her child. She would not ignore her baby. She would not desert it. She would never hit her child, never make it feel like a mistake. No. She would not do any of the things her own mother had done to her.

This child would be loved. And this child would know it. Every day of her life, Shallie would make certain of that.

Shaking her head, she fought for control when she realized that Mac's worried gaze was focused intently on her. She didn't deserve his concern. But he did deserve the truth. At least, as much of the truth that she could bear to tell him.

"I'm pregnant," she said, figuring she'd just as well blurt it out and get it over with. Her heart beat like crazy while she waited for his reaction. When it came, it was the last one she'd expected.

"I know. I'm thinking about three months along?"

Her gaze shot to his. "How did you *know?*"

He lifted the laptop. Shrugged, trying to hide his concern. She saw it anyway. Along with the merest thread of anger...and worse. Disappointment. "I've been reading. You should be out of the morning sickness stage soon."

"No. I mean, how did you know I was pregnant?"

"Lucky guess?"

Shallie was horrified. "Is it that obvious?"

"Only to someone who knows you. Shallie," he said gently, "you refused pain medication last night for one thing. I wondered about it then. I mean, I know you're tough, but that went a little beyond making sense to me. And you turned down my best wine. Nobody turns down my wine."

He was trying to make her smile, but she just didn't have it in her at the moment.

"As for this morning," he continued, "I remember that cast-iron stomach of yours. When we were kids, I'd be barfing my guts out with the flu and you wouldn't so much as burp. So you and a case of the flu at nine in the morning didn't really seem like a good bet."

She sat in silence, waiting for questions or recriminations or something. Instead he seemed to be waiting for her to talk. So she did.

"This is the part where you're supposed to say something like, how could you be so careless? For Pete's sake, Shallie. Ever heard of birth control? Or—"

He cut her off with a raised hand. Seemed to gather

himself. Shrugged. "Like I said. I'm your friend. Not your judge. Now what can I do to help?"

She should have known that he'd respond with generosity instead of giving her grief. But then, he didn't know the whole story. If he did, he might not feel so generous.

Because of that…and because he was who he was—solid, steady and true—she felt like crying and laughing at the same time. So she did that, too.

"You could get me some of that tiramisu," she said after she'd dried her eyes.

He rose with a forced grin. He paused by her chair for a moment, then gently ruffled her hair as he walked by her on his way to the kitchen. "One order of tiramisu comin' right up."

"Better?" Mac sat across his kitchen's island counter and watched Shallie clean up the rich chocolate and butter finger dessert.

"Much. Chocolate *always* works."

He scooted off his stool and retrieved a carton of milk from the fridge. "Then I'm your man because there's lots more where that came from. In the meantime, drink some more milk. Good for you and for the kid."

"Yeah," she agreed. "Good for me and for the kid."

"The baby…it's okay and everything, right? I mean, hitting that snowbank. It didn't jar something loose, or hurt the baby?"

"Oh, Mac."

She must have been able to tell from his voice how much he'd been worried about that possibility, because she looked sad for him.

"No. Don't worry about the baby. The doctor checked me out. Everything's fine."

"Thank God." He heaved a breath of relief. It was bad enough he'd been responsible for breaking her wrist. If he'd caused any harm to her baby, well, he didn't know if he could live with that, too.

Just like he didn't know how he was going to live with the idea that she was probably still in love with the baby's father. After all, she'd cared enough about the guy to sleep with him. The Shallie he knew would have to care—even love a man—to get that deeply involved. And yet, she was here—which meant the jerk wasn't the man she'd thought he was.

Poor kid. And poor him.

Pipe dreams. Last night had been one big pipe dream.

She lapsed into silence while he made a big show of wiping down the counter. He needed something to do with his hands. He was determined to wait for her to talk—about the baby, about the father, who he'd already decided was a lying, cheating lowlife or she wouldn't have had a need to come back to Montana.

Yeah, he'd wait and see if she needed to talk about it. Or, if she wanted to just be quiet, that would be okay, too.

His resolve lasted all of a minute. "Okay," he said, turning back to her with a scowl. "So, where's the father? Why isn't he here? With you? Taking care of you?"

Nothing. Unless you counted the fact that her shoulders stiffened. That told him the issue of the father was a lot more than nothing.

"Is there some jerk out there somewhere who needs his lights punched out? Because I'm just the man to do it."

Her brown eyes met his over the glass of milk. She smiled, but it was a sad smile and it made his chest feel all squishy. "Thanks for offering."

Which meant, yeah, there was some creep who'd broken her heart and left her in a bad way. But she wasn't ready to share that piece of information with him. Probably because she knew he wasn't blowing smoke. Seeing her this way—miserable and pregnant and on her own—he was pretty much in love with the idea of making the guy pay with a little blood loss for leaving her in this fix.

Her mother hadn't given her anything but pain when she was a little girl. She didn't deserve more of it. Not from some guy who wasn't smart enough to know what he was giving up.

"Know anyplace that would be willing to hire a one-armed, pregnant woman?"

Okay. So he'd let her change the subject. Even though he still wanted, in the worst way, to ask if she was in love with the bastard.

"You're not going back to your teaching job?"

She flashed a tight smile. "Yeah. Well. Here's the deal. I…I fudged a little on that. There's no job to go back to."

He frowned. "You wanna run that by me again?"

She raised a shoulder, looked toward the window where the sun was glinting off the foot or so of new snow. "I no longer have a job."

"You got fired?" Even as he asked, he couldn't believe that was possible.

"Kind of came down to that, yeah."

Now he was really ticked. "Because you're pregnant?"

"Because I'm not *married* and pregnant. It's okay," she added, evidently seeing just how ticked he was.

And he was ticked. And at the same time relieved.

She wasn't married to the jerk. She wasn't *married*. He shouldn't have felt so much relief. He felt guilty because he did. And confused. Most of all confused because the truth was, he didn't figure into her situation in any way other than a shoulder to lean on.

That's what she needed from him now. That's what he'd be.

"I know I could fight it. And I'd probably win. The truth is, I don't want to fight. I don't want to go back there."

Her gaze drifted to the window. "I need to start fresh, you know? Me and my baby."

She smiled again, plucky to the bone. "Hadn't planned on job hunting with only one good wing, though."

Yeah. There was that. Guilt settled on his shoulders, as heavy as last night's snowfall. "Thanks to me."

"Oh—I didn't mean that. It was just the luck of the draw. Don't worry about it. I've got a little savings stashed away. I'll get by until I can work again. It won't be *that* long."

Mac rose, poured himself a cup of coffee and thought about the idea that suddenly popped into his head. "Tell you what," he said, deciding it was the perfect solution. "I know where there's a place available. The rent should be cheap, too."

She perked right up. "Yeah? Where?"

"The old Fremont cabin," he said, figuring she didn't

need to know he owned it, because knowing Shallie she'd figure she would be taking advantage of him if she stayed there.

"Ah. You mean *your* cabin."

He scowled over his mug. So much for her not knowing he owned the cabin. "Bob Coleman really has got a big mouth."

"Your name is on the mailbox."

Oops. "Right. Forgot about that. Regardless, the only reason I bought it was so I'd have a place to sleep when I'm in Sundown, working on the Dusk to Dawn. You'd actually be doing me a favor if you stayed there. Keep an eye on things, you know? This way I won't have to worry if the electricity goes off or the furnace goes on the fritz."

"You're worried about the furnace?"

"Okay, well, no. I had a new one put in this fall, but winter is winter. You never know."

She shook her head. "You're fabricating excuses to make me feel like I'm not imposing. Look, Mac, this is very sweet—and so are you," she added, her eyes soft, "but I'm not going to take advantage of your friendship—"

"Take advantage…please," he pleaded giving up on the pretense of her doing him a favor. He wanted her close. He didn't want her so close, however—like in the bedroom across the hall—that he'd be tempted to…hell. What would he be tempted to do?

She was pregnant. And he was probably right—she was most likely still in love with the creep who was responsible—and if she was, Mac really didn't want to know.

The hell he didn't.

And that realization added a bone-deep ache, to go with the anger that was knotting his gut.

"Look," he said, just to keep things in perspective, "the cabin is just sitting there empty most of the time. I rarely use it, and if I need to stay there sometime, it's not like there isn't room for both of us."

"But it's *home*."

He lifted a hand in a gesture that encompassed the kitchen. "*This* is my home. The cabin is a convenience. I only bought it because I knew I'd be splitting my time between Sundown and Bozeman until I got the Dusk to Dawn running the way I want it."

He expelled a patient breath. "Now at the risk of sounding redundant, you are my friend. Let me do this for you. Come on," he wheedled, flashing his most persuasive smile. "Just say yes, for Pete's sake. I'm dying of guilt, here, for putting you in that cast."

She frowned into her glass of milk. But he could tell she was coming around.

"You have to let me pay you something."

Like hell. "Fine. Whatever. We'll work that out later."

"Okay," she said finally. "But just until I'm released to do some kind of work."

"We'll worry about that later, too."

She studied her fingers as she ran them up and down the glass of milk. "That's something I've gotten pretty good at—worrying about things later. One of these days, I'm going to have to figure something out."

Poor little short-stack, Mac thought. She really has had a lot on her plate to deal with.

"Well, that day isn't today," he said softly. "Today is all about you getting rested up and me making sure that you do."

One corner of her mouth tipped up. "Anyone ever tell you you've got a major mother complex?"

"Bite your tongue. I'm all man. And I've got the tools to prove it." He shook a finger at her when her burst of surprised laughter told him the direction her mind had taken on that one.

"*Hand* tools, Malone. They're in the drawer right next to my aprons."

She laughed again when he opened a drawer and pulled out a hammer and an apron with Kiss the Cook splashed across the front in bold red letters.

"God, I've missed you," she said in a voice that was warm with affection and a little sad with regret.

Yeah. He'd missed her, too. Just like it looked as if he'd missed his chance with her.

He pushed his little self-pity moment aside. She was the one with problems. He had the means to help her out. And making her smile was one of them. "You'll get over that soon enough. I'll make you sick of me in no time."

"Not likely."

No. It wasn't likely, Mac thought. He sure as hell knew he wasn't going to get sick of seeing her. Stressed over seeing her, he realized when, despite the disclosure of her pregnancy, she lifted her arms over her head and stretched, and her breasts pressed against that baggie red sweater. A sharp, direct tug of lust pulled straight from his chest to his groin.

That sweater. It was old and ratty and obviously well-worn and well loved. And until that uncalculated stretch, she looked about as shapeless as a sack of spuds in it.

But he knew that wasn't the case. He knew that her breasts were soft and full and warm underneath it. And as he watched her now, he had an in-your-face visual reminder.

"Mac?"

His name registered on a level that told him she might be repeating it.

"Yeah? Hmm? What?"

He dragged a hand over his face and avoided her questioning brown eyes.

Smooth, McDonald. Real smooth.

"Where'd you go?" she asked with a curious grin as she slipped off the stool that flanked the island.

"Maui," he said, deadpan. "Those quick trips do wonders for cabin fever. What did I miss while I was gone?"

Another smile. "I asked you how long you've had Spaghetti Western."

"Tell you what. You go sit by the fire. Since chocolate seems to settle, I'll make us some cocoa and be right with you. I'll tell you all about it."

And while she was in the living room, he'd putzed around making that cocoa until he had his head back on his shoulders where it belonged—instead of in his pants where it was giving him ten kinds of trouble.

Four

Half an hour later, Shallie hugged one arm around her waist and sipped her cocoa while she stood by Mac's huge picture window and watched him clean off his driveway. Snow flew in a big, high arc as the snow blower cut through the foot-deep snow and ate an ever-widening path on the concrete.

She couldn't help but smile. He was right about the all-man part. He was out there working in his jeans, a plaid flannel shirt and a black down vest. Boots and a pair of gloves were the only other concessions he'd made to the cold. Nothing on his head. No scarf around his neck. No jacket to cut the bitter winter cold.

His nose and cheeks were red with it. Frost puffed out of his mouth like smoke as he worked his way back and forth on the driveway. The women must still drool all over him, she thought, remembering the way the girls used to swarm around him in high school. Mac and J.T. both, with their rugged good looks and quick, teasing grins, had broken more hearts than Montana had mountain peaks.

He had that undeniable air of competent male about him. It was there in the way he carried himself. In the way he smiled. In the way he related to people. Competent, confident, in charge. And he had integrity to spare. He was a guy's guy. And he was a woman's dream man.

Why hadn't Jason been like Mac? Honest. Credible. Fun. True blue. And why had she had to meet Brad? Who cheated on his wife.

She always fell for the losers. And now she was one, too.

Mac was so much a winner. She'd bet he was still breaking hearts—then had the proof of her suspicions when his phone rang. She was about to open the door and tell him he had a call when the message on his answering machine kicked on.

"Hey, it's Mac. Leave a message."

"Hi, sexy man. It's Lana. I was hoping I'd catch you at home."

The voice was seductive and kitten soft and had Shallie rolling her eyes and feeling like an eavesdropper. Which she was. She was also very curious and—now here was an admission that shocked her—a little jealous.

She should leave the room, she thought, glancing over her shoulder at the phone. But she couldn't quite make herself move as the voice purred on.

"Anyway, you haven't called in ages," Lana continued, sounding a little pouty, "so I thought I'd see what you've been up to. We could do drinks sometime. I'm dying to see your new place."

Oh, I'll just bet you are, Shallie thought with a snort.

"Hey," Lana of the midnight-velvet voice continued, "here's a thought. New Year's Eve is just four days away. So, call me, baby. We could ring in the New Year together. I'll show you a real good time, I promise. Bye-ee."

"Bye-ee," Shallie mimicked, picturing Lana as a voluptuous, if slightly needy, blonde and wondering if she was one of Mac's half-a-brain dates.

That thought was funny for all of a moment.

Speaking of half-a-brain. Who was she to judge?

She was twenty-seven years old. She was broke. She was three months pregnant and on the run from a relationship that never should have been.

In short, she was not exactly living the lofty dream she'd had when she'd left Sundown ten years ago. She had been going to be somebody. She had been going to make a difference.

And look at her now.

Shallie looked down at her still-flat tummy and gently covered it with her good hand. "So, what do you think of your momma so far, little one?"

I'm guessing, not so much, she thought on a deep sigh.

"Don't you worry, baby mine," she promised in a soft whisper. "We've just hit a little bump in the road. It'll be okay. We'll be okay. I promise. I'm not going to let you down."

And that's how Mac found her.

She was standing in a shaft of light that angled in from his front window. The sun kissed the rim of her cheek-bones, cast glossy highlights on her soft-brown curls.

Her hand covered her tummy. Her voice was whisper soft and reassuring.

He must have cleared his throat or something because, startled, she turned her head abruptly to look at him. Her brown eyes were bright, her lips tipped up into a smile that said she was happy to see him.

And, damn, he thought, as his heart kicked him a couple of good ones in the chest, if she wasn't one of the prettiest sights he'd ever seen.

"Hey, hard-working man," she said, her eyes filling with a wicked light. "You got a phone call while you were outside."

He tucked his gloves into his hip pockets then shrugged out of his vest. "Who was it?"

"La-na," she said, drawing out the name on a breathy, theatrical sigh. "She left a message. Sounds like you're gonna get lucky. She promised you a reallll gooood time."

Mac snorted. "Lana promises everybody a real good time," he said, wishing he'd never gotten involved with her last year. You live. You learn.

"You up for a ride?" he asked, wanting to change the subject. Lana, like most of the women he'd dated, left a lot to be desired in the "real person" department. Why did women have to play so many games? Why couldn't they just be themselves? Be honest, for Pete's sake instead of devious to the point of deceitful? You couldn't trust one of them. Even his own mother, it turned out, had been a liar and a cheat.

Shallie. Now, there was a woman you could count on. Too bad she didn't want to count on him for anything more than friendship.

"Most of the main streets should be cleared by now," he said, damn grateful that the woman sharing his house at the moment didn't have a deceitful bone in her body. "I need to check on some things at the restaurant. We can have lunch while we're there."

"You can't go on feeding me."

"Why not? I feed half of Bozeman on a good weekend."

"Half of Bozeman *pays* for the pleasure."

"Half of Bozeman is not my good friend. What's the point of having a restaurant if I can't feed my friends?

"Look," he added when he could see she wasn't convinced, "if you were gainfully employed—which you aren't, thanks to yours truly—and you could pay your way, it would be different."

She walked into the kitchen and rinsed her cup in the sink. "Would it?"

"No, actually, it wouldn't," he admitted. "I'd still want to feed you for free, only you wouldn't think anything of it."

She glanced at him over her shoulder, then laughed. It was a great sound.

"Your logic totally escapes me," she said turning back to him.

"It's only when a person is unable to do something that they feel like they need to do it," he explained. "So, following that logic, if you were flush, and paying for dinner wasn't a problem, you wouldn't feel bad about accepting it free."

She opened her mouth. Shut it. Shook her head. "I'm not going to win this argument, am I?"

"Now you've got it," he said, and, acting on impulse, turned her around to face him and plopped a kiss on her forehead. She smelled fresh and warm and new. And sexy as ever-loving sin.

Pregnant, he reminded himself. The lady is pregnant.

"So…are you up for it?" he asked again. "And just so you know, the answer to that question is yes."

"Well then, yes," she said on a laugh.

"Cool," he said. "Whenever you're ready."

"Umm—" she made a gesture toward the phone "—what about La-na?"

He shrugged back into his vest. "What about her?"

"Aren't you going to call her back?"

"I'll get around to it…one of these days."

She grinned.

He'd like to think that maybe it was because Shallie was a little pleased that he wasn't going to call Lana back. Wishful thinking, McDonald.

"You're a bad man, Brett McDonald."

"I'm a *single* man," he stated with playful conviction. Shallie had spoiled him for any other woman. "And in spite of Lana's agenda, I plan to stay that way." Because the woman he wanted didn't have a clue that he loved her.

It hurt suddenly. Accepting that, after all these years, he still loved Shallie Malone, and the possibility of her loving him back was the same now as it had been back then. Zip.

"Besides, I'm going to be an uncle," he added, gently patting her tummy to project the illusion that all was fine and dandy in his world. "I'll have duties. No time for wild women because I'll be taking the little guy to the park, teaching him how to fish."

He could see in her eyes that she'd needed that small assurance that she wasn't going to be going through this alone. That he was going to be there for her and for her baby.

And he would be. He made that promise to himself as much as to her right then and there.

"Him?" she asked, her brown eyes glistening with speculation.

"Him. Her. Doesn't matter. Kid still needs to know how to fish. Now, come on. Grab your jacket and let's boogie. We'll talk about names on the way. I'm kind of partial to Heathcliff and Gertrude. Whadaya think?"

"Oh, man." Three nights later Mac sat back from his dining room table with a blissful look on his face. "Shallie, you give me the recipe for this cheesecake and not only will that running tab you insist on keeping, of what you think you owe me, be wiped clean, I'll end up owing *you* money."

Sitting at Mac's huge mission oak dining room table, three whole days after she'd arrived, Shallie grinned, watching him polish off the cheesecake she'd topped with a sugary raspberry sauce. "I'm thinking that means you like it."

"Like it? Honey, I'm crazy for it. What a proud moment. My little short-stack grew up and learned how to make something other than PBJs."

He was good at making her smile. He was just plain good for her, Shallie thought, not for the first time since she'd been staying with him.

And not for the first time she thought about what it would be like to be Brett McDonald's woman. The word *easy* came to mind. And just like that, the thought went away.

Don't trust *easy*, she mentally repeated the mantra that had proven itself true too many times in her life.

"I'm serious," he continued. "I'd kill for this recipe. How did you manage it, anyway—not just dessert but the entire dinner, which was awesome, by the way. How did you do it? I mean, with your arm and all?"

Grilling the salmon and making a salad hadn't been that difficult. And while it had been a bit of a trick to whip up the cheesecake with only one fully functional hand, Shallie had learned how to manage a lot of things in the past three days.

"It's all about leverage," she said. "And determination. Oh, yeah—and your state-of-the-art kitchen, gadgetman."

He leaned back in his chair, balancing on two of its legs, and waggled his eyebrows. "Like my toys, do ya?"

She laughed. "Oh, yeah. I like your *kitchen* toys." And she was happy that he'd enjoyed the meal she'd prepared for him. She'd been determined to make him something special after all he'd done for her.

"As to the recipe, it's all yours," she told him. "And small payment for such exceptional room and board."

He let his chair drop back down to all fours. Gave her a stern look. "Okay. Let's not spoil this kick-ass meal by forcing me to go into lecture mode. You owe me nothing. Nada. Zip. As a matter of fact, you just did me a huge favor. I was going to go back to the restaurant and work tonight, but now that I'm feeling full and lazy, I think I'll knock off for the night."

"You work too hard," she said.

"Damn straight," he agreed without any real conviction, unclipped his cell phone from his belt and punched in a number. "Cara. Hi. It's Mac. What's happening?"

Shallie watched while he nodded, answered some questions from Cara Brown, his night manager.

He did work too hard, whether he wanted to admit it or not. Mac, she'd discovered, was a very hands-on manager. Did everything from cooking to bartending to maintenance, if the need arose. He put in a lot of hours at the restaurant during the past three days she'd been staying with him.

Three days. Amazing. Shallie wasn't sure how it had happened, but the time had passed in a blur. She'd rested and was recovering from not only the broken wrist but from the past few months of stress and worry about her future.

Mac had a way of making everything but the moment seem to be in another realm. A realm that was not really part of the here and now. Like tonight, for instance.

He'd breezed in the door about six, after calling and telling her he'd come to pick her up and take her to the restaurant for dinner, as he had every night. When they'd gone grocery shopping that morning, she hadn't told him that she'd made certain to pick up the items for this surprise, special dinner.

"Sounds like you've got things well in hand," Shallie heard him say after he and his manager had apparently covered all the bases. "Listen. I'm going to call it a day. Give me a ring if something comes up. I can be there in five minutes. Yeah. Thanks. G'night."

"Done deal," he said after he'd hung up. "I'm yours for the night."

She shook her head at his big grin. And fought the urge to wish she really was his. He was so special, this man. Funny. Sexy. Tender, and yet as alpha as they came.

The question was out before she could stop it. "So why aren't you someone *else's* for the night? Someone like Lana?" she added with a teasing waggle of her eyebrows to hide how curious she really was.

"Don't you worry about Lana. The fact is, she's just not my type." He rose and started clearing up the table. And, if she didn't miss her guess, to run away from this line of questioning. Interesting.

"You cooked," he said, gathering dishes for the dishwasher, "I'll clean up."

Shallie stood, too, and followed him into the kitchen with her plate and silverware. And her seriously piqued curiosity. "So what kind of woman *is* your type?"

He shot a glance over his shoulder. "Anyone ever tell you that you're nosy, Ms. Malone?" He sounded more amused at her line of questioning than upset by it—and maybe he also sounded a little nervous. Interesting.

"More than one. You'd think I'd learn. So, why *isn't*

there a special woman in your life, *Mr.* McDonald?" She couldn't help it. Now that she'd opened up this channel, she wanted to know. "I mean, it's not like you're mud ugly or anything—"

"Aw shucks, thank you, ma'am." He winked at her as he opened the dishwasher and stacked their plates.

"And then there's that humble bumpkin thing you've got going for you," she added with a smile. "Plus, you're a nice guy. You're financially solvent—and then some—and unless you've switched teams while I've been gone, you're arrow straight."

"Same team," he assured her and made a show of flexing his bicep. "I jus' *luvs* the ladies."

She laughed. "And I'm sure the ladies jus *luvs* you. So, really—why haven't you gotten married? And don't give me that ring-in-the-nose bit because I'm not buying it."

He waited long enough that she was beginning to wonder if he was going to tell her to take a hike. Finally he turned back to her.

"Okay, here's the deal," he said, tossing a dish towel over his shoulder. Leaning back against the counter, he crossed his ankles then folded his arms over his broad chest. "I like my life. I like calling my own shots. I like doing what I want to do, when I want to do it. I like not having to be responsible for anyone but me. And most of the women I know, well, let's just say they leave a lot to be desired in many areas," he added, his eyes growing hard. "Besides, from my perspective, marriage, as an institution, isn't all it's cracked up to be."

She figured he was referring to his parents. Figured also—more from what he hadn't said than what he had said—that their divorce may have soured him. But the Mac she knew was also a cockeyed optimist. It was hard to believe he'd just written off marriage.

She eased a hip onto a bar stool, leaned her elbow on the granite countertop. "How do you know that, if you don't give it a chance?"

He considered, then pinned her with a look. "Did you? Did you give the institution of marriage a chance?"

Okay. Ouch. Not only had she not given marriage a chance, she'd almost been responsible for breaking up one. And that was something she would always have to live with.

A familiar sinking nausea accompanied that reality—and it had nothing to do with a biological reaction from her pregnant hormones. It was about shame. About being stupid and needy and so blinded by the humiliation Jared had caused her that she'd rushed headlong into a situation with Brad that added mortification to the mix.

She was not a home wrecker. And as soon as she'd found out she was pregnant, she'd made up her mind that Brad would never know about the baby. This baby was hers. She would raise it. Love it. Take care of it.

"Shallie? You okay?"

When she realized she'd been a couple of thousand miles and two months ago away, she pulled herself back to the moment. What was done was done. She couldn't undo it. But she could not bring herself to level with Mac about the truth surrounding her baby's conception. She knew that he assumed the father had abandoned her. She knew it was wrong the let him continue to think it. But she couldn't bear to see the disappointment in his eyes if he knew the whole story.

Which meant that she really needed to stop prying into his business since she hadn't confided the whole truth about hers to him.

"I'm fine—other than being a prying bore. Sorry. Your love life is none of my business."

An odd look that she couldn't read crossed his face.

"Tell you what," he said, tossing the dish towel over the edge of the sink and pushing away from the counter, "what do you say we let our relationship issues drop and see if we can find a movie on pay per view? I bought that monster of a flat screen when I moved in and I don't think I've watched it for more than an hour total—and that's been in fits and starts."

"Deal," she said, because she really did want him to just kick back and relax since that's what a night off should be about. "Just no blood-and-gore flick, okay?"

"You used to *love* blood and gore," he pointed out with a disappointed frown.

"And I will again—just not at this particular stage of my pregnancy."

"Ah. Got it. Does that mean we have to watch a chick flick?"

"Not my cuppa, either, at the moment."

In the end they compromised. They found an old Steve Martin comedy and, snuggled on the couch with a fire glowing in the hearth and a very light snow feathering down, laughed their way through it.

* * *

When Mac woke up several hours later, his arm was asleep. His neck had a crick in it. The TV droned softly, and a soft, warm and amazingly sexy woman was snuggled up against him.

Shallie.

For a long moment he just lay there, absorbing her heat, enjoying the moment. He didn't remember falling asleep. He sure didn't remember stretching out full length on the sofa and taking sleeping beauty with him for the ride.

But evidently he had, because he was flat on his back and Shallie was plastered against his side like a second skin, the weight of her cast lying heavily on his chest. The weight of her thigh, however slight, was settled with a much more pronounced effect across his lap. A lap that was suddenly reacting to all this soft woman heat sleeping by his side.

Perfect. Be a guy. Embarrass the hell out of both of us.

Or fix it. Fast, lunkhead.

So, as he'd sometimes had to make himself do the past three days when he found himself caught up in some unsolicited and inappropriate sexual fantasy about Shallie, he thought of anything but all that heat.

Tax audits. Quarterly payments. The waitress schedule. The reservation for the Simpsons' wedding rehearsal dinner that was going to be a nightmare to pull together. The leaky roof at the Dusk to Dawn that was going to cost a small fortune to fix.

And let's not forget, this is a pregnant woman you're holding in your arms.

Okay. That helped. Enough, at least, that he could draw another breath—but not an easy one.

Careful not to disturb her, he yawned hugely, then checked his watch. Holy cow. It was almost 2:00 a.m. He needed to get her to bed where she could get some quality rest. But then she stirred, and his arm automatically tightened around her back, sliding instinctively down her hip to hold her so she wouldn't tumble to the floor.

Lordy, she was small. Slight, fine bones. Slim, lean curves. But curves, just the same. Why had he never realized before how fragile she was?

Because of her grit, that's why. Tough. Shallie Malone had always been tough. She'd had to be.

He remembered the first time he'd ever seen her. She'd been all of eleven years old. She'd shown up at school near the end of the spring semester. Her clothes had been worn and patched and not all that clean. Her hair had been just as curly then as it was now, only it had stuck out around her face like a Raggedy Ann doll.

The Griener twins had cornered her on the playground at recess and had been giving her the new-kid-in-town third-degree.

"Where'd ya get them jeans? Looks like a clown wore 'em they've got so many patches," Billy Griener had said, acting superior and mean.

"Yeah," Willie had chimed in. "Got clown hair, too. Do a trick, clown."

"Yeah, clown, do a trick," Billie ordered on a mean laugh.

"I'll do a trick," the new girl had said. "See how you

like this one." Then she'd walked up to Willie and kneed him in the groin.

Mac smiled into the dark, remembering. Willie had howled like a scalded dog all the way to the teacher, who had promptly dragged Shallie to the principal's office.

Mac and J.T. had been waiting for her on the steps when school got out that day.

"What do you want?" she'd snarled, her little hands clenched into fists at her sides, the set of her mouth telling him she was ready to take on the world if she had to.

Mac had only been a kid himself, but he'd figured out then and there that Shallie Malone had probably taken on the world several times already in her short life. And if he hadn't already fallen in love with her, he did right then.

"I want to shake the hand of the girl who put wailing Willie to his knees," he'd said.

She'd looked suspicious at first, but then he'd grinned at her and stuck out his hand. "And I want to make sure I'm on your good side, 'cause I don't ever want to see your knee comin' at me the way it came at Willie."

Still uncertain, she drew back her shoulders but cautiously shook his hand.

"What about you?" She'd turned a dark look on J.T.

"You play baseball?" J.T. asked with a matching scowl.

"I can play circles around you," she'd said, her chin notching up, daring him to dispute her claim.

J.T. had grinned. "Cool. Let's go to the park and get us a game going. We'll whump the snot out of anyone who thinks they can beat us. You'll be our ringer."

That was all it had taken to melt her ice block of resistance. And aside from it being his first puppy love crush, the three of them had been fast friends from that day on.

If anyone ever needed a friend, it had been Shallie. Joyce Malone, Shallie's mom, had drifted into town, Mac had heard eavesdropping one day at the Dusk to Dawn, because she'd needed a place to hide out from a string of bad debts and bad relationships.

For whatever reason, Joyce had taken a liking to Sundown, and that's where she and Shallie had stayed, until Shallie had graduated from high school. Shortly after Shallie left, Joyce hooked up with a trucker and took off, too.

Mac had never liked Joyce Malone. Not just because of the physical bruises she sometimes put on Shallie. The emotional bruises were just as hard for his little short-stack to deal with. Both his mom and J.T.'s mom had always had time for the three of them underfoot. They'd always had cookies, too. And hugs when they'd needed them. Most likely they were the only hugs Shallie had ever gotten, Mac figured, because Shallie never took them home to see *her* mother. And she never had much to say about her.

"She's workin'," Shallie would say with a look that dared anyone to dispute it.

Truth was, Mac had figured out when he was old enough to learn the way it was with women like Shallie's mom, that in between her job at the dry cleaners,

Joyce Malone did a lot of work on her back. On more then one occasion, he or J.T. had had to wipe a smirk off one of their brainless buddies' faces when they'd suggested that maybe Shallie did a little back work herself for Mac and J.T.

She stirred again, and the warmth of her breath tickled his throat. His body reacted when her thigh slid across his lap. The sweet friction almost made him groan. And when the swell of her breast pressed oh, so sweetly against his chest, he thought he might dive right off the deep end.

Okay. Time to nip this little disaster-in-the-making in the bud.

Five

"Shallie." Mac whispered softly so he wouldn't startle her. "Sweetheart. Wake up. We need to hit the sack."

She sighed and nestled closer, her cheek resting on his shoulder. "Mmm. Okay. In a minute."

He lay rock still. Except for his heart, which was pounding so hard in reaction to her silky sigh and soft body that he was certain the reverberation would wake her up.

But she was asleep again. Or so said her deep, even breaths.

He was far from asleep. He'd dreamed about holding her like this for years. And now here she was. In his arms—yet just as unattainable as she had been all those years ago.

Lord help him.

"Shallie," he whispered, determined to do the right

thing. "Come on, sleepyhead. You're going to get all stiff and sore lying mashed against me like this."

"Comfy," she breathed, and shifted again and damned if all of her didn't somehow end up on top of all of him. "So...comfy."

Well, hell. Because the trouble was, it *was* comfy. Damn comfy. He could feel so much more of her now, and the weight was wonderful. Her breasts pressed firmly against his chest, and with a little imagination he could picture her nipples pressing against her bra. And of course that picture stirred up more and more pictures. Like the two of them skin on skin and him sinking deep inside of her.

He wasn't just rock still now, he was rock hard, too. And, Lord help him, she had to be able to notice.

She'd kill him. She'd flat-out kill him. Neuter him with that lethal knee if nothing else. And he'd deserve it.

He held his breath. Waited for her to lift her head, glare at him and tell him to grow up.

But she didn't. She did something else, instead. And he had to believe she was still half-asleep because never in a million years would a wide-awake and alert Shallie start moving her thigh back and forth along his erection as if she not only didn't hate that it had sprung up between them, but like she liked—more than liked—the way it felt against her.

Sweet heaven, he needed some of the blood that had shot to his groin to find its way north and fuel a little gray matter.

"Shallie," he groaned, feeling himself losing the battle with his better judgment.

She moved again with an answering little sigh, pushing herself higher, rubbing her breasts and her belly against him as she lifted her head and touched her mouth to his.

Mother.

He needed to push her away. Clearly, she didn't know what she was doing. Except she sure *acted* as if she knew, and she was doing it damn well. Maybe she was awake after all. Maybe…maybe she did feel something for him. Maybe she was as hot for him as he was for her.

Her lips were sure as hell hot, and so incredibly soft against his. And when that tentative contact of her closed mouth slowly transitioned to the sound of a yearning sigh and she opened for him, he ran out of reason and will to fight it.

He was only so strong. How could he not welcome her open kiss? Devour her questing tongue when she slid it along his teeth, then slipped inside.

Hunger. Yearning. Need. It was all there. And he fed it. His and hers. Catered to it. Built on it, wrapping her tightly against him and fusing his mouth to hers.

Heaven above, she tasted fine. Felt even better. The inside of her mouth was hot and slick. Her body was both lean and lush; her hair was like silk when he buried one hand in her tangled curls. And he was barely aware of his own actions as he slipped the other up and under her sweater.

More heat. Heat to the point of burn when skin met skin and she arched into his hand. Before he knew what he was doing, he slid his hand up along her ribs and higher to find the weight of a full, heavy breast. He swallowed her gasp of pleasure when he gently squeezed. And when he flicked his thumb over the lace that covered her nipple, she pressed into his touch, driving him deeper into her fire. So deep, he rolled her beneath him and settled his weight fully on top of her.

He wedged his knee between her thighs, simply had to get closer. He had to touch more. He had to... *Whoa.*

He had to stop. That's what he had to do.

This was insane.

This was Shallie. Half-asleep. Totally vulnerable. Completely off-limits.

Pregnant.

He didn't know where he found the strength, but he slowly dragged his hand out from under her sweater. Slower still, he pulled his mouth away from hers, fighting her kitten sounds of protest.

Fueled by guilt and desire, his heart was pulsing at about one hundred per when he pressed her face against his neck and held her. Just held her, groping for brotherly thoughts, praying she wouldn't hate him when she came fully awake and realized what had just happened.

Maybe he'd get lucky, he thought, gently stroking her hair. Maybe she'd slept through the entire thing and she wouldn't even remember.

But then he felt her stiffen beneath him. Felt the flutter of her eyelashes against his throat and knew he could kiss that notion goodbye.

"Well." Her voice sounded husky; her breath was kind of thready. "This is…awkward."

Awkward. Good word.

So was *incredible.*

Amazing.

Hot.

Oh, and here was a word: *suicidal.* At least it would be if he pulled that train of thought any further. Time for a little diversionary drivel to get the train back on the right track.

He lifted his head. Frowned down at her. "Okay, lady. Who are you? And what have you done with my friend, Shallie?"

Thank you, God, her mouth turned up in a smile.

"I'm going to start counting," she said in her best hypnotist's voice, gamely playing along, "and when I reach ten, you will wake up, no longer have the urge to quack like a duck, and you will forget this ever happened."

Not damn likely.

Still, he forced a grin. She was cool with this. They were cool. Well, technically he was still hot, but he'd deal with that later.

"Okay. Just one last quack. Maybe two," he said then pushed out two very anemic quacks that actually had her giggling. "Now that I got that out of my system…umm…damn, Shall. I am so, so sorry."

"You should be sorry. No self-respecting duck sounds like that."

He pushed out a snort. "I was referring to what happened between us just now."

Her eyes softened. "I know."

He watched her face, looking for anger, relieved when he saw none. "I really *am* sorry."

He would go to hell for lying, too, because the truth was, he couldn't muster up the necessary regret to be sorry about anything right now. The kiss had been incredible. "Guess we…uh, both fell asleep."

"And woke up next to a warm, snuggly body," she added with a nod.

"And naturally, instinct took over—"

"And what with our weakened mental capacity and all," she continued.

"The next thing you know…yada, yada, yada." He was doing his damnedest to keep this light, when the situation was anything but. It was explosive, but again she kept the fire from burning out of control when she smiled. "Or something like that."

She searched his eyes for the longest time. "For the record, McDonald, you yada very well when you're asleep."

Ah. So that was why she was being so forgiving. She thought *he'd* been sleeping when this started, too.

It was a straw and he grasped it.

"Right back atcha, kid," he said lamely, shoving back the guilt, and finally had the presence of mind to haul his sorry self off her.

Maybe it was because he was tired. Maybe it was because, like most men, he was born horny. Maybe he was just a jerk. Whatever the reason, as he stood there looking down on her, he was fresh out of reasons why he shouldn't just pile back on top of her sweet, soft body and finish what her sleepy, sexy eyes told him she wouldn't mind finishing. And that was probably just more wishful thinking on his part.

So he did what any self-respecting jerk would do in this situation. He bailed.

"Before this gets any weirder…I'm hitting the sack. You sure you're okay with…uh…you know?"

She nodded. "I'm okay."

"All right. Well. G'night, then, short-stack. See you tomorrow."

Then he hightailed it the hell away from her before yada, yada, yada turned into hotter, hotter, hotter and they both woke up naked and way more than embarrassed in the morning.

The next night was New Year's Eve. Spaghetti Western was standing-room only. Had been since about 6:00 p.m. when locals and out-of-towners had decided to start their evening early with a nice dinner before they either went on to parties or home to watch the crystal ball drop in Times Square on TV.

And finally, finally, Shallie was able to do something to help Mac out. His regular hostess was down with a bad sinus infection. His back-up was on a ski trip to Steamboat. And Mac had already pressed any additional staff into action to help cover the rush.

"I can do it," Shallie had said that morning, sitting at the island in the kitchen after she'd overheard Mac on the phone to his day manager. "I can fill in as hostess," she told him when he'd hung up.

"I can't ask you to do that," he'd insisted.

"Why? Because I'm pregnant? Sorry. That's a nonissue. Because of my wrist? Another nonissue. I don't need two hands to keep track of seating charts and to seat people."

He'd frowned, but she could tell he was considering the idea.

"If it's experience you're worried about," she'd continued, determined to do this for him, "I paid my way through college working in restaurants. I've done everything from cooking to waiting tables to busboy chores to playing hostess. And I've spent enough time around SW these past few days that I have a pretty good feel for how things flow there.

"Besides," she'd added, resorting to the big guns when he'd still looked dubious, "I'm bored. Let me help. It'll be fun."

"I don't know." He'd still hedged.

"Please," she'd wheedled in a really good imitation of a woman about to throw a little temper tantrum.

"Oh, for Pete's sake. If you're going to get all sulky about it."

She'd seen the grin through his grousing and rushed over to give him a one-armed hug. "Thanks. It'll be great. You'll see."

It was the first time they'd touched since the "nocturnal kissing" incident the night before. And since then, Mac had made it a point to keep his distance. Shallie had done the same. Which was silly, she thought now, as, despite her cast, she felt festive and even a little pretty in her red velvet holiday dress, while she ushered an elderly couple to a table.

"Enjoy your meal," she said with a smile, and handed them their menus.

So they'd fallen asleep, woken up in each other's arms and let their bodies do the talking before their brains had engaged, she thought, walking back to the hostess station. It wasn't as if it had been planned.

And it was silly to be thinking about that kiss now, Shallie told herself as she caught a glimpse of Mac. He was currently dug in behind the bar helping the bartender who was overrun with orders.

Still, it was hard for her not to think about it. He was an amazing kisser, her friend, Brett McDonald. His lips were so soft and skilled. And his body—Lord. She'd known he was in great shape. One look was all it had taken to figure that out. Chest to chest, hip to hip, however…well, tactile contact was much more telling than visual.

Much more telling, she thought, and actually felt her face flame hot when she remembered the feel of his hand on her breast and his very impressive erection pressing against her belly.

"You okay?" Cara, Mac's assistant manager, asked making a point to check on Shallie as she hurried by on the way to the dining room.

"Fine. Great," Shallie said quickly.

"Okay," Cara said with a concerned look. "You look a little flushed."

"Has Mac been telling you to watch out for me?" Shallie asked, all of a sudden more concerned that he might have inadvertently spilled the beans about her pregnancy than she was alarmed by the turn of her thoughts.

"Mac? He hasn't told me anything. You have a broken wrist. Seems to me that's enough reason to be a little concerned about you. Thought maybe you might have bumped it or something."

"Oh. Sorry." Shallie forced a smile. "I'm fine. No problems, really." Unless you count the fact that she was having a sexual fantasy about her best friend, which was about as left field as waking up in his arms and thinking about kissing him every time she saw him. "I'm having a good time. Am I doing okay?"

"You're doing great. In fact, you've been a godsend. We'll have three tables bussed and ready in a couple of minutes."

As Cara took off at a fast walk, Shallie glanced at the crush by the door and in the waiting area. They were talking and laughing, enjoying the complimentary champagne Mac had made available. No one seemed to mind the wait. Probably because they all knew a meal at SW was worth waiting for.

The rest of the night flew by. Shallie only caught glimpses of Mac as he worked the dining room, making certain everyone was happy and well fed and covered whatever base needed covering to make certain everything went smoothly. Yet every time their eyes met she felt a sharp little zing of arousal flashing between them.

It was unsettling and pulse-altering and...well, exciting. And she was totally wrong to be thinking about the possibility of something more happening between them.

She'd made a big enough mess of her life. She wasn't

going to mess it up further—or mess his up in the process. She made it a point to avoid eye contact the rest of the night and finally, around ten-thirty, the crowd had thinned to a few tables and the kitchen was in the process of shutting down. Shallie had just bidden two couples good-night and happy New Year when she realized Mac had slipped up beside her.

"Hey," he said with a tired smile. "How you holding up?"

"I'm great. Okay," she confessed when he narrowed his eyes, "my feet hurt a little. But it's been fun. Really. I enjoyed myself tonight."

"We couldn't have made it through the crush without you."

"You're overstating, but thanks for that."

"What do you say I grab something from the kitchen and we take it home to ring in the New Year with a late dinner?"

It was her turn to question him—first with a look, then with an admonishment. "It's New Year's Eve," she pointed out. "You don't have to babysit me."

"What are you talking about?"

"Don't you have a party or something to go to? A date waiting with a bottle of wine and a come-hither smile?" She didn't much like the idea that a woman might be waiting for him, but the truth was, it would be better all around if one was.

He grunted. "I've got a date with my sofa, and that's about as much action as I want after taking care of this crowd tonight."

"Really?" She felt too much relief over that news, but

pushed gamely on. "Because I'm okay if you just drop me off at the house."

"I'm not dropping you anywhere," he assured her. "Sit tight. I'll go raid the kitchen and tell Cara we're out of here. Be right back."

Shallie's nerves zinged like the zephyrs of wind that whisked powdery snow into tall, swirling gusts beneath the streetlights as Mac drove through town on deserted, winter-cold streets.

Get a grip, she told herself mentally. Just because this was New Year's Eve, the date night of all date nights, and she and Mac were together, it didn't mean anything.

But there are implications, the suddenly insane side of her personality reminded her.

Okay, *normally* there would be implications when two single people decided to spend one of the biggest holidays of the year together. There shouldn't, however, be any of that stuff in the mix between them.

And there wouldn't have been—except that last night had happened. Last night when they'd more than kissed. That spelled *implications* with a capital *I*. At least, it did from her perspective. Mac, however, didn't seem to be affected by the kiss at all.

Shallie glanced at him across the darkened cab of his truck. Nope. He seemed oblivious to her thoughts. Thoughts that had her looking at him through new eyes. The eyes of a woman as opposed to the eyes of a friend. And with a new awareness and appreciation of just how much of a man he was.

Careful, she warned herself. You've forgotten about

the *easy* factor. *Easy* spelled disaster for her. No matter how appealing this amazing man was.

He drove, she realized now, the way he did everything else. With confidence and complete control. Just as he was in complete control of whatever awkwardness he could have shown around her.

He was still quick with his smiles. Still attentive to a fault. And she hadn't seen a flicker of a notion that he felt any discomfort left over from last night.

Which was good, Shallie assured herself. It was a very good thing that one of them had their wits about them, she thought and, indulging herself in a wistful look at his poster-boy profile, she told herself to give it a rest.

She chalked up her lingering fascination with Mac, the man, to haywire hormones. It was the only logical explanation. She normally didn't cry, and she normally didn't have attacks of the hots for her best friend—who very clearly had forgotten all about the kiss that she was going to do her darnedest to put out of *her* mind, too.

She had much more critical items on her agenda, anyway. Items like finding a job and taking care of herself and her baby. And she'd made enough mistakes lately. She wasn't going to make a mistake with Mac— and if she repeated that particular mantra often enough, she just might pull it off.

If he didn't get his act together, Mac thought as he set the table for their late New Year's Eve dinner, he was going to fool around and screw up their friendship.

He may have been acting like a fool but he *wasn't*

one—at least, not normally. Well, damn, that dress she had on tonight didn't help matters any.

It was bright-red velvet—a holiday dress—with long sleeves that covered her cast, a deep-vee neckline and a fitted and flirty short skirt. Man, he'd almost swallowed his tongue when she'd walked into the living room with a smile and an "Will this be dressy enough for the hostess at the hottest spot in Bozeman on New Year's Eve?"

Oh, yeah. It was dressy enough. The hottest spot in Bozeman that night, however had been anywhere she had been. Her full breasts pressed provocatively against the red velvet. Her tummy was still flat. And she had the most amazing legs, not to mention sweet, curvy hips that had had him salivating over the wet bar way too often for a man his age.

He shook off the wallop of seeing her that way. Good thing Shallie had her full wits about her. Half-wit was about the most he could lay claim to, because he'd been thinking about her in a totally man-woman way for the better part last night and today.

All because of that kiss, she hadn't even been aware that she'd initiated and then taken way beyond the initiation stage before he'd managed to put the skids on his wayward libido. And before things had gotten completely out of hand.

It was the out-of-hand part he hadn't been able to get out of his head. Another few minutes and he'd have had her sweater off her. And damn it all…he'd been thinking about that possibility way too much, also.

Well, it was clear that *she* wasn't thinking about it.

He was guessing the only thing she was thinking was that she was glad to be off her feet, that she was hungry as a bear and that it was way past time he fed her.

"You're stupid squared, that's what you are," he muttered while he debated—then against his better judgment—went ahead and lit the candles.

"Soup's on," he said as he walked into the great room where he'd ordered her to sit down in front of the fire with her feet up while he set out their meal.

"Smells like heaven," she said following him into the dining room. She stopped just inside the arched double doorway. "Oh. Oh, Mac. This looks wonderful."

"Let's hope it tastes good, too," he said, experiencing another one of those punches of lust when she smiled for him.

"For the lady." He made a grand gesture with a sweep of his hand and held her chair out for her. "Spinach salad, asparagus with cheese sauce and succulent Maine lobster. And for dessert, tiramisu. Oh," he added uncapping a bottle of sparkling white grape juice, "and a little nonalcoholic bubbly just for you to ring in the New Year."

Okay, he thought as he watched her face light up. Now he knew what it meant when someone said a woman looked radiant. Her eyes sparkled, her cheeks had turned a beautiful shade of carnation pink and, as tired as she had to be, there was a glow about her that made it appear she'd bathed in champagne.

And maybe he should have bitten the bullet and taken Lana up on her offer of a "really good time" because it was getting damn hot in here and he didn't have cooking privileges in Shallie's kitchen.

"This is all so special," Shallie said looking from her wineglass to the candles, then to him as he sat down across from her.

"It's New Year's Eve," he said with a brightness that he hoped to hell she didn't see through as his having a case of the hots for a woman he had no business being hot for. "And a special one at that when two old friends get together. So I figured we'd do it up right. Plus I thought you might be tired of eating Italian."

"I don't think I'd ever tire of the menu at SW," she said kindly. "You were so thoughtful to do this. As usual, it's too much."

"It's just right," he said, and snapped his napkin onto his lap. "Now, eat before it gets cold."

Cold. He should be so lucky.

"So," Mac said as they settled into the great room, him on the sofa, Shallie folded a safe distance away from him in a side chair, "my turn to play twenty questions."

She blinked, puzzled. "Your turn? When did I have *my* turn?"

"'What kind of woman is your type?' 'Why aren't you settled down?' 'Why aren't you married?'" he reminded her, mimicking her tone from the other day.

"Oh. *That* was my turn. I didn't know that. And I didn't know we were keeping track, but fair's fair." She grinned at him. "Okay. Shoot."

Oh, he planned to. During dinner he'd made some decisions. One: things had gotten just plain crazy from his perspective. So she was a gorgeous woman. So he'd always had a thing for her. Okay, more than a thing. So he'd always loved her. Still did, but that didn't really matter now. He had to cut it out. The overriding factor here was that all she needed him to be for her was a friend. So that's what he'd be. Period. Done deal.

Two: this sort of undercut the first issue, but he was now very interested in knowing what kind of man flipped her switch. And it wasn't a pride thing, he assured himself. He was curious, that was all. It wasn't as if his ego had taken a hit, knowing that the only time he had any male-female effect on her was when she was sleeping.

Okay. So maybe it *was* an ego thing. And maybe he didn't like knowing that he was jealous as hell of a man he didn't know. A man she was probably still in love with.

"You said something about a question?"

He looked up to see her waiting, with a curious and expectant look on her face.

"Why haven't you ever been married?" he asked finally, deciding to go for broke.

"Wow. Didn't see that one coming." Her feigned look of surprise made it clear she'd seen it a mile away.

Just that fast, however, she sobered. "Okay. The truth is, I came close. Well, at least I thought I was close. Turned out he wasn't close at all."

She fiddled with the sling supporting her wrist, and he had more thoughts of murder and mayhem when he saw the pain in her eyes.

"Only, he never made that little difference in life plans known to me. I still might not know if I hadn't caught him—" She paused, shot him a brittle smile.

"Well, if I hadn't *caught* him. In the interest of keeping this conversation civil, let's just leave it at that."

Bastard, Mac thought. So the guy had led her on, gotten her pregnant, then cheated on her. And Mac had the horrible feeling there might be more to this story than she was letting on.

"He's not only a jerk, he's a fool," Mac said. "I'm sorry. Really sorry he did that to you."

She raised a shoulder, as if it was no big deal, but he saw the hurt and something that even looked like shame in her eyes before she looked away. And, for making her feel that way about herself, Mac hated the guy even more.

"Yeah, well. It's all behind me now."

The plasma screen was on in the background. Times Square was packed as New Year's Rockin' Eve gave a minute-by-minute countdown to the stroke of midnight.

"Hey," she said, her attention suddenly caught by the music. "Remember that band? Oh, my gosh. I love that song."

Mac leaned over and snagged the remote, punching up the volume a couple notches. "Oh, man. I used to make out to that song with Wynona Gray."

She pushed out a laugh. "You used to make out to that song with everyone."

"Just the everyones who wore skirts," he corrected her, then on impulse stood and held out his hand. "Come on. Let's dance out the old year."

If there was hesitation on her part, it was as brief as her surprise. She laughed and took his hand. "Why not."

Oh, he could tell her why not, Mac realized the minute he pulled her into his arms.

Mistake.

Big, big mistake, he thought, liking far too much the way her heat nestled next to his. Hell. She wasn't even aware of what she was doing to him. But she'd know soon enough if he didn't do some serious maneuvering.

"We're going to take you to Times Square now, folks," the TV announcer said as the network cut away from the inside party and scanned the crowd gathered in the street. "The countdown to the new year is about to begin."

They stopped dancing and turned to watch the scene on the screen where the crystal ball had started to descend.

"Ten, nine, eight…"

Mac felt Shallie lean into him a little.

"Five, four, three…"

He turned away from the TV to look down at her…and realized she was looking up at him.

"Two, one! Happy New Year!"

A riot of noise erupted from the television as they stood in the suddenly close silence of his living room, eyes locked, smiles tentative.

"Happy New Year, Mac," she whispered.

"Happy New Year, Shall," Mac said just as softly, and knew, without a doubt that he absolutely should not kiss her.

But it was New Year's Eve.

It was tradition to kiss the one you were with at the stroke of midnight.

And he was just plain nuts. Because he lowered his head. Touched his mouth to hers and realized he wasn't really surprised that she'd lifted her face up to meet him.

It was soft, that kiss. It was sweet. And it was infused with a wary and tentative awareness. Awareness of the heat. Awareness of the little sparks of electricity arcing between them.

Awareness that they both knew what they were doing this time and where it could lead if they dared take it a little farther.

And oddly, Mac sensed the rightness of it all. In the gentleness in which their lips met. In the honesty of affection that passed between them.

The surprise came after. After he had slowly pulled away. After he'd searched her deep-brown eyes and had finally seen what all this awareness between them was really about.

It was one of those "it all became crystal clear" moments. One of those, "why hadn't he seen this before?" revelations.

What was going on here—it wasn't all about attraction. It wasn't all about need—although both were heavily seeded into the mix.

It was about being alone in the middle of a cold winter night when it appeared that the rest of the world was made of couples. It was about being lonely when both of them did their damnedest to never let that show.

Yeah, he realized as he lifted his hand and gently cupped her cheek. Both of them. He was lonely, too…only, he'd never really realized it until now.

For Shallie he suspected it was also more. It was about being afraid. His Shallie was afraid. Afraid of her future. Afraid of the mistakes of her past. Afraid that what she had now was all there was. And she was afraid she would accept and adjust and miss out on something special because of it.

He saw all of that in her eyes. And he saw it clearly because there wasn't a fear or an emotion that he didn't feel himself.

He was weary of the singles scene. Weary of the shallowness of it all, of the game playing and the sport so many made it. Did he expect to find lasting love? No. Not unless it was with Shallie.

That wasn't going to happen. She was still in pain from another relationship. Another man who had let her down. Left her pregnant and alone.

Alone. Like him. He didn't want to spend the rest of his life alone. And he didn't want mistakes he'd made or mistakes his parents had made to harden him and deprive him of something good.

Here was something good. Something like love. At least on his part. Oh, he knew she didn't love him the same way—not the earth-shattering, can't-live-without-you love. But she loved him just the same.

And he had always loved Shallie.

Would it be so bad, he wondered, to let her know that?

In this moment in time, alone together, could he share that with her? If for no other reason than to prove to her she wasn't alone. That she didn't have to be single in a world full of couples.

He kissed her again. And when she kissed him back, less tentatively now, more giving than guarded as she leaned into him and wrapped her arms around his neck, he knew that he was right on target.

There was power in her give, strength in his take. And there was understanding. Unspoken, unselfish and undeniable.

But most of all…most of all, he realized, there was vulnerability. She was so, so vulnerable.

And the real kicker? So was he—except he'd never realized it until right now.

Maybe he needed to think about this. Really think about whether he was willing to spill his guts and possibly settle for an "I love you but I'm not in love with you" apology.

From the look on her face when he pulled away, she needed some think time, too.

"That way lies trouble," he said with a smile meant to reassure yet make known that they were about to tread a potentially dangerous path if they continued doing what they were doing.

She searched his eyes, finally nodded with a tight, sad smile. "Yeah. That way lies trouble."

He expelled a heavy breath. It wasn't exactly relief he felt that she, too, saw the potential pitfalls if they took this further. It wasn't exactly regret. It was something in between. Enough of something that he knew he really had to think about what was happening here.

He pulled back, tipped her face to his with a finger under her chin. "Okay, then. Once again, we avert disaster."

She smiled, he suspected, because he did. "Once again."

He squeezed her arm. "Go to bed, short-stack. We might actually need to talk about this in the morning."

She nodded, turned to leave, then stopped and, stretching up on her toes, kissed his cheek. Her fingertips trailed across his jaw as she left him.

Six

Morning came. And they didn't talk about it. *It* being what they'd both wanted to do last night. *It* being the fact that they'd both spent restless nights alone in their respective beds thinking about *it*.

Seems they were both big talkers after the sun went down and took a day's worth of inhibitions with it, Shallie thought as she sat in the front seat of Mac's truck as they headed down the highway toward Sundown. But in broad daylight, with a sleepless night behind them and the uncertainty of their relationship looming between them, it was easier not to talk about it at all.

Lord knows, they'd both done enough thinking about it. At least she had.

Mostly what she was thinking was, thank God Mac was the man he was or she might have made the biggest mistake of her life last night. Considering some of the mistakes she'd already made, that was saying something.

She didn't want to lose him. Not her friend. And friends and lovers…well, sooner or later you lost one or the other or both. He must have considered the same outcome because, like her, he didn't bring *it* up.

Instead when they'd gotten up, he'd asked her if she'd like to take a trip to Sundown, check out the cabin and if she liked it, move in.

And out of his hair, she thought as the miles flew by. Yeah. Maybe it was time she got out of his hair and out from under foot. She could use the distance, too. To figure out what she was going to do next. And what exactly she was feeling for Mac.

So, to keep their feelings firmly in check, they talked about the size of the snowdrifts along the highway. About the antelope bounding across the fields beside them. They talked about her broken wrist and about the plans he had for the Dusk to Dawn. They talked about anything but last night, like maybe if the subject didn't come up, it had never happened.

The games people play, she thought with a rueful smile.

"And there she is," Mac said as they descended into the valley and turned the final corner that led to town.

Sundown. Sleepy. Serene. Blanketed in white.

A peaceful stillness settled over her. And then she laughed.

"Oh, my gosh. I see progress has hit the great American West. Sundown's gone from a one-horse town to a one-stoplight town. When did they put the stoplight in?"

"This here ain't no Podunk Hicksville no more, missy," Mac said, launching into his best cowboy geezer voice. "Why, we even got us some o' them whatchacallits...some indoor outhouses." He pretended to spit tobacco out the window, wiped his mouth with his sleeve. "Yessiree, Bob. Up and comin'. That's what's happening here."

They were both grinning when he pulled the truck up in front of the Dusk to Dawn. It was a long building in the middle of the block on Main. The white clapboard siding was weathered but the sign above the double glass doors proclaiming it Dusk to Dawn in bold, shamrock-green letters was crisp and new.

Shallie could see a light on and hear the muffled sound of voices and laughter coming from inside when Mac came around and helped her out of the truck.

"It's open today?"

"Yeah, I decided to open up at noon for anyone who wanted to watch a New Year's Day bowl game."

Judging by the trucks parked outside the bar and restaurant, several people were doing just that.

"Hold on," Mac said when she couldn't figure out the best way get around the three-foot snowbank the plows had pushed up against the curb. "Here's how we'll handle this."

He picked her up, hefted her in his arms and scaled the drift with his long legs.

"He cooks, he does dishes—and he's got a white knight complex," she said batting her eyes at him when he set her down by the front door. "You're a handy man to have around, macaroon."

He laughed as he tugged open the door. "Macaroon. Haven't heard that in an age or two."

And she hadn't *ever* heard the chorus of, "Welcome home!" that greeted her when he set her down inside.

It had been the exact right thing to do, Mac thought, stepping back and watching Shallie become engulfed in a series of hugs and warm welcomes. After he'd made the call to J.T. a couple days ago suggesting they stage a surprise welcome-home party for Shallie, he'd started having second thoughts. Maybe she was a little too fragile right now. Maybe it would be rushing her.

But as he saw her smile of surprise and unqualified happiness as old friends surrounded her, he was glad he'd gone with his gut instinct. And he was glad he'd put J.T. in charge of contacting all the Sundown locals. J.T. was well liked and persuasive. Looked as if it was going to be a helluva party.

Besides the usual suspects who were always up for a party, J.T. and his wife, Ali, and Cutter and Peg Reno and their two kids, Shelby and little Dawson, were here. Among many others, Lee and Ellie Savage had driven in from Shiloh ranch to join the festivities. Crystal and Sam Perkins and their brood were here, too. Even old Snake Gibson, Joe Gilman and the Griener twins had shown up with their wives and kids.

Mac slipped behind the bar to help his manager, Colt Smith, mix another batch of punch for the kids and tap a keg for the adults who wanted something a little more celebratory to commemorate not only Shallie's return but the first day of the New Year.

"You are a sneaky snake," Shallie accused him an hour or so later as she wandered happily up to the bar and plopped on a stool.

"Guilty as charged." He slid a glass of punch across the bar to her as a whoop went up from across the room when someone's favorite team made a touchdown.

"You never said a word." She smiled over the top of her glass.

It was a good smile. A great smile. A smile that said she was happy as hell.

He wiped a bar rag over the worn and scarred oak surface, set a bowl of peanuts in front of her. "Wouldn't have been much of a surprise party if I had."

It had been fun watching her get reacquainted with her friends, Mac thought. But when her head went down—right after he swore he saw a tear, panic hit him like a brick.

"What? What's wrong?"

She shook her head and when she met his eyes again she was smiling and wiping tears at the same time. "This is the…the nicest thing anyone has ever done for me."

Relief was as sweet as the joy in her eyes.

"Thanks, Mac. I mean…really. Thanks for this. It's great."

While he was moved by her words, it was the look on her face that really got to him. He wanted to vault over the bar, gather up in his arms and tell her that if this was the nicest thing anyone had ever done for her, she'd been hanging with the wrong people.

And he might have done just that if J.T. hadn't shown up right then.

"I've been going to tell you that I know a good lawyer," J.T. said with an ornery grin as he slung an arm over Shallie's shoulders. "I figure you could take this no-count busboy to court and end up with everything but his shirt for breaking your arm. Probably get the shirt, too, if you wanted it, but ugly as it is, I'd take a pass."

"Hey, hey," Mac said affecting a wounded look, "don't be giving her any ideas. And you're in a helluva position to be insulting my taste in clothes. Although, now that Ali is picking yours out for you, there has been improvement."

"Just give me a beer, McDonald. I can do without the lip."

"*You* can do without the lip? See what I have to put up with?" Mac appealed to Shallie, who was grinning at the good-natured banter. "And in my own place."

"Yeah, well, you're just lucky we're a tolerant bunch of folks," J.T. continued, accepting his beer with a nod of thanks, "or we'd have run you out of town by now. Come on, Shall. They're about to crank up the karaoke machine."

"I don't care if you drink in here Tyler, but for God's sake, please don't sing."

"You ever see anyone so jealous of natural talent?" J.T. asked over his shoulder as he herded a giggling Shallie toward the stage.

God, it was good to see her smiling so much, Mac thought, resting both hands on the bar as he watched them walk away. Reminded him of when she was a girl and he and J.T. used to talk smack to each other just to make her laugh.

Hadn't seen all that much of her smile since she'd shown up a few days ago, Mac realized, grinning when J.T. dragged her reluctantly up onstage and shoved a mike in her hand to the enthusiastic cheers of the crowd.

No. He hadn't seen her smile all that much. At least not this kind of smile. Spontaneous, not forced. Truly happy, not an attempt to make him think she was happy. He was damn glad he'd had a hand in making her smile today.

And he'd decided he was also glad he'd put a skid on things between them last night and suggested she move into the cabin today. He'd had a moment of weakness. So had she. She was allowed; he wasn't.

She was pregnant, on her own and about as vulnerable as a body could be. She didn't need him sniffing around, putting on the moves and complicating her life even more.

She needed him to be solid and steady and supportive. End of story.

It was going to be hard, though, he thought as he watched her gamely sing along to an old Dolly Parton song. Her cheeks were flushed with embarrassment; her gaze sought him out in a "help me" plea. She looked so happy and so pretty it did all sorts of weird things to his heartbeat.

He made himself grin and gave her a thumb's-up. Then he went back to the kitchen where he could get a firmer grip on his equilibrium and left her in J.T.'s capable hands.

* * *

It was close to five and almost dark by the time Mac pulled his truck up in front of the weathered log cabin in the woods south of Sundown.

"Stay put," he ordered, jumping out from behind the wheel.

When he rounded the truck and opened her door, Shallie understood why. The snow was knee-deep. Only because his truck had four-wheel drive had they made it up the long lane after they'd left the main road.

"You're going to hurt your back hauling me around," she protested as he hefted her into his arms and carried her up the snow-laden steps to the front door.

"I expect insults from J.T. but not from you—not after I threw you a surprise party," he said, grinning.

"How was that an insult?"

"You obviously underestimate my virile manhood if you think that a lightweight like you could—oh. Ouch. Did I say lightweight? How much did you eat today, anyway?"

She cuffed him on the shoulder. "Okay. Okay. Point taken. I won't insult your supermacho ego, and you won't insult my new and piglike eating habits."

"There you go. Key's in my breast pocket," he said with a nod of his chin. "Fish it out, would ya?"

"Or you could just put me down now."

"I could, but the snow on the porch is ankle-deep so all this show of strength would have been for nothing. Now get the key, woman, and let's get out of the cold."

With a shake of her head, Shallie tugged off her glove and dug into his jacket pocket until she came up with the key. He angled her close to the door so she could slip it in the lock.

"Success," he said brightly, then shouldered open the door and deposited her on a bright, woven rug in the small entryway.

"Oh, Mac," she said when he'd flipped on a light switch. "This is charming."

"Okay, we're going to have that semantics problem again, I see. It's supposed to be rustic."

"Charming. Rustic. Whatever. Don't worry your tender sensibilities. It's very masculine. And very homey. I love it."

The cabin wasn't nearly as large as his new house in Bozeman but it was everything a mountain cabin should be. Lots of warm, aged pine covered the walls of a great room that was living room, dining and kitchen all rolled into one. The tall peaked ceiling was crisscrossed with open beams of aged, native pine and hosted a loft at the far end with yet more natural pine railing. A massive stone fireplace commanded the center of the north wall, the fire well deep enough and tall enough to roast half a beef if need be. A wide, four-shelf bookcase loaded with paperbacks, CDs and DVDs filled the wall space between the living and the kitchen area.

"I know people who would kill to spend a single night in a place like this," she said, spotting more and more touches around the cabin that charmed her. Like the ancient webbed snowshoes crisscrossed above a mantel laden with thick, chunky candles. On the brick hearth sat an ornate iron fire-screen molded in the shape of a bear. Comfy mission oak furniture with cushions covered in Native American prints and colors flanked the fireplace.

Outside the cabin was a world of deep greens and winter whites and darkening sky as snow swirled, weighed down pine bows and drifted onto the corners of the multipaned windows. Inside, woven rugs in pallets of reds and blues and greens warmed the great room while Mac struck a match to a fire already laid out in the hearth.

The dry tinder caught quickly, and soon the licking flames of a toasty fire crackled to life, scenting the cabin of pine tinged with the pleasant aroma of wood smoke.

"Not that Sundown or even Bozeman are hubs of urban activity," Shallie said, forgoing a comfy-looking mission oak sofa and rocker to ease down on a soft rug in front of the fire so she could feel the warmth of it heat her cheeks, "but doesn't it feel a little like we passed through a time warp when we closed the cabin door behind us? I mean—I can almost get a feel for what it was like a hundred or so years ago."

"And what's your interpretation of how it felt?" he asked, walking over to a wall and turning up a thermostat that had obviously been set just warm enough to keep water pipes from freezing.

She raised both shoulders, held her hands out to the fire. "Isolated but cozy. Exciting and a little scary. And on a night like this…romantic," she said.

The minute that thought popped out, she wished she could snatch it back. *Romantic* was not a good thought to express at the moment. Not with the two of them alone again and all those unsettled feelings held over from last night.

And definitely not with her still trying to deal with the way it felt to be held in his arms when he'd carried her to the cabin. He made her feel small and feminine. Protected and cared for. And it made her ache—more than a little—to be held by him again, as he'd held her in his arms last night and kissed her.

She was swamped by a heavy wave of confusion. She didn't want to think of Mac in those terms. She had no business thinking of him that way. And yet…and yet he'd kissed her. Twice. How could she not think about it?

"Yeah," he said, snapping her out of her thoughts, "the prospect of ducking out of the cabin in the middle of a night like this to use the facility that, in those days, would have been twenty or so yards from the cabin, does have a romantic ring to it."

She turned to smile at him. Good thing one of them had things in perspective. Romance clearly wasn't on his mind. His next statement cinched it.

"But then, the prospect of hustling out in the cold again in the morning to hunt us up a possum for breakfast, now, that conjures all kinds of romantic thoughts."

She laughed. "Okay. So I may have glossed over a few of the hardships," she conceded. "Still, you have to admit, this place does take you back in time."

"Yeah," he finally agreed. "It's pretty cool. But speaking of possum," he snagged his jacket, "I'd better get those groceries out of the truck before they freeze or I *will* be hunting up our breakfast in the morning."

When he went outside Shallie rose and explored the

rest of the cabin. Besides the great room and the kitchen, there were two roomy bedrooms with a shared bath between them on the main level. Upstairs, in the loft, was a small sitting area and an open bedroom.

She heard the door open, then Mac's voice boom up the stairs. "Where'd you go?"

"I'm up here."

She started back down the stairs as Mac kicked the door shut behind him, stomped the snow off his shoes, then headed for the kitchen area with his arms full of groceries.

To the fire scents, he added the smell of winter— cool, crisp air and night. It clung to his jacket as she joined him and dug, one-handed, into a sack to help him put the groceries away.

It all felt very homey and domestic. As well as cozy and warm and…right. Just like it felt right to be standing beside him and feeling a warm and encompassing glow.

"Are you planning on feeding a football team?"

"A woman who's eating for two," he said, reaching behind her to open the refrigerator door and stow a carton of milk. "Can't have you going hungry just in case we get stranded out here."

She glanced out the window over the sink where the snow was still swirling. "You think that's a possibility?"

"Not in the next week or so. What you see moving around out there is the wind blowing snow off the trees— but you never know, so I wanted you to be well stocked."

He shoved a dozen eggs and some lunch meat into the fridge. "Before I leave for Bozeman tomorrow I'll put the blade on the truck and clear the lane. There's a four-wheel-drive Jeep in the garage you can use when you want to go into town. It's an automatic so you shouldn't have any trouble driving it."

She felt the tears before she even knew she was going to cry. They just welled up out of nowhere. And so fast, she couldn't hide them.

"Hey. Hey," Mac said so softly when he realized what was going on that it made her cry harder. "What's this? What's wrong? Is it your wrist? Are you hurting?"

Horrified by her outburst, she shook her head, then looked away from him, trying to hide her embarrassment over the sudden attack of waterworks. He wasn't having it.

"Come 'ere," he said gently and, tucking her under his broad shoulder, walked her into the living area and sat her down with him on the sofa. "Tell Daddy all about it."

She pushed out a weak laugh, then sniffed and buried her face in his neck. He still smelled of winter and a little like the Dusk to Dawn and a lot like Mac. Subtly spicy, warm male heat, comfort and strength.

"Come on," he coaxed when she couldn't find the words to express what she was feeling. He cupped her head in his big hand, lightly tapped a finger. "What's going on in there?"

And the dam broke. One moment she couldn't articulate a thing, the next, she was spilling out her feelings like water spilling over a broken dike.

"How did I get myself in this fix? How did I get to the point where I have to rely on the generosity of friends to feed me, to put a roof over my head? To shore up my bruised and battered ego by throwing me a party to take my mind off the fact that I'm without income, without prospects and without a father for this poor little child who never asked to be born to a woman who doesn't have the good sense to take care of herself?"

She stopped long enough to wipe her nose with the tissue he handed her. "I hate it. I hate taking advantage of you. I hate blubbering like a sissy every time my hormones get a little out of whack. I hate lying to Peg and J.T.—at least lying by omission—and not telling them about the baby. I hate thinking that all my life I was ashamed of my mother for relying on cheap men to make her happy, for not loving me enough to make her happy, for…for making such awful judgments in her life. And now…here I am. I'm just like her."

"You are nothing like your mother," he said, her white knight defending her honor. "You're kind and you're smart and I've already seen that you want and love this baby. And you'll love and care for your child. That's something your mother never did for you."

She sniffed again, snuggled closer into the sheltering warmth he offered and felt more hot tears track down her cheeks. "Why couldn't she love me, Mac? What was wrong with me that made it so hard for her to love me?"

His strong arms wrapped her even tighter. "Nothing was wrong with you. Nothing *is* wrong with you. Nothing, you got that?" he added adamantly. "The problem was with her.

"Who knows," he added after a moment. "Who knows what happens to some people to make them the way they are. Maybe she was abused when she was a kid. Maybe she was giving you the best she knew how to give. I don't know," he said quietly. "I don't know what made her tick. But I do know about you. I know what you're made of, short-stack. I knew it the first time I saw you standing up to the Griener boys."

She sniffed again, tipped her head back so she could see his face. "The Griener boys?"

He smiled, all sleepy and slow. "You don't remember?"

"I remember attempting to neuter one of them with my knee."

"I know. I saw it. And I was in awe."

His exaggerated, awestruck look made her grin. "You were afraid you were next, is more like it."

"That, too," he confessed, "but more than that, I saw someone who knew how to take care of herself. And I saw someone I admired. I still see someone I admire," he added before she could make a case for him thinking otherwise.

"You get up, Shallie," he said, tucking her head under his chin. "You take a hit and you get up. You always have. You always will. That's a lot to admire in a person. And that's one of the things I admire about you."

She didn't see much to admire. She saw a lot of mistakes, and they felt too heavy on her shoulders to move her out from under the sense of failure that had settled in for the night.

"You're tired," he said. "You've had a big day. Lots of emotions flowing, right?"

She sniffed. "Stop being so nice to me. I'll just get all blubbery again." She sat up and wiped her eyes. "God. I *hate* this. And don't look at me. I'm a mess."

"So's my shirt," he said, tugging the wet cloth away from his shoulder with such an exaggerated frown he made her laugh. Which, of course, is what he wanted her to do.

"Thanks," she said.

"For being a friend? Hey, you'd do the same for me."

"I don't know," she said, finally mustering up enough spunk to feel a little ornery, "if you threw a hissy fit like that, I'd probably tell you to take a pill."

"See, there's that respect thing again," he groused, even though his grin said he was glad to see her rallying. "I don't get any from J.T., and now I'm not getting any from you."

Shallie woke to the sound of silence. The sunshine slanting in through the cabin window was so brilliant and bright it was almost blinding. The plump down comforter covering her was warm and cocooning. She felt as if she was lying in a nest of feathers, all soft and snug and sheltering. And if it weren't for the demands of her bladder, she'd simply lie there for, oh, another decade or two, and wallow in all this homespun comfort.

The cabin was empty when she tiptoed out of the bathroom a few minutes later. She smelled coffee and followed her nose to the kitchen where, typical of Mac, he'd set food out for her. Chocolate-covered donuts, chocolate iced éclairs, and according to the note he'd set on the counter beside them, there was also tiramisu in the fridge.

She felt a smile crawl across her face. "That man would see me as plump as a Christmas goose if I'm not careful."

It was cute the way he coddled her. Took care of her. Made certain she had her daily chocolate hits. And if she wasn't careful in that area, she told herself as she filled a mug with coffee and wandered toward the big window in the living area that overlooked the forest, all this TLC could become addictive.

In particular, all this TLC from a *man* could become a habit. She'd never had a father to turn to while growing up. Jared had been her only steady relationship, and even before he'd gotten violent, he hadn't been the attentive or coddling kind. In fact, she realized now as she caught a glimpse of Mac behind the wheel of his big black truck, pushing snow with a blade attached to the front of the vehicle, Jared hadn't contributed much of anything in the TLC department. He'd been silent and stoic and, well, she could see now, he'd been a user.

Hmm. Funny how time and distance could add a little perspective. Too bad she hadn't had this kind of perspective when she'd gone "looking for love in all the wrong places" that night three months ago, she thought with a heavy sigh. She wouldn't be in this fix—depending on Mac. Living a lie.

She took a sip of her coffee; Mac made the best coffee.

As she watched him through the window, a fresh wave of guilt swamped her. She should tell him about the baby's conception.

She should tell him.

He looked up from his work about then, spotted her watching him and shot her a big sexy grin and a wave.

She waved back, and that wave of guilt gained weight and settled like a five-hundred-pound monkey on her back.

Yeah. She should tell him. But she just couldn't bear to see the look on his face when he found out the truth. At the moment he was the only stable, caring element in her life. In the short span of a few days, he had become everything to her. Provider. Friend. Family.

She'd always considered herself a strong person. She'd survived a childhood without a father, without the love of her mother. From the time she could remember, she felt as if she'd been on her own.

And now here was Mac. And now she couldn't imagine getting through this point in her life without him.

So no, she wouldn't tell him, because right now, this moment in time, as guilty as it made her feel, she needed him. Needed what he gave her. And of all the things he provided—food, shelter, transportation—it was his friendship, his unbridled affection for her that she needed most.

If she told him, she'd lose him.

"Oh, by the way this baby's father didn't leave me, like you think. No, this baby's father is a married man. Yeah. That's right. I slept with a married man. A man who has children of his own who need their daddy, rat-bastard that he is. He doesn't even know about the baby. He'll never know. At least, he wouldn't find out from me because he doesn't deserve to know."

And because I will not be responsible for breaking up a family, she vowed firmly. It was a little late to think about those particular consequences of her stupidity, but on that count she would not budge.

Mac waved at her again and shot her another big, goofy grin.

No. She would not tell him. Because she would not, could not, lose him.

Seven

"Shouldn't you be wearing your sling?" Mac came in from shoveling and pushing snow to find Shallie dressed and putting the finishing touches on toasted cheese sandwiches and tomato soup.

She was wearing a pair of worn jeans and a pretty pink sweater that made her cheeks look pink, too.

"Doctor said to use my own judgment. And right now it's in my way."

"You didn't have to do this," he said, slipping out of his vest and hanging it on a coat hook by the kitchen door.

"But I wanted to," she said with a smile. "A hardworking man's got to have something warm to eat when he comes in from the cold."

"Hardworking? I'll let you in on a little secret. Any

time I get to play with something with that much horse-power, I'm literally playing, not working."

"Boys and their power tools," she said with an exaggerated indulgent look.

He made a grunting, he-man sound and beat on his chest. "Me love horsepower and snow blades."

She laughed. He loved the sound.

"All right, tool man, take time out from the macho stuff and refuel, will ya? Eat while everything's hot."

"You shouldn't have any trouble getting out of the lane and into town now," he said, washing his hands at the sink. "I pushed snow all the way to the road, and the weather forecast calls for clear skies and light winds the next few days so there shouldn't be any drifting."

"I can't imagine that I'll need to go anywhere. There's enough food to last for a month, you've got a library that would take a speed reader a decade to plow through and enough movies to start a rental business. Besides. This cabin is like something out of a fairy tale. I don't think I ever want to leave it."

"Just the same, I'll feel better knowing that you can get out if you need or want to. Um. Good," he added, sitting down at the table and digging into his lunch.

"So, you're heading back to Bozeman?" she asked, oh, so casually as she sat down across from him at the small table.

Mac wasn't certain if he heard a little disappointment in her question. Wasn't certain if he was glad or concerned that she might miss him.

"Yeah," he said, "I need to get back to the restaurant.

I promised Cara a few days off this week, and I'll need to cover for her."

Then something else occurred to him. Maybe it wasn't the prospect of missing him that made her seem a little reluctant to see him go. "Hey, short-stack. In spite of all this talk of loving the cabin, are you worried about being out here all by yourself?"

"Absolutely not. And I do love the cabin."

"So, you're going to be okay on your own?"

"Mac. I've been on my own for a long time now. I'll be fine."

She'd been on her own too long, Mac thought when he left her an hour later as he drove down the highway toward Bozeman. Maybe that's why it had been hard for him to leave her there.

Maybe that's why he kept thinking about turning around, telling her to repack her bag and come back to Bozeman with him.

The truth was, he was going to miss her like hell. How could that be? Until last week he hadn't seen her for ten years. How could you miss someone who hadn't even been in your life for a decade?

How? Because he'd loved her all that time, that's how. And he'd missed her all that time, too.

He thought about her way too much during the next few days. Called her several times a day because he wanted to make sure she was doing okay.

And because he wondered what she was doing. If she was curled up with her nose in a book or doing something homey around the cabin.

He thought about how quiet his new house seemed

when he came home after a day at SW—which didn't make a lick of sense because he'd lived alone for almost ten years now, if you didn't count his college days when he'd lived first in a dorm, then in a frat house.

It wasn't as if he'd ever had a woman live with him, yet all of a sudden he missed the softness one could bring to a room. And the scent. Shallie definitely had a scent. In the middle of winter she smelled like spring flowers. Funny, he thought as he checked with his chef over the evening's specials. Funny how he thought of that now. With marinara sauce bubbling on the stove and garlic bread baking in the oven, he thought of spring flowers and Shallie.

"Phone call, Mac," his bookkeeper said, poking her head out of the office.

"Who is it?"

"Don't know. She's got a nice voice, though," she said with a grin.

His spirits dropped when it was a salesperson on the other end of the line instead of Shallie.

And it was then he decided he'd had enough of missing her. He was wired for sound when he pulled into the drive at the cabin and saw Shallie bundled up in her jacket and waving at him from the front porch.

It had been four days since he'd left her there. Since he'd scooped out the lane, shoveled the porch and left her with orders to call him if she needed anything. He'd also left J.T.'s and Peg's phone numbers with her in case she needed someone close and in a hurry.

Well, he'd come in a hurry—whether she needed him or not. And he'd be damned if he knew exactly what he had in mind now that he was here.

* * *

"What do you think?" Shallie asked, surveying her handiwork. Well, technically, it was her idea but Mac's work.

"I like it," he said, studying the new furniture arrangement with a critical eye. "Should have been this way all along. And I like that wreath over the mantel, too. What I don't like is thinking about how you managed to get it up there."

"No ladders involved, I promise," she said, plopping down on the sofa that now faced the fire and the TV, which sat on a stand to the left of the hearth. "I got it down with a hoe I found in the shed. Then I propped it on the mantel and used the hoe again to lift it from there and slid it on the hook."

"Very resourceful," Mac said, sitting down beside her. "Now hand over that popcorn."

It was funny, Shallie thought as they sat there and one of the DVDs began to play. He'd been gone four days.

She'd thought she would enjoy the solitude. And she had, but she'd also found herself waiting for the phone to ring, knowing when it did that it would be Mac. And it had rung. Often. And they would talk—sometimes for an hour or more. She couldn't remember now what they'd found to talk about. Nothing, mostly. But they'd laughed a lot and he'd fussed over whether she was taking care of herself, and she'd taken great pleasure in telling him that yes, she was being a good girl.

Silly banter. Necessary contact.

And now the contact was physical.

His thigh brushed hers as they sat side by side. She

tried really hard not to notice how strong that thigh was. How much heat his big body generated or how good he smelled. Just like she tried not to make a big deal of it when their fingers tangled, then dueled in the bowl of popcorn she'd popped for the "pseudo movie theater experience" as she'd told him.

"I can't believe these movies hold up after all these years."

They'd loved *Star Wars* when they were kids. They loved it now. Mostly she loved that Mac was back in Sundown and that he planned to spend the night at the cabin.

Truth was, she loved it a little too much.

Since he'd left her four days ago, she'd had a lot of time to think about that kiss New Year's Eve. A lot of time alone. A lot of time wishing they might have talked about it as they'd planned.

She wondered if he thought about it, too.

Beside her he smelled warm and wintry at the same time. She glanced sideways at him. The fire glow did incredible things to his profile as he slouched back on the sofa, his gaze locked on the TV.

Too much of a good thing. Now Shallie knew what that cliché meant. Mac was too much of everything. Too handsome. Too sexy. And tonight probably too close for comfort, given the haywire state of her hormones, which had chosen tonight to remind her she was a woman, with woman's needs.

She had to back away from that line of thought. She had to keep things on an even keel. So when he lifted his hand to dig into the popcorn bowl, she inched it away from him and prepared to shift into good-ol'-buddy sparring mode.

When he felt blindly around for the bowl, she moved it again until she had set it all the way to her left side. Since he was sitting on her right, it finally dawned on him that something was amiss.

"Hey," he squawked when he finally tore his gaze from the movie and discovered that she'd deliberately moved the popcorn out of his reach. "What's the deal?"

"No deal," she said with a shrug.

"Then give me some popcorn before you find yourself in some trouble."

"You want popcorn? Open your mouth."

He was on to her game but went along with it, anyway. "Bet you can't hit it," he challenged and opened wide.

She laughed and, taking aim, tossed one his way.

"That's the best you got?" he taunted, when she missed.

"I can do this," she insisted and tried again. And missed again, several times.

They were both laughing when he reached for the bowl. "A man could starve while you take potshots. Now gimme some of that popcorn."

"No problem." She pelted him with a handful.

He opened his mouth. Shut it. Narrowed his eyes.

"Okay. Now you've done it," he warned, and with a quick, deft move, managed to swipe the bowl away from her.

"Hey, give that back."

"My pleasure." Digging a big hand into the bowl, he fired a handful and hit her full in the face.

She fell back against the sofa cushions, laughing as popcorn cascaded over her head and shoulders. "I don't believe you did that."

"Believe it. You didn't really think you were going to get the best of me," he said, holding the bowl above his head and out of her reach.

"But I'm incapacitated," she wailed between giggles and plucked popcorn out of her hair. "You're supposed to let me win."

"You obviously have never read the bully's handbook. Now hold still," he said, swinging his leg over her lap, then straddling her with his knees dug into the cushions on either side of her hips. "You're about to get full payback for making me suffer through popcorn deprivation."

She shrieked and held up her cast to ward off the attack—not that it did any good.

He dumped the bowl over her head. Popcorn rained down all over her.

"You are crazy!"

"You started it."

So she had.

And as the room suddenly became very quiet, except for the war of spaceships going on in the background, she realized that Mac had become very quiet, too.

He wasn't laughing anymore, either.

Neither was she.

In fact, she was barely breathing…yet very aware of every breath. His as much as hers.

His chest was broad and hard beneath a thick navy-blue sweater. She could see the rise and fall of it so very close in front of her.

She chanced a glance up to meet his eyes, had to lean her head back on the sofa cushion to make eye contact as he stood on his knees poised over her.

He was watching her with eyes that had gone dark and searching. And testing. And asking the same thing she was thinking.

If he lowered his mouth, would she let him kiss her?

She heard a soft plunk, realized he'd tossed the empty bowl beside them on the sofa. Very slowly he lowered his hands to the cushion on either side of her head.

He searched her face, slowly shook his head. "You are one fine mess, Shallie Malone."

Oh, yeah. She was a mess all right. And not just from the popcorn. Her heart was knocking like an air hammer. Her breath was short and choppy. And if she got any hotter, she was going to have to take off some clothes.

Yikes. The look in his eyes told her he was thinking along the same lines.

"You…you made me this way," she managed on a faint, thready breath.

"Messy?" he asked, his voice whisper soft and spring-water deep.

She swallowed, slowly nodded. Messy. Yeah. And hot. And bothered and, man—

"Guess I'll just have to clean you up, then."

Before she could even gulp, he was doing an impro-vised pushup, lowering his upper body toward her and—oh, sweet heaven above—nibbling popcorn off her shoulders.

"I...um..."

"Shh. Hold still," he whispered, working his mouth along her collarbone, "this is man's work. I need to concentrate."

"Oh. Oh...okay," was the best she could do as he moved back and forth, his mouth gentle, his breath July hot against her throat, against her jaw...against the corner of her mouth.

"Umm. Salty," he murmured taking his time and licking her bottom lip. "And very, very sweet."

His lips felt incredible as they cruised over her face. She could feel the slight abrasive scrape of a day's growth of beard, smell the subtle scent of his after-shave. And, oh, my, she thought as the touch of his lips on the tender skin behind her earlobe made her shiver, she could very easily lose herself in the overwhelming sensuality of what he was doing to her.

Don't stop, she thought. Please, don't stop this time. To make certain he didn't, she lifted her right arm, buried her fingers in the coarse silk of his hair.

"Shallie." His voice sounded raspy, tightly reined. He closed his eyes. Pressed his forehead to hers. "We might be in a little trouble here again. We definitely should have that talk."

"Don't want to talk," she whispered, and lifted her mouth up to his, chasing it when he pulled away.

"Be sure," he said, more plea than warning, "Be very, very sure this is what you want."

She was sure. She was sure she was lost. So very,

very lost in the promise of his kisses, in the tenderness of his touch. And she trusted him. To make everything be all right between them. To make this one of the best experiences of her life.

"I want," she whispered and pulled him back down to her mouth for a long, hungry kiss.

And it was hunger she felt. Hunger to be held. Hunger to be loved. Hunger to believe that finally, finally, she was with a man—a good man—she could trust to always be honest with her.

Honest with his passion. Honest with his expectations. Honest with his love.

And Mac did love her. Just like she loved him. It was the best kind of love. The kind that came without complications. The kind that came from being friends. And this friend would take special care to make things good. To make things right.

She couldn't even call it surrender when he stood, lifted her in his arms and carried her to his bedroom. And she definitely couldn't call it defeat. What she could call it was wonderful as he laid her down on his big bed and then tugged his sweater up and over his head.

Mac knew he shouldn't be doing this. He knew he should be the one to stop it. And if she said the word, he would. In a heartbeat.

But she hadn't said stop. She'd said go. In the thick, rapid beat of her heart. In the long, burning look in her eyes.

He bent over her, kissed her long and deep. And felt one final tug of conscience.

"You sure you're up for this?"

She closed her eyes. And damned if all of her certainty didn't dissolve into a misty panic. "Am I making a fool of myself?"

Oh, God. "For making love with me?"

She swallowed. "For thinking…for wanting…" She hesitated. Looked away.

"For wanting something more for yourself?" he finished for her.

When she nodded, he cupped her jaw, gently turned her head back so she had to look at him. "Not a fool. You're just a little lonely. Just like me," he admitted, then smiled when he saw the disbelief in her eyes.

"Where's the harm, Shallie? We're both unattached, healthy adults who care deeply about each other. I trust you. You trust me. What could possibly be wrong with making each other feel good?"

"Nothing," she whispered. "Nothing at all."

"So we won't be sorry in the morning?"

All her hesitation had faded. She smiled for him. "I've been sorry for a lot of things in my life. I can't imagine that spending a night with you would be one of them."

He breathed a huge breath of relief. "Friends and lovers. Has a nice ring to it." He reached for the hem of her sweater.

"Who knew," he said when he'd helped her out of her clothes and she lay before him in nothing but a pair of lilac bikini panties. "Who knew my little short-stack was so…well…stacked," he finished, because he knew it would make her smile and because she was even more than he'd imagined beneath her jeans and sweaters.

Soft and full. Feminine and beautiful. He lowered his head, bussed his nose around a velvet-soft nipple.

"Are you sensitive?" he asked, remembering that he'd read a pregnant woman's nipples could be very sensitive and sore.

"A little," she admitted.

"Then you'll tell me if I'm too rough," he said just before he surrounded all that velvety softness with his mouth. He suckled her with special care, laved her budding nipple with his tongue and knew from the way she arched into his mouth that she liked it.

That was good. He liked it, too. Liked the way she tasted. Loved the texture and the heat and the plump fullness of her in his mouth. Loved it so much, his sex knotted tight when she moaned and sighed and urged him with the touch of her hand to the back of his head to take her deeper.

He did it gladly. Beneath his hands she felt like silk. All supple, graceful limbs, and skin as fluid as water, as hot as a winter fire.

Her hips were slim. Her tummy still flat, and while he'd seen her legs a hundred times when they'd been kids in the summer, he'd never touched her. The length of her calf. The inside of her knee. The tender flesh where her thighs joined, and a damp scrap of lilac lace—the only barrier between them.

"Okay?" he whispered against her breast when he slipped his fingers inside her panties and met with damp curls.

"Mmm."

He chuckled. "I'll take that as a yes."

"Mmm." She expelled a deep, restless breath when his finger found her wet and slick and swollen and open for him.

A very sensual woman was one Ms. Shallie Malone, Mac thought as he teased her with long strokes just so he could hear that delicious sigh, just so he could feel that quivering little eddy of shock ripple through her.

She was so special to him, he thought, pulling away from her long enough to shuck his jeans and briefs then skim her panties down her hips.

"Tell me what you like, Shall," he whispered, laving attention on her breast again when he'd lie back down beside her. Her skin burned his where they met, naked and needy for the very first time.

"Everything." She lifted her good arm and touched him, experimentally stroking his chest, the line of his hip, searching for his erection between them. Finding. Caressing. Making him moan. "I like everything you're doing to me."

"Oh, sweet woman. I haven't even got started."

"Seriously?" she asked with such a sober look that he laughed. Until she added, "In my experience, by this point in the process, anything to do with me as something other than a receptacle is pretty much over."

He scowled down at her. He didn't want to think about the guy who had cheated on her. He didn't want to bring him into this bed. But he was there just the same. And all Mac could think was the guy was not only a cheating bastard, he was a *selfish* cheating bastard.

"Well hang on, darlin'," he whispered, working his mouth along the fragile line of her rib cage, stopping to indulge in the delectable little dent of her navel. "Before I'm through with you, we're going to reinvent that process."

"I...um...we are?"

She hiked herself up on her elbows, looked down at him as he eased down the bed and made a comfy place for himself between her thighs.

"You...umm...really?" Her words came out on a quivering sigh when he lowered his mouth to her damp curls and kissed her there.

"Me. Umm. Yeah. Really."

And then he proceeded to really, really take her someplace she'd evidently never been before.

She tasted amazing. She made sounds of stunned wonder. And when she finally decided she could relax and let him have his way with her, she opened for him like a flower, came in his mouth with a shattered cry and collapsed back onto the mattress with a serrated gasp.

He was smiling when he crawled back up the bed and settled carefully over her slack and sated body.

"Well?" He nuzzled her neck, licked the salt of her sweat from her skin.

"I always thought," she said breathlessly as she raised a limp hand and cupped his face, "that *necessity* was the mother of invention. Here it was sex. Who knew?"

He chuckled and kissed her.

"Mac." She broke the kiss, made sure he was looking at her. "Thank you. That was...incredible."

"*You* are incredible," he said and, wedging his knee between her thighs, eased himself inside her giving warmth. "Now let's try for amazing."

It *was* amazing. The way she took him in. The way she gloved him, held him and became for him everything he needed her to be.

Supple strength. Sensual woman.

It touched him, the way she gave. Destroyed him, the way she clung then rode with him to a place they'd never been together.

Eight

This was the part where she should be feeling remorse, Shallie thought as Mac slept beside her. This is the part where she should be thinking, Oh my God. What have I done?

But as this big, gorgeous and sensitive man lay with his head on her breast, his arm slung over her waist and his muscled thigh thrown across hers, all she could do was smile.

Who knew? Who knew sex could be about more than giving? Not that giving to Mac wasn't wonderful, but, oh, wow. Taking was a whole new experience for her. And he made it so easy.

He made it so…amazing.

He made it so good, that for the first time she under-stood what all the fuss was about. Just like she understood she'd been looking for something with Jared that she was never going to find. He hadn't been capable of this kind of generosity.

"You're awfully quiet."

Mac's voice, deep and sleepy, roused her from her thoughts.

"That's because I'm very relaxed."

"Relaxed? Not regretful?"

"No." She lifted her hand and touched his hair. "I'm not regretful. What about you?"

He hiked himself up on an elbow, smiled down at her in the pale lamplight. "Does this face look like the face of a man feeling regret?"

She smiled back, stroked his hair. "Actually, it looks like the face of a very generous, very sensitive lover."

"We aim to please," he said capturing her hand in his, then pressing a kiss to her palm.

"You've got great aim there Mr.…what did you say your name was again?"

He grinned up at her from beneath sinfully thick lashes. "Lucky. My friends call me Lucky. And what can I call you?"

"Satisfied," she said on a sigh, then stretched in contentment when he kissed his way down the length of her arm, lingering at her inner elbow.

She liked this. This peaceful, easy feeling. This playful sexy banter. But most of all she liked the way he made her feel.

She especially liked the way she felt right now. She was tired, sated and, thanks to the tender attention he was paying to the under side of her arm, which just happened to be in close proximity to her right breast, she was feeling very achy and anxious again.

"You have a beautiful body, short-stack," he murmured as he kissed a circle around her breast, his lips gentle, his breath warm, his tongue skilled, as he lapped at her nipple and brought it to a tight, aching peak.

"You're pretty gorgeous yourself," she said, running her hand down the lean, ropey muscles of his back.

"You do," he said, lifting his head, "have a problem," biting her gently on the chin, "with semantics."

She laughed when he rolled to his back and brought her with him. "Okay," she conceded as she straddled his lap, "not gorgeous. Handsome. Manly. Muy macho. And…oh," she gasped as he settled her over his heat and eased her down onto him.

"You were saying?" He was doing a little gasping, too, as his big hands grasped her hips and moved her slowly up and down.

"Hmm? Mmm. What?"

She couldn't think for the way he felt so deep inside of her. Could barely catch a breath and he expected her to talk?

Her breasts felt heavy. Her heart felt light. And the ache building low in her belly where they met and parted, met and parted, grew to a want so huge, a yearning so vast, it consumed her. Body. Soul. Spirit.

And if she wasn't careful, she thought moments later as she sprawled exhausted and sweaty and spent on his heaving chest, her heart was also going to take a fall.

But she wasn't going to think about that now. She

wasn't going to think about anything but the moment. This special, magical moment where she could give with total trust, take without inhibition. A moment that was hers.

She'd had too much taken away from her in her life. Nothing was going to take this away.

Mac was just debating about mixing up some pancake batter when Shallie, bundled from chin to shin in his navy-blue terry cloth bathrobe and wearing a pair of his wool socks, came padding into the kitchen.

Love hit him smack in the chest like a bullet. God, he loved this woman. It had taken every ounce of restraint not to tell her exactly that when he took her to bed. But he knew his Shallie. The *L* word would have scared her off.

Hell. It scared him and he was the one who wanted to say it.

"Your thermostat running a little on the cold side this morning?" he asked, leaning a hip against the kitchen counter and grinning at the house-frau picture she made.

Her hands were lost in the sleeves of the robe as she shuffled over to the counter and poured coffee into a mug he'd set out for her. "Seems I slept cuddled up to a furnace last night. I haven't acclimated to the loss of the heat source just yet."

"Hmm. How about I make the transition a little easier?" He walked up to her, wrapped his arms around her and pulled her close. "How's that?"

She nestled her head on his shoulder. "I'd say that's just about perfect."

Feeling more contentment that he figured he should

be feeling, Mac just held her that way for a while. She didn't seem to mind. And when he started to sway back and forth—just a little—she started humming. The next thing you knew, they were doing a little slow dance in place, her in his ratty robe, him in his bare feet and jeans.

And damn, if all didn't seem right with his world.

He needed to make sure, though, that things were truly okay in hers. "So, we're good, right?" He tucked his chin to look down at her.

"I'd say we're pretty damn spectacular," she said looking mighty pleased with herself.

"Yeah," he agreed with a final squeeze. "We are."

So. Everything was good. Everything was fine. They'd both scratched an itch. They'd given and received affection and pleasure. And they weren't going to make a big deal of it in the morning.

But later he planned to make a very big deal of it. Later, when she got used to the idea of him and her together. And during the night, when he wasn't making love to her or sleeping, he thought he'd come up with a way to make palatable for her the idea of the two of them together forever.

"How's that cast-iron stomach of yours doing? You up for some pancakes?"

"Don't you ever get tired of cooking for me?" She took her coffee to the table and sat down.

"I'm in the wrong business if cooking tires me out."

"That's what I mean. You shouldn't have to cook when you're away from the restaurant."

"Unless I want to," he pointed out. "And I want to."

"What can I do?"

"Just sit there and look hungry."

"Ha. I can do that without working up a sweat. Speaking of sweat," she unknotted the belt of his robe. "Thanks for warming me up."

"My pleasure."

And it truly had been. All night long.

They were snuggled up on the sofa later that afternoon, sipping hot chocolate, making stabs at reading, but mostly watching the fire and the falling snow. Mac's back was at one end of the sofa and Shallie's at the other; they'd been playing a hit-and-miss game of footsie beneath an old patchwork quilt when Shallie realized Mac was watching her.

She looked up over her open book. "What?"

His expression was thoughtful, searching. "We should get married."

She considered his statement, decided he was just being silly and went back to her mystery novel. "Sure. Okay. Whatever."

The silence from the other end of the sofa lasted a little too long, prompting her to look up again. Her heart kicked her a couple of good ones when she realized he was still watching her. And that he was serious.

"Think about it," he said as if he *had* been doing a lot of thinking about it. "We're not kids, Shall. We're not looking for storybook, fairy-tale love. We're not foolish enough to think that it even exists. Hell. Look at my parents. They were wild, crazy in love when they got married. Seems that ten years later, neither one of them remembered what the fuss was about. The next ten years they just stuck it out because they were too stubborn to fix it…or too mired in their own misery to do anything about it."

He leaned forward, all earnest eyes and handsome face. "I never knew. Never knew they weren't happy together. Never knew that Mom wanted to travel and Dad refused to go any farther than Bozeman. She wanted excitement. He wanted status quo. They were miserable.

"Anyway, Mom finally left him." He tried to sound casual, but his face had grown hard. "I understood that part. More or less, anyway. But it was how she did it that I'll never be able to forgive."

A sinking sensation swamped Shallie as she waited for him to explain. She had a horrible feeling that she didn't want to hear the rest. She was right.

"She had an affair. Some guy from Bozeman. A married man."

Shallie's heart dropped like a stone.

"How…uh, how are they doing…um, now, I mean, since the divorce?" she finally managed to ask, while his words rattled around in her head: an affair…with a married man…never be able to forgive.

He lifted a shoulder. "Dad's doing okay, I guess. It's been five years now. He more or less buries himself in work, lets the rest of the world go by."

"And your mom?" she asked softly while her heart pounded so loud it almost drowned out her question.

Another shrug. A disinterested look that didn't quite ring true. "No clue. Haven't seen or talked to her since she left him."

"Oh, Mac." Shallie could hear the hurt in his voice.

The disillusion. She ached for him. He'd loved his mother. Adored her. And Carol McDonald had adored her son. It broke her heart to hear they had lost contact.

She suspected that it broke his, too, because he quickly moved on.

"The point is, I've got a ton of friends in the same boat as they were. Either trapped in a marriage they no longer have a stomach for or divorced and looking to make the same mistake all over again."

She shot him a concerned look. "So now you want to join the ranks? Make your own mistake?" she asked, hoping to help him realize he was talking nonsense.

"See, that's the thing. We wouldn't be making the same mistakes they did. We know going in what we are to each other. You're my best friend."

"And you're mine," she agreed, "but—"

"No wait. What better foundation could you build a marriage on? Friendship. Respect. Trust. Most important, trust and honesty. We could make this work.

"Plus we've got this damn hot chemistry going on," he added with a grin. "And the baby. I don't want you raising this baby by yourself. It's not fair to you. It's not fair to little Heathcliff. Or little Gertrude," he added with another soft smile.

She studied his beautiful, sincere face. Yes, there was friendship. Yes, there was respect. And the chemistry was incredible. But trust? She trusted him, absolutely. But that coin didn't flip both ways. She didn't deserve *his* trust. She'd lied to him. And God help her, she would continue to lie to him about the baby's father because she just couldn't bear to see the look in his eyes if he knew the whole truth. Especially now that she knew how he felt about his mother.

"Unless," he said, a deep crease forming between his brows, "are you still in love with him, Shallie?"

Oh, it hurt to see that compassion in his eyes. And while it would have been her out—she could flat out lie to him and tell him that yes, she was in love with the father and he would probably back away—she just couldn't do it.

"No. I'm not in love with him. I don't think I ever was," she realized as she thought about Jared. "I just wanted to be."

"See," he scooted forward, looking unreasonably happy. He wrapped his arms around her raised knees and rested his chin on them, "that's what I mean. We all think we want something that doesn't exist. So why not take advantage of something that does?"

When she continued to frown at him, he let out a deep sigh, smiled. "Think about it, okay? Just think about it."

"Okay. I'll think about it. But you'd better think about it, too, friend of mine. Think about why you want to do this. Ask yourself if any of the reasons have anything to do with what *you* want or if they're all about this white knight thing you've got going on. I don't want you offering yourself up for a lifetime commitment for my sake. Not even for the baby's sake."

"Fair enough," he said after another long, searching look. "I'll give it some more thought—providing you seriously consider it, too."

"Do I have to be serious about it right now?" she felt an almost-panicky need to lighten the tension his suggestion had knotted tight in the room. "'Cause the only thing I'd like to get serious about is a nap."

One corner of his beautiful mouth turned up in a crooked grin. "I could go for a nap. Want some company?"

"Depends."

"On?"

"On whether we're going to take this nap with our clothes on or off."

His eyes flickered with fire. "I vote for off."

"Then it's unanimous," she said, and let him draw her into his arms for a long, hot kiss.

"Who knew we'd be so good at this together?" he said, after they'd done everything but nap.

"Yeah," she murmured on contented sigh, just before she nodded off. "Who knew."

She couldn't quite define the feeling. But she liked it, Shallie thought a few days later while she sat in a corner booth at the Dusk to Dawn watching Mac and J.T. give each other grief.

Maybe it was that sense of belonging she'd been looking for when she'd made the decision to return to Sundown. Maybe it was just being around these wonderful people who had welcomed her back—or in Ali's case, had accepted her as a friend.

She finally felt like she was a part of something. Something solid. Something good—which was a rare and special feeling for her.

"You'd think they would run out of insults after a while," Ali Tyler, J.T.'s wife and Sundown's veterinarian, said with a shake of her head as the guys chomped down burgers and the women shared a basket of fries. "I'll never understand that about men. The closer they are, the more smack they dish out."

"I read somewhere that it's a chromosome thing," Shallie said.

She'd liked Ali the first time she'd met her on New Year's day at her welcome-home party. Her opinion of the pretty blonde hadn't changed. It was a plus that she obviously made J.T. a happy man, but Ali's warm, open friendship didn't hurt, either.

"Really?" Ali gave Shallie a wide-eyed look.

"Well, no," Shallie admitted, "but I figure it's as good an explanation as any—and who knows. Someone might have done a study."

Ali laughed and nibbled on a French fry. "You're probably right. What a pair."

"You should have seen them when they were kids."

"Tell me," Ali begged, leaning over the booth top. "I could use some dirt on that man of mine."

"Oh, no," J.T. said with a waggle of his finger, suddenly tuning into the women's conversation. "Shallie. Remember our pact."

"Pact?" Ali grinned from J.T. to Shallie.

"They made me swear in blood," Shallie said.

Ali gasped. "You didn't."

"'Fraid so," Mac admitted, and winked at Shallie. "We've got enough dirt on each other that not one of us would dare open up that can of worms."

"You were kids," Ali protested. "How bad could it have been?"

J.T. glanced at Mac, who glanced at Shallie, who glanced at J.T. They all burst out laughing. Shallie figured they were thinking of the goat that disappeared from Clement Haskins's ranch and ended up in the town library. Or maybe the beautifully gift-wrapped boxful of horse manure that mysteriously showed up on Principal Cooper's desk. Or any one of a number of harmless, juvenile pranks that no one had ever owned up to but that the three of them were behind.

"I'll get it out of you," Ali promised J.T. with a wicked look.

J.T. made a show of looking worried. "She does have her ways," he admitted. "I may break under the plea-sure…I mean *pressure*."

"There are words for men like you," Mac sputtered.

"Yeah," J.T. said, caressing Ali with a very private look. "Happy." Then he leaned over and kissed his wife. "Should we tell them?" he asked, holding her gaze as he pulled away.

She nodded, then turned to Mac with a huge smile. "We're pregnant."

Shallie felt herself stiffen. She quickly recovered and gave them both a huge smile. "That's wonderful! Congratulations. When are you due?"

She heard all the animated and happy chatter as a blur of noise as Ali and J.T. filled them in on all the details. She made herself smile. She knew she was smiling because her face felt as if it was about to crack.

And she was aware of Mac watching her, his eyes filled with understanding and concern.

It should be this way for her, Shallie thought,

nodding her head, concentrating to keep her smile firmly in place. She should be able to announce to the world that she was pregnant, that she was thrilled about the prospect of having a baby to take care of and love and provide for.

But she couldn't. At least, she couldn't enjoy the sharing process the way Ali and J.T. deserved to enjoy it. Their baby would be raised in a warm and loving home. With a mother and a father to adore it and each other.

"You okay?" Mac asked quietly after Ali and J.T. had left for home.

"Sure." She flashed him a bright-eyed grin. "Great news for them, huh? They're so excited."

"Yeah. They are. I'm sorry, Shallie. I know that was hard on you."

"Don't be silly. I'm happy for them. They deserve to be excited."

"So do you," he said, wrapping an arm around her shoulders. "You deserve to be happy, too."

"I am," she insisted, and blinked hard and fast to hold back a waterfall of tears. Lord, she hated the way pregnant hormones messed with her emotions. "I am happy."

He pulled back. Cupped her shoulders between his big hands and gave her a little shake so she'd look up at him. "This guy. Whoever he is. He doesn't deserve your tears. And he doesn't deserve you. Or the baby."

And I don't deserve you, she thought when Mac hugged her again. But she was thankful, so thankful, for having him back in her life.

"I've got to go back to Bozeman tomorrow," he said after a moment. "Why don't you come with me? You need to have your cast checked about now, anyway. While you're there, we could find you an OB doc. And we could go to the courthouse. Pick up a marriage license."

He hadn't let the idea of getting married drop. He wasn't pushy about it. Just sneaky. He'd bring it up at the darnedest times. Like when she was feeling most vulnerable. Like now.

"You're kind of like a dog with a bone, aren't you?"

"Bow-wow."

She shook her head. "Mac." And took his hand. "What J.T. and Ali have…well, it's special. Peg and Cutter have it, too. It's proof, you know, that there is such a thing as over-the-moon in love. When two people have that, it's magical. You deserve that for yourself. You won't get that marrying me."

He looked down at their joined hands, absently rubbed his thumb back and forth across her knuckles. "Do you know the odds of two people finding that kind of connection? Approximately slim and none. Okay. Agreed. Our friends have it. But what that does is pretty much cut the possibility of it happening to either one of us down to nil."

"One of the things I've always loved about you is your optimism," she teased in reference to his gloom-and-doom prediction.

"I *am* an optimist, short-stack. But I'm also a realist. So let's be real here, okay?"

"Do we have to?" In the interest of trying to stall this conversation, she attempted to lighten the mood with a pout.

"Yes. I think we do."

He looked so serious suddenly that she sobered, too.

"Raising a baby on your own is not going to be easy. Sundown's a small town. Yeah. You've got good friends who will stand beside you…but do you really want to subject your little one to the small-town gossip?"

Her heart did a little stutter step. She hadn't wanted to think that far ahead. Most of all, she hadn't wanted to remember how it had been for her growing up. Kids were often unkind. And she'd been on the receiving end of snide remarks about more than her hair and her ragged clothes: "How come you don't have a dad? He get one look at that brillo pad hair of yours and hit the road? How come your momma has so many 'friends' comin' in and out of your house?"

"Shallie…honey?"

She looked up, realized she'd zoned out on Mac.

"I'm sorry," he said. "I didn't mean to hurt you."

"No. No, you didn't. You just said something that really hit home, is all. It just…really hit home."

She searched the face of this man who offered her the chance to save her own child from that kind of torment. Who offered her so much more than she really deserved.

And he looked so sweet. And so kind. And so determined that he had the right answer for both of them.

"You're really sure about this?" she asked, making it clear she was asking him if he was sure he really wanted to marry her and if he was sure he knew what he was giving up.

"Last I knew, life doesn't come with money-back guarantees, Shallie Mae. But I come with a few basic promises. I'll take care of you and the baby. I'll be your friend. I'll always be true. And you'll never have a reason not to trust me."

Trust. There was that word again. He promised that she could trust him. And she knew she could. Just like she knew she should trust him with the total truth surrounding her baby's conception.

Yet every time she screwed up her courage to tell him, something stopped her. Something like panic. Something like shame. Something that was too strong to make her do the one thing she knew was right.

So she said the one thing that made it easier, instead.

"Okay," she said, feeling like she was diving off a high board even though she knew that Mac would be there to catch her. "Let's go get that license."

He squinted, searched her eyes. "For real?"

She pushed out a laugh. "For as real as it gets, Brett McDonald, so you'd better be sure you're up for this."

When he smiled at her that way, she could almost believe he loved her. And when her chest filled with a sweet, aching joy, she could almost believe she loved him. Not just a best-friends-for-life-I'll-always-be-there-for-you kind of love.

The other kind. The kind that Ali and J.T. had. The kind the Peg and Cutter had.

Yeah. She could almost believe it. And if Mac hadn't been right about the odds of that happening being slim to none, she might have believed it. Lord knew, she wanted to.

Nine

"**Y**ou dog, you!" J.T. railed at Mac a day later, even though he was grinning broadly. "I can't believe you didn't tell me.

"And you." J.T. turned an accusatory glare on Shallie now that he was done scolding Mac. "I'm your friend and you kept this a secret!"

Mac grinned from J.T. to Shallie, who was looking a little shell-shocked by J.T.'s reaction to the news that they were getting married.

The truth was, she'd looked a little dazed ever since they'd cut the deal. And he'd felt a little dazed himself. Okay. A lot dazed.

He had a shot. A real shot at making this work. She didn't love the guy. He'd been bouncing off the walls ever since that night he'd asked her, "Do you still love him, Shall?"

Not only did she not still love the creep, she was pretty certain she never had.

It was all he'd needed to charge full steam ahead. And he had—and done his damnedest to take it easy with her. They'd talked about the reality of getting married several times, and she'd insisted she was happy with her decision. And the closer the big day came, Mac realized he was more than happy. Yeah, the prospect of marrying Shallie made him grin. Made him feel mature. Settled. And it was time.

That's why he'd called J.T. and asked him to meet him and Shallie in Sundown. Since they'd wanted to talk with Ali, too, and she couldn't leave the office today because she was short-handed, they met at her vet practice instead of the Dusk to Dawn.

"I believe the correct response to our announcement is, congratulations," Mac said as, careful of her cast, J.T. wrapped Shallie in a big bear hug.

Ali did the same with Mac. "Congratulations!"

"You have my condolences, sweetheart," J.T. said, dropping a kiss on Shallie's cheek. "And I've got to tell you, I'm a little disappointed in you. I always thought you were so much smarter than to get hooked up with a no-account like this."

"Smartest woman in the world," Mac assured his buddy, who turned to him and extended a hand.

"Congratulations, man," J.T. said, serious now. "Really. This is great. Just damn great. I couldn't be happier for you."

"So, I'm in the market for a best man. Since the pickin's around here are pretty slim, what are you doing a week from Saturday?"

J.T. blinked. "No kidding? That soon?"

"Can't think of a reason to wait," Mac said. And he *couldn't* think of any good reason. Even Shallie seemed to want to make it official as soon as possible. Whether it was for fear that she'd back out or actual excitement, he didn't know.

All he knew was that his plan to play it loose and easy and slow had worked. She hadn't shied. She hadn't spooked. She'd said yes.

And he'd damn near blown a gasket.

She'd said yes. And he was determined that someday in the near future she'd say yes again to another question. One that went something like "Do you love me, Shallie?"

"Well, I'm your man, then," J.T. said, beaming. "Just tell me where and what time."

"Ali?" Shallie turned to her new friend. "I know we haven't known each other for long, but—"

Ali actually squealed. "I would be honored," she said, interrupting Shallie before she'd finished asking her to be matron of honor. "Oh, this is so exciting."

Mac loved the look that crossed Shallie's face when Ali responded with such excitement. He'd known she was hesitant to ask Ali to stand up with her, and on some level he understood the reason why.

He'd never had a doubt that Ali would be thrilled. Shallie had had doubts, though, and he figured it stemmed from the way she'd felt about herself from the time he could remember. Hell, when your own mother didn't want much to do with you, it was a leap of faith to think anyone else would. And Shallie didn't leap toward anything. She picked her way very carefully.

Ali's open and excited reaction was exactly what Shallie needed. It had been a major hurdle for her to let down her defenses enough to trust that someone might actually want to be a part of her life.

Yeah. It had been a major hurdle. And, judging by the look on Shallie's face, she was glad that she'd taken the chance on Ali.

The woman he saw right now was a happy one. And he liked it.

"Have you bought your dress yet?" Ali asked.

"My dress?" A look of minor panic replaced Shallie's smile. "I'm afraid I haven't gotten that far."

"Great. Then we can go shopping together."

God bless Ali Tyler, Mac thought later, as he and Shallie headed for the cabin. The two women had gotten their heads together to plan a shopping trip to Bozeman. Mac and J.T. had shot the breeze, occasionally warned the ladies with the bright eyes and excited smiles not to get too carried away and grinned because Mac knew he'd indulge Shallie in about anything she wanted to do to pull off her idea of the perfect wedding.

Well, not perfect, he realized. They couldn't do perfect in a week. But they could come pretty damn close, he'd decided and had already set the wheels in motion to make sure they threw one of the biggest, fanciest receptions the Dusk to Dawn had ever seen.

"You know," Shallie said, standing by the hearth one night after Mac had rebuilt the fire. "It would have been a lot easier if we'd just driven to Nevada and done this in a civil ceremony."

"Oh, boy. Here we go again. Haven't we had this discussion once or twice already and nixed the idea?"

"You nixed the idea," she pointed out.

"Come 'ere," he said and patted the sofa cushion beside him. "Let me explain this to you one more time."

With a self-conscious smile she eased down beside him, let her head fall back on his shoulder when he draped his arm around her.

"Comfy?"

She nodded and turned into him, snuggling close. He loved that she was so comfortable touching him now. Loved that they were so easy with each other.

"Now listen very carefully. We are not going to Nevada for a quickie civil ceremony. We're going to get married in the company of our good friends, and then we're going to throw the biggest reception Sundown has ever seen. Why? Because a woman deserves to have a special day to remember and tell her children and grandchildren about."

He ran his hand up and down her arm in a slow caress. "And because a man wants to have a memory of his wife all dressed up and pretty for him when he thinks back on that day."

"I hate to break this to you McDonald, but in spite of your big talk to the contrary, you're a romantic, you know that? Even though you claim you don't believe in fairy-tale love."

Yeah. He was a romantic, all right. And someday he'd let her know exactly how romantic he was.

"What I am," he said choosing his words carefully, because for some reason he was suddenly having a hard time picking the right ones, "is a man who cares very much for a certain woman. I want to make you happy, Shall. And I want to start out by giving you a special day."

She tipped her head way back so she could look up at him. Her eyes were a misty, shimmering brown, and they were brimming with something that gave him a little lump, right in the center of his throat, and made it hard to swallow.

"You are such a good man," she whispered, touching his face with her fingertips, touching his heart with her smile.

They made love slow and easy, then. With the fire crackling in the hearth and the sun sinking low in the horizon.

"I'll do right by you, Shallie," he promised, moving in and out of her as she clung and arched and gave herself over to his loving.

"I'll do right by you and the baby."

"I know," she whispered back. "I...know."

When it was over she cried. His tough Shallie who never cried when someone hurt her. He held her close and stroked her hair and told himself it was all about those hormones she was always cussing. He pressed a soft kiss to the top of her head. Bless her, those hormones did give her fits.

She had to tell him, Shallie thought as she lay awake well into the night that night. He was so good.

So kind. And so trusting that she was the person he needed her to be.

She had to tell him. And in the morning she would. Maybe he'd understand. Maybe he'd forgive her.

Like he forgave his mother? she wondered, and snuggled closer to her future husband's side.

It didn't matter. Somehow, some way, she had to screw up the courage to tell him about her one night-stand with a married man.

She cringed, just thinking about it. Even so, even if he saw her for the horrible, deceitful person she was and he changed his mind about marrying her, she couldn't live with herself if she didn't come clean. And she had to do it before the wedding, which was only five days away.

He stirred in his sleep and pulled her closer to his side. And she realized, with a horrible ache in her heart, how much she was going to lose if she lost him.

She was going to lose the best thing that had ever happened to her. She was going to lose the one person who had ever really cared about making her happy. And, surprise, surprise, she *was* happy. Really happy.

With distance from her old life and the physical surroundings of her failures and with Mac's tender support, she was actually more happy than worried about the prospect of being a mother. She'd needed someone to love for so long. Someone to love her. She'd thought it would be just her and her baby. She'd thought she could make it enough.

But now there was Mac. And now she knew he truly did make her life complete.

That was the biggest revelation of all. She'd been determined to classify their relationship as friendship. She'd been determined they were marrying for convenience. For the sake of the child. And because Mac was ready for a family and had given up on love.

Well, guess what? She hadn't. She'd thought she had. She'd thought there wasn't a chance on earth that she'd ever fall in love again.

Turns out she was wrong. Turns out she'd never been in love at all. Not really.

Well, she was now. For the first time.

Mac. She loved him. Loved him for being there for her. Loved him for wanting to take care of her. Loved him for being the kind of man he was.

But most of all, over the course of the past week and a half, she'd fallen in love with him as she'd never loved another man.

It was more than love now. At least, it was more than any love she'd ever known. She couldn't wait to see him every morning. Couldn't imagine going to bed without him at night. Adored it when he touched her, kissed her, made love to her like she was the most special woman in the world. No one had ever given her that before. No one.

Her macaroon. Her white knight.

And because she loved him, she had to tell him in the morning, she reminded herself, sobering in the dark.

But when morning came, he was gone. She found a note tucked under a plate of chocolate-glazed long johns:

Hey, Shall,
You were sleeping so sound I didn't want to wake you. Cara's got a problem with the refrigeration

at SW so I had to head back to Bozeman. I'll call
you later, okay?
XOXOs, Mac.

Shallie slowly folded the note. And felt a relief too big
to be anything but cowardice. She'd been given a reprieve.
And she was grateful.

Tonight, she promised herself, walking over to the
kitchen window to watch a vibrant red cardinal eat
cracked corn from a feeder Mac had put up, for her as
much as for the birds. She would tell him tonight.

But he didn't make it back to Sundown that night.
The refrigeration problem had become a dilemma and
he'd had to drive to Helena for parts.

During the course of the week, a dozen things dis-
rupted their communication flow. Even when Shallie
and Ali spent a day in Bozeman shopping for their
dresses and they stopped into SW for lunch, Shallie
couldn't find the right time to talk to him.

The next thing she knew it was Saturday, their wedding
day, and, for a number of reasons, she still hadn't told him.

More to the point, she'd started to believe there might
be a valid reason that "life" kept interrupting her good
intentions.

Maybe fate was intervening on her behalf. Maybe it
was okay that he didn't know. Maybe it was okay to
leave her past in the past and start this new life with Mac
without the weight of her mistake hanging over them.

And maybe, just maybe, she deserved to have him
think of her the way he wanted to think of her, not the
way he would be forced to think of her if he knew.

Whatever the reason as she slipped into her wedding dress and put the final touches on her makeup, the only thing she was certain she was going to say to Brett McDonald this afternoon, was "I do."

Besides Mac and Shallie, only J.T. and Ali and Mac's dad, Alex, witnessed the vows as Preacher Davis performed the ceremony at the Sundown Congregational Church where they were pronounced man and wife.

The reception, however, was a different story. They wanted *all* of their friends at the reception.

The Dusk to Dawn was packed. From the bar to the eating area to the dance floor, it was party room only.

And for Sundown it was the party of the decade.

"How'd a couple of duds like us rate women like them?" J.T. asked Mac as they stood, beers in hand, watching Ali and Shallie dancing with the Griener twins.

Mac grinned and shook his head. "Beats the hell out of me. Sometimes it's best not to question good luck."

"Amen to that. Hey…there's Lee and Ellie Savage. I've got to go say hello. Be right back."

Mac was barely aware of J.T. leaving. Hadn't been aware of much of anything except Shallie since he'd caught sight of her walking down the aisle toward him at four o'clock this afternoon.

Shallie had always been a looker. She had that wholesome, girl-next-door-with-an-attitude look that had always made him think of a modern-day Annie Oakley. *Grit* was a word that always came to mind when he'd thought of her.

It wasn't the word that came to mind today. A lot of others did, though.

Beautiful, for one.

Special, for another.

Mine, however, topped the list.

As of today, Shallie Malone was Shallie McDonald. And she was his. To take care of. To share with. To have and to hold and to love and to cherish.

He'd meant every word when he'd said them. It wasn't that he hadn't expected their vows to have meaning. He just hadn't expected them to mean so much.

He grinned as Billie Griener twirled Shallie across the dance floor and she threw Mac a look that clearly cried, Help!

Setting his beer on the bar, he set off through the crowd to rescue his very own damsel in distress.

"I'll be taking my wife back now," he said, tapping Billie on the shoulder.

"Yeah, I saw the way you were watching us," Billie teased. "Figured you'd get to worrying 'bout me beating your time."

Mac grinned at Billie's receding hairline and to-bacco-stained teeth and pulled Shallie into his arms. "You read me right, man. Now give me some room to work here so I can make her forget all about you."

With a chuckle, Billie slapped him on the shoulder and headed for the bar.

"So," Mac said, slowing things down to an intimate, easy sway even though the band he'd hired was rocking to a Montgomery Gentry song, "you having a good time?"

"The best." When she looked up at him, her smile was so huge and bright it staggered him. "And even better now. Thanks for the rescue mission. I don't think my feet could have taken one more hit from Billie's boots."

"God, you're pretty," he said because he just couldn't hold it in. She'd done something special with her hair. Nothing too fancy. Nothing too much could be done with those short, springy curls, but she'd tamed them some and tucked a little sprig of flowers above her right ear, and damned if she didn't make him think of some kind of a forest nymph.

There was a little extra pink in her cheeks, a shimmery gloss on her lips—probably the dress had something to do with it, too. He didn't have a clue what it was. Silk maybe. And pale pink with long sleeves that covered the smaller cast the doctor had put on just yesterday. She looked sleek and slim and soft. Felt that way, too.

"You don't look so bad yourself, cowboy."

Just for her, because she'd remarked how sexy J.T. had looked at his and Ali's wedding—Ali had had them for dinner last night, and Shallie had spotted the picture on the wall—Mac had dressed in a black western-cut suit.

"Yeah, well. Told you I cleaned up pretty good."

"That you do," she agreed with the softest smile. The kind of smile that made him feel all full inside.

This was going to work, he told himself as the band changed gears and launched into a ballad. This marriage was going to work. Everything felt right about it.

More right, even, than he'd thought it would. He felt it

more and more every day. And seeing Shallie today, glowing and happy and knowing he was in part responsible for that happiness, he'd started to feel something else.

He could make her fall in love with him. He smiled to himself and lowered his head so he could nuzzle her ear and get a whiff of that amazing scent she was wearing.

Yeah. He could make her fall in love with him. This woman who was the antithesis of almost every woman he'd ever been involved with. A woman who didn't play games. Whose life didn't revolve around how she looked. A woman who wasn't after him for his money and wasn't overly impressed by his success.

She was fun and funny and sincere.

And she didn't have a deceitful bone in her body.

She was just Shallie. Honest. And real. And true. In short, she was perfect.

Any man would be lucky to have her. And as he held her in his arms and she snuggled up against him, he counted himself as one damn lucky man.

"What I'd like to know," Mac murmured as they cuddled under the big quilt on the floor in front of the fireplace later that night, "is what kind of woman prefers winter in an old cabin in the mountains to a condo on Maui for a honeymoon destination?"

Shallie snuggled closer, loving the feel of Mac's big naked body pressed against hers, sharing his heat with her. "I don't need Maui."

"I'm not talking about need. I'm talking about what you want."

"I want what I've got. And it's right here."

"Six-foot snowdrifts, Arctic winds, the possibility of power outages—"

She cut him off with a finger pressed to his lips. He promptly sucked it inside his mouth, gently latched on. "I want a home, Mac," she said, hearing her voice clog with emotion.

He heard it, too. Let go of her finger and looked into her eyes.

"I want a home," she repeated softly. "It's all I've ever wanted. You've given it to me." She searched his beautiful face, cupped his strong, hard jaw in her palm. "What more could a woman want?"

He was quiet for a long moment before he slowly shook his head. "You're one of a kind, short-stack."

"Broke the mold, all right," she agreed, giving him a smile.

"No. I mean it." He kissed her forehead, then her brow, then her cheeks. "I don't know anyone like you. Unassuming. Unspoiled. Honest."

She felt those damn tears well up again. Not just from the tender way he kissed her, not just from the sincerity of his words, but from the guilt over just how dishonest she had been with him.

"Mac," she began, overcome by an urge to blurt out the truth about the baby. Get it off her chest.

He shook his head. "No, wait. I'm not finished. There's something I need to say to you. Something I should have said before today but didn't have the guts."

She swallowed hard, her heart pounding, her nerves shredded as she waited him out. She'd let him have his say. Then she'd tell him.

"You know that notion of love and happily ever after I've been speaking out against?"

Heart in her throat, she nodded.

"Well, the deal is, I didn't know what I was talking about."

Her heart stopped then. Flat-out, still as stone, stopped.

"I want happily ever after with you, Shall. I want love with you. And I'm thinking maybe I'm going to get it."

"Mac—"

"There you go," he scolded, a smile in his voice, "Interrupting me again. I love you, Shallie. I've always loved you. Honest to God, head-over-heels, love you. There. I'm done. Now you can talk."

Like she could talk. Joy rolled over trepidation. Hope won out over guilt. She threw her arms around his neck, clunked him on the back of her head with her cast and made them both laugh. And then she just hung on. To this man. This beautiful, amazing man who thought he loved her.

"Hey. Hey, hey," he soothed. "Are you crying again?"

She laughed, pressing her face against his neck. "How do you think I'm going to react to a statement like that?" she sniffed.

"Oh, I don't know. I was kind of hoping you might tell me how *you* felt about the idea of love and happily ever after and stuff."

She sniffed again. "Stuff, huh?"

"Well, mostly about the love part."

She pulled back so she could look into his beautiful gentle eyes. "I really, really like the love part. In fact, I'm pretty much in love with the love part."

He smiled and her world went one hundred percent right again. "Pretty much?"

She nodded.

"How pretty much?"

And laughed. "Pretty much pretty sure that I pretty much love you, too."

He looked so happy. Not just the usual, good-natured, Mac-the-good-guy happy. But a-man-in-love happy.

"Lots of pretties in there."

"Yeah. Lots."

"So," he said, stroking a hand along her hip beneath the quilt. "This is like a good thing, right?"

"Yeah." She laughed again. "It's like a good thing."

He watched her face for the longest time, then turned serious as he slid his hand around and covered her stomach with his big palm.

It felt warm and gentle and protective against her.

"I want this to be *our* baby, Shallie. I want to raise this baby as mine. Yours and mine."

Her eyes blurred and burned and it felt like her heart was going to push its way out of her body through her throat. "Mac."

His big hand slowly caressed her there, where the baby slept and grew. "Our baby, Shallie. Okay?"

How could she say no to this gift he was giving her child? A gift that should be a birthright. A right she'd never had. How could she deny it to her child?

And how could she tell him the truth now and risk losing it all?

"Okay," she managed to whisper between trembling lips. "That is so very, very okay."

Ten

While the last of the women who had attended her baby shower said their goodbyes, Shallie bounced little six-month-old Jacob Savage on her knee. The baby drooled and grinned and made Shallie's heart swell with anticipation of her own baby's arrival in less than four months.

"He's such a sweetheart," she said to the baby's mother, Ellie Savage.

"He's our little miracle," Ellie agreed, beaming as she helped Peg Lathrop tidy up the Dusk to Dawn which had been closed today for the private shower.

Ali and Shallie started to show about the same time a couple of months ago. Shallie was sure people had wondered about the timing of her pregnancy but they were too kind to say anything. It was about that same time that Peg Reno and Ellie decided it would be a fine time for a joint baby shower.

They'd done it up right, too. Shallie was overwhelmed by the generosity of the Sundown women—some of them she barely knew. Judging from the look on Ali's face as she organized her gifts so J.T. could help her haul them home, Ali was pretty amazed, as well.

They were wonderful people, these new friends of hers. Shallie had gotten to know Lee and Ellie well during the past couple of months since she and Mac had gotten married. During that time, she'd grown to admire the young woman who struggled with epilepsy, yet didn't let it keep her from enjoying life to the fullest. Even if it had meant risking her own health to conceive and deliver this amazing child.

"Your momma thinks you're a miracle, baby boy," Shallie said, lifting Jacob to her shoulder and snuggling him close. "I have to agree. You're such a good baby," she murmured, rubbing his back and inhaling the wonderful scent of baby and powder and thinking that it wouldn't be long now until she held her own baby.

Hers and Mac's. And that's exactly how she thought of the life growing inside of her. Mac's child.

"I think that pretty much covers it," Peg said, looking around at the tidy room.

"You guys are too much," Ali said, her look encompassing both Peg and Ellie.

"Agreed," Shallie chimed in as Ali held her arms out so she could have a turn at cuddling Jacob before everyone headed for home.

"Any excuse for a party," Peg said with a grin just as the front door opened.

"Did someone say party?" J.T. beamed as he walked into the Dusk to Dawn followed by Mac, Cutter Reno and Lee Savage.

"Sorry, guys. It's all over but the heavy lifting." Ellie handed the diaper bag to Lee, then pried Jacob out of Ali's arms so she could bundle him into his little snowsuit.

"And what did you four troublemakers find to do to keep yourself busy for the last few hours?" Peg asked, grabbing her coat.

Cutter hurried over and helped her into it. "Just a friendly little card game."

"Friendly?" Mac snorted. "It was cutthroat."

Lee slapped him on the back and addressed the room in general as J.T. gathered up an armload of baby gifts and winked at Shallie. "Treat him with kid gloves tonight, Shallie. The man had a little string of bad luck."

"Card sharks, is what they are," Mac grumbled.

"Poker face is what he isn't," J.T. pointed out with a nod in Mac's direction. "But he *is* a sore loser."

"Har. Har." Mac walked over to Shallie, sat down in a huff.

"What's the matter, sweetie? Did those mean boys pick on you today?" She patted his hand with staged sympathy while the other guys looked anything but sympathetic.

"They beat me out of my lunch money, Mom," he whined, playing for a laugh—which he got along with a few more jabs from the guys before they all collected their women and headed out the door with a chorus of goodbyes.

"Thought they'd never leave," Mac said, urging her onto his lap. He kissed her. Smiled. "So, did you and Heathcliff rake in lots of loot?"

She laughed. "Me and *Gertrude* did pretty darn good. Wait until you see all this stuff."

"Had a good time, did you?"

She nodded. "Had a great time. These people…well, they're wonderful."

He kissed her again. "So are you. Now, what do you say we get this stuff loaded up and head for home?"

"Sounds good to me. I'm beat. Opening presents is very exhausting."

"Your wrist hurting?"

"No. Oh, no," she said quickly seeing the concern in his eyes. He'd been that way ever since she'd had the cast removed a month ago. "Will you quit worrying about my wrist? It's fine. Perfect. I was kidding, okay? Now, let's start loading up so we can go home."

"You will load nothing. I'll handle it. I don't want you lifting one thing."

That was another thing about Mac. He was a protector. If he had his way, he'd keep her in a glass cage where nothing could get at her. No germs, no possibility of accidents.

The independent side of her would complain, but he was so cute about it she couldn't bear to burst his bubble.

"Sit tight for a second," he said, sliding her off his lap. "I need to check on some things in the kitchen. Be back in about five minutes, and then I'll load this major haul into the truck."

"I'm not going anywhere," Shallie said, and watched him disappear into the kitchen.

Life, she decided, lifting a little yellow sleeper out of a box, just couldn't get any better. The past two months since they'd gotten married had been the best of her life. Mac was sweet and gentle and so much fun to be with. And he was an inventive and selfless lover. She got a little chill just thinking about the way he made her feel when he made love to her.

Yeah, she thought, holding the little sleeper to her breast. Life just couldn't get any better. For the first time in her life she had a home—a complete home. She had someone who loved her. Her. Just as she was, in the form of a man she still couldn't believe she'd been lucky enough to want to be a part of her life.

Yeah. Life was perfect.

And then the front door opened with a cool rush of mid-March air.

A man's silhouette filled the dark doorway.

"Hello, Shallie." He stepped into the light.

And Shallie felt her perfect world slip out from under her like a sinkhole.

"Jared."

Mac took a little longer than he'd thought, stocking the cooler for the bar action that the Dusk to Dawn was sure to see tonight when they opened back up to the public at six.

He was afraid Shallie might have given up on him when he finally shut the kitchen door behind him and headed for the main room.

"I told you to leave," he heard Shallie say before he saw her and every protective instinct in his body went on red alert.

She was standing and she looked agitated, and whoever was the cause of that agitation was some guy who looked about as determined to stay as she was for him to go.

"Damn it, Shallie, I didn't spend five months hunting you down, then drive two thousand miles to find you, just to turn around and go back to Georgia without you. I made a mistake, all right? I realize that. I said I was sorry. So quit talking nonsense and get in the car."

"I believe the lady said she wanted you to leave." Mac walked up behind Shallie, put his hands on her shoulders and gently set her behind him.

"Mac. It's okay. I can handle this," she said quickly.

The guy glared at Mac. "Who the hell are you?"

He was about Mac's height and weight. His eyes were a mean brown, his attitude superior as hell. And Mac didn't much care for the way his fists were clenched at his side.

He also didn't care for the implications. This had to be the guy. The guy who'd cheated on Shallie and left her pregnant.

Mac's gut clenched as he sized him up. He hated him on sight. Hated to think of this guy touching Shallie. Hated to think of him having anything to do with her. And rumbling through it all was a growing and consuming concern that he might be here to stake some claim on the baby. The baby Mac had come to think of as his own.

"I'm the guy," Mac ground out, "who's going to

invite you real nice-like to do as my wife says and get the hell off my property."

"Wife?" His dark gaze shifted from Mac to Shallie who had moved out from behind Mac and was trying to insinuate herself between them. He grunted, threw her a look of disgust. "Well, it didn't take you long to find another bed to crawl into, did it?"

"One more word," Mac ground out, pushing past Shallie and grabbing the guy's jacket in his fist and twisting, "and I'll kick your ass from here back to Georgia."

"Stop it!" Shallie reached for Mac's arm, tried to push him away. "Please. Stop. Mac. Don't. He's not worth it.

"Jared," she said, turning to the guy as Mac reluctantly let him go. "Leave. Now."

Jared gave a macho shrug of his shoulders, shot Shallie a glare. "This is what you want?" He lifted a hand toward Mac. "You want to be stuck out here in the boonies with cowboy Bob here?"

"Look, you're the one who screwed up, okay?" Mac was pissed now. Royally pissed. He shoved Jared hard in the middle of his chest, knocked him a step backward. "What kind of man makes promises to a woman then cheats on her? What kind of a man walks away from his own baby?"

Jared staggered when Mac shoved him, caught his balance and glared from Mac to Shallie. "Baby? What the hell are you talking about?"

"I'm talking about how you got her pregnant and then walked out on her."

"Whoa. Whoa." Jared lifted his hands beside his head

in a show of supplication. "I don't know anything about a baby. Is that what she told you? That I got her pregnant?"

"Figures you wouldn't own up," Mac said with a snarl.

"Own up? Hell, cowboy," Jared said with a cocky and ugly smile, "I'd own up if it was true, but the fact is, I'm shooting blanks, man."

Mac narrowed his eyes.

"Vasectomy," Jared supplied, looking smug. "Three years ago. I don't want any little bastards running around costing me money."

Mac glanced at Shallie. She'd gone statue still. Ghost white.

She closed her eyes. Swallowed. "You need to leave now, Jared," she said in a voice that sounded hollow and weary and empty of conviction.

Jared looked from Shallie to Mac then smiled a nasty smile. "Looks like maybe I do. My mistake, cowboy," he said, backing toward the door. "She's all yours. Her and the brat."

The silence that rang in the wake of his departure could have filled the Grand Canyon.

Mac was aware of Shallie suffering beside him. Aware but unable to do anything about it.

He felt as if he'd been gutted. He felt as if he'd been strung out, hung out, stripped of everything he thought he knew. About her. About them.

She'd lied. Shallie had lied to him.

It didn't compute. It didn't add up to what he knew about who she was and what she was.

And it left him feeling so fractured and confused he didn't know what to say. How to handle the sense of betrayal, the surge of anger that had him glued to the spot, his gaze stuck on the door that had shut behind the man who had just changed his life forever.

"Mac—"

He held up a hand. Shook his head. "Don't."

"Please." There were tears in her voice. No doubt, in her eyes as well. For once it didn't affect him. He didn't want to hear what she had to say. Didn't want to look at her.

"Let's get these things into the truck," he said, and started stacking boxes and grabbing sacks.

He walked around her where she stood in the middle of the room, looking helpless, looking hopeless.

"It was after I caught Jared cheating," she said and he stopped cold in his tracks. Back stiff. Shoulders back.

"He'd hurt me, you know? And I don't mean just hurt me because he cheated. He, um, he hit me."

All the muscles in Mac's body clenched tight. His gut knotted. And for a second, there, he thought he was going to be sick.

"That was it for me. I left him. And then I wallowed. If you can imagine, now that you've had the pleasure, I actually felt like I'd lost something other than my self-respect. For a month I threw one big pity party. Poor Shallie. Nobody loves me. Nobody wants me."

Mac swallowed. Lowered his head. And still he couldn't turn to her.

"Anyway," she said, sounding weary and resigned, "a couple of the girls I worked with dragged me with them to a bar one night. Just to make me get out. You know. Crawl out of my cave. This…this guy…"

She stopped, her voice trembling.

"This guy," she began again after she'd collected herself, "he was so…nice to me, you know? Made me feel worth something again. He was charming. And he charmed me."

Another pause, as if she was working up the courage to go on.

"Shallie," he finally said, needing to stop her. He didn't want to hear any more.

"It wasn't until the next time I saw him a week later that I found out he was married," she finished with a truckload of guilt weighing down her words.

Married. She'd slept with a married man.

Something inside of him went stone-cold dead.

"I didn't know. I swear I didn't know. And after… after that night, after I found out, he…he kept after me no matter how often and how vehemently I told him no. And when…when I found out I was pregnant. Well. I'm not a home wrecker, Mac. He has a wife. Kids.

"Anyway," she said after the moment it took her to compose herself, "I had to get away from there. And that's why I ended up here."

Mac drew a deep breath, let it out, thought of his mother who had cheated on his dad with a married man. And couldn't find it in himself to sort one situation from another.

"I meant to tell you."

"Then why didn't you?" he asked, finally finding his voice and with it the hard edge of anger.

"I…I tried. I really tried. But it was just so easy to let things get in the way of the truth. You…you made it so easy."

"Ah. So it's my fault."

"No. That's not what I meant. Mac—"

"Look. Let's just get out of here. I don't want to talk about it. I don't want to hear about it. It's over. It's done. Nothing's changed. You're still pregnant. We're still married. Let's just leave it at that."

Even as he said the words, he knew they were lies.

Everything had changed.

Everything.

Winter was almost over, but Shallie had never felt so cold. Cold outside. Cold inside.

A silence the size of a glacier radiated from Mac like an Arctic chill as they rode from Sundown to Bozeman.

She understood. She understood his anger. Understood his disappointment. In her. In who he'd thought she was.

And it was no one's fault but her own. She was the one who'd made the mistakes. She couldn't even blame Jared for showing up out of the blue and exposing her.

She still couldn't believe he'd tracked her down. No. She wasn't foolish enough to believe he'd taken the time and the trouble to find her out any sense of love or guilt. With Jared, it was about control. Possession. Evidently, he'd decided he missed that aspect of their relationship.

She didn't.

But she did miss what she'd just lost.

So much for happily-ever-after, she thought, as Mac

pulled into his garage and without a word and started unloading baby gifts.

So much for things finally being easy.

Three weeks passed in numbing, miserable silence. Shallie felt Mac pull farther and farther away from her. Farther and farther into himself.

He didn't act angry. If he had, maybe she could have handled it better. Instead, he acted indifferent. She was more than familiar with indifference. It's the best that she'd ever gotten from her mother. Indifference meant there would be no hitting, true, but the pain that lack of caring implied had almost been worse than a physical blow when she was a child. And the effect hung around much longer than a bruise.

It hurt as badly now.

So many times she wanted to ask him to say something. Anything. Curse. Belittle her. Berate her. Anything but this tepid, polite apathy. Anything but a cool good-night as he went to bed in the guest room and shut the door behind him.

No hugs. No kisses. No chocolate. She missed the chocolate most of all because it had become such a symbol of his love for her.

They were now husband and wife in name only. But he did his duty, this disillusioned husband of hers. He did what he had promised to do. He took care of her. He didn't have it in him to do anything else.

"Do you need anything from the supermarket?"

"When's your next doctor's appointment? Do you need me to take you?"

"I'll be at SW. Call me if you need anything."

That was about the extent of their conversation these days.

And it was slowly killing her right along with their marriage.

Tonight, when he came home from SW, was just another night in a string of nights where their communication consisted of short, guilty looks. He looked tired and haunted when he said a quiet, "Good night," and walked right past her without ever meeting her eyes.

That's probably the part that got to her most. She missed those smiling eyes. Missed the mischief. Missed the fun.

She'd done that to him. And it was this night that she'd finally had enough of dealing with the fallout.

With her heart in her throat she walked to the guest bedroom door. Knocked.

A few seconds passed before it opened.

Mac stood there in his bare feet, his shirt unbuttoned and tugged out of his pants.

"I give up," she said, before he could ask her what she wanted and make her feel even more of a pariah than she already felt.

He looked at her then. She'd given him little choice. All she saw was fatigue. Maybe a hint of anger.

It was the first real emotion she'd seen since that fateful day in March—and it spurred a surprising arch of anger in her.

"I'm sorry," she said. "It's too little. I know. But what else can I say? What else can I do?"

His jaw clenched and he looked away.

"Yeah. That's right. Look away. I'm sorry about that, too. That you can't even stand to look at me."

He scrubbed a weary hand over his jaw. "Look. I'm tired, okay? And I don't see what good this is doing."

"No. Of course you don't see. Your idea of dealing with what I've done to screw up *your* life is to ignore it.

"I've waited, Mac," she said, her voice rising in accusation. "I've waited. I've given you room. Hoped that with time you might talk to me. Might be able to forgive me. A lot to ask, I know. And why should you? I can't forgive myself. At least, I haven't been able to. But you know what? That stops right here. Right now. Tonight."

She was shaking now as almost a month of tightly wrapped emotions uncoiled like a spring inside her. She pushed past him, walked to the bed. Sat down on the edge of the mattress and braced her palms on either side of her hips.

"I made a mistake, okay? It was a horrible mistake. It wasn't my first. It probably won't be my last, but you know what, Mac? That doesn't make me a horrible person. A horrible person wouldn't have beat herself up over this. A horrible person wouldn't have left Georgia to avoid one mistake compounding into another."

"You're not a horrible person," he said with a grim reluctance that told her he wasn't one hundred percent convinced of that.

"Then why are you treating me like I am?" she implored, hearing the heartache, the humiliation, the disappointment in her voice and knowing he heard it, too.

He met her eyes, looked away. Again. Shook his

head. Again. "I don't know. Honest to God, Shallie. I don't know."

"I think you do," she said reacting to something she saw in that brief glimpse of his eyes. "I think you know exactly why. You just don't want to come to terms with it."

"Well. If you've got all the answers, by all means, enlighten me, then, will you?" There was just enough bite in his tone to let her know that the anger he'd bottled up all this time was near the bursting point.

Good. Because she was right there with him.

"I think the problem is that I'm not the same needy little girl who left here ten years ago. And you wanted me to be. You wanted me to be needy and perfect and a victim—just like I was back then."

"You let me think you were," he accused.

"Yeah," she said quietly. "Yeah. I did. I did because intuitively, I knew that's what you wanted me to be. I didn't want to let you down, Mac. From that first day we met when you were waiting for me on the school steps, I made it my mission to never let you down.

"And now I have," she said with her chin up. "And you reacted exactly the way I was always afraid you would. You turned away. You tuned me out."

"You lied to me," he said, a wealth of pain and defense in those four little words. "The last thing I expected from you was deceit."

"You think I don't know that? You think that wasn't a huge part of what stopped me from telling you the truth about the baby? I didn't want to disappoint you. You, the one person who always loved me.

"And now—" she lifted a hand, let it drop "—now I

have this chance for you to love not only me but my baby, too. Do you know what that means to me to know that my baby would actually have a father? A father like I never had? To have the *family* I never had?"

She felt tears push. She pushed back, determined not to give in to them now. "Did I lie? Yes. Was it wrong? Of course it was. Did I use you? Yes again. But I did something else, too, Mac. I loved you. There was nothing dishonest about that. It's all I had to give. It's all I've *ever* had to give anyone. And until you, it had never been enough."

She paused, met his eyes. "And you wonder why I lied? I lied because I was afraid of exactly what happened. I lied because I was afraid that like everyone else, my love wouldn't be enough for you, either. Turns out I had more than enough reason to be afraid."

When he said nothing, she knew it was over. She stood slowly, walked past him to the bedroom door. "Look…I got a response to the résumés I sent out a couple of weeks ago."

She stopped just inside the room, still hoping he'd say something, knowing in her heart that he wouldn't. "Actually got a job offer. So here's the deal. You won't have to worry about taking care of me anymore. But I would like a little time. A couple of weeks to find an apartment if that's okay. Then I'll be out of your hair."

She didn't expect him to follow her. And he didn't.

She walked to the bedroom they used to share, undressed in the dark and crawled under the covers. Tried not to remember the loving and the laughing they'd shared in this bed. Tried to reprogram, regroup and gear up for the next hurdle. Because that's what life was really all about. And that's what she always did to get by.

She'd be okay. She and her baby. They'd be fine. Just the two of them together.

Because that was the way it was going to be.

But she'd always be sorry. Always and forever be sorry that her love was never enough.

Eleven

Mac watched Shallie walk out the bedroom door. He had a lump in his throat the size of a football. Big enough anyway, that he blamed it for his silence.

Big enough that he blamed it for the burning going on behind his eyelids.

Feeling weary to the bone and as hollow as an empty well, he dragged his fingers through his hair. Flopped down on his back on the bed and stared at the ceiling.

What a mess. What a big, screwed-up mess.

Shallie's words kept replaying in his head, along with a litany of her sins.

He checked them off one by one, just as he'd been doing for days, rewinding and replaying and using them to distance himself from her emotionally.

She'd lied. She'd used. She'd deceived.

She'd slept with a married man.

Of all the transgressions he'd stacked up against her, the last one was the one that had been hanging him up the most. She'd committed adultery—just like his mother.

Yeah. He'd slogged around, knee-deep in those sins she'd committed against him for weeks now. Letting them build. Let them breed one on top of the other until he couldn't even look at her because that's all he saw. A liar. A cheater. A user.

But he had some new words to think about now. Words she'd delivered like a promise. A promise he knew she would keep.

Give me a couple of weeks. Then I'll be out of your hair. Out of your hair...out of your hair...out of—

He sat up straight. Felt the kick of his heart. Felt the flood of panic spread through his chest.

She was leaving. She was letting him off the hook.

So, what did you think would happen, Einstein? Did you think she'd just hang around, like the ball and chain you'd decided she would always be? Just wear you down with the weight of her sins?

Out of your hair...out of your hair...

He swore into the darkness.

She'd do it, too. She'd leave him. For his sake. Because that was her true nature.

It all became so clear then. The accusation wheels stopped spinning in endless circles. What he hadn't been able to sort out in damn near a month slipped into place with the ease of the right combination on a safe lock.

All because her words made him realize what he'd be losing if he let her walk out that door.

God, he was a fool. The worst kind. The kind who couldn't see the beauty of a wildflower because his book of rules labeled it a noxious weed.

He rose, walked to the bedroom door. He had to fix this. He had to fix everything.

But it wouldn't be tonight, he realized when he carefully opened his master bedroom door and found her sleeping.

"Make it good," he told himself, and pulled on his shoes and socks. "Make it damn good."

And with that mission in mind, he slipped out of the house and started laying the groundwork for undoing the harm he'd done.

It was late the next morning when Shallie slipped out of the bedroom and ventured toward the kitchen. She hadn't slept well. She felt as rested as if she'd spent the night standing up in a corner—like a bad girl should, she thought morosely as she walked into the kitchen.

And stopped dead in her tracks.

Chocolate. There was chocolate everywhere.

Éclairs. Cake. Cookies. Candy. Tiramisu. Boxes and cartons and plates and trays of chocolate desserts of every size and description covered every inch of available counter space, some of it stacked layers deep.

"Thought you might have missed this, too."

Mac's voice startled her. She turned to see him standing just inside the kitchen, his fingers tucked in his back pockets, his hair a mess, his eyes blurry, as if he hadn't slept all night.

"I, um," She lifted a hand toward the mountains of chocolate. "I don't…understand."

But she hoped she did. She hoped with all her heart that the guilt she read in his eyes, the fact that he was looking at her, that he'd evidently bought the entire city of Bozeman out of chocolate by ten o'clock in the morning, meant that she understood perfectly what it meant.

Hope, it seemed, was stronger than despair. Because all he had to do was take a step toward her, hold out his hand and she was in his arms.

Clinging. Crying. Thanking God and her lucky stars and anything she could think of that she was in his arms again.

"I'm so sorry," he murmured into her hair. "So sorry for shutting you out."

"It's okay. It's okay," she whispered, beyond caring about how badly she'd hurt the past three weeks, only caring that he'd forgiven her.

"It's not okay," he said rocking her back and forth, holding her tight. "It's not okay at all.

"Come on," he said with a gentle squeeze. "Let's go into the living room. There are things I need to say to you."

She sniffed as, with his arm over her shoulders, he walked her to the sofa and sat her down.

"Nobody's perfect," he said, taking her hands in his and meeting her eyes. "And you were right. I wanted you to be. I expected you to be. And it wasn't until you pointed it out that I realized what a jerk I was."

"You weren't a jerk. I hurt you."

He shook his head. "I was a jerk," he restated emphatically. "Hell, Shall—I was a *perfect* jerk. Perfect life. Perfect business. Perfect woman for me to take care of and play perfect husband for."

He made a face that told of his self-disgust. "That's what happens when Peter Pan grows up to be a man. He expects the status quo. And he can't handle it when something happens that doesn't fit his standard, so he cuts it out of his life."

He wanted to talk, so she let him. Knew, instinctively that he was working his way through his thoughts very carefully.

"Well, life's not perfect. And you know what happens to a man who expects perfection? He loses out on some of the best things in his life." His gaze dropped to their joined hands before meeting her eyes again. "I don't want to lose you, Shallie. I don't want to lose what we had. I don't want to lose the most important thing that ever happened to me. Don't go. Please don't go."

Well, damn. She was crying again. "I'm not going anywhere," she managed to whisper between the tears. "You're stuck with me, Mac. You just try and shake me loose. See what happens."

"I love you, Shallie. I love you so much."

She wrapped herself around him. Held him close. "That's enough for me. That will always be enough."

And for the first time in her life she knew that what she had to offer—her love—was finally enough, too.

Epilogue

Ella Margaret McDonald came screaming and kicking into the world at 3:26 a.m. on June 9.

"Just like her momma," Mac whispered as he snuggled his baby daughter in his arms three hours later while Shallie dozed in her hospital bed.

"She's beautiful, Mac," his mother said with tears in her eyes and with a love he had missed for too many years.

Yeah, Mr. Perfect had learned a lot from his scrapper of a wife. He'd learned to forgive. And he'd learned that picking up the phone and calling his mother wasn't such a hard thing to do after all. In fact, next to marrying Shallie, it was one of the easiest and the best things he'd ever done.

Hearing the joy in his mother's voice when she'd realized he was letting her back in his life again took some of the bite out of the guilt he felt over turning away from her.

He'd told his dad first, of course. Told him that it was time for both of them to get on with life and learn to live with the truth of it. Yeah, it had hurt his dad at first, but he was a fair man. Of course, the fact that Widow Hammel had started making him pot roast on Sundays and keeping him company a couple of nights a week also helped.

"Hi, sleepyhead," Mac murmured when Shallie opened her eyes and blinked up at him.

"Hey. How's our girl?"

"Little Gertrude is doing just fine," he teased, knowing he'd get a grin out of her. "How's her momma?"

"Good," she said, shifting gingerly. "I'm good."

Mac leaned down and kissed her. "You're better than good, short-stack. In my book, you're *almost* perfect."

And that, Mac knew, was the best anyone could ever hope to be.

* * * * *

A SPLENDID OBSESSION

by
Cathleen Galitz

CATHLEEN GALITZ,

a Wyoming native, teaches English in a rural school that houses primary and secondary students in the same building. She feels blessed to have married a man who is both supportive and patient. When she's not busy writing, teaching or chauffeuring her sons to and from various activities, she can most likely be found indulging in her favourite pastime – reading.

For Casey – who inspires me every day
with his courage

One

She was going to get fired.

It was the last thing Kayanne could afford at the moment. Financially or emotionally. She could think of nothing more unfair after working so hard to pull herself out of the gutter and back up on her own two feet than proving to be a failure her very first day on the job.

Unless, of course, it was endangering another person's life....

Where could that crazy old lady have wandered off to?

Kayanne scoured the perimeter of the nursing-home grounds one more time and tried to calm herself.

Still no sign of Rose.

Maybe she had just gone for a little unauthorized walk. Kayanne couldn't blame anyone for wanting to escape the bland horror that was the Evening Star Retirement Manor. She just didn't want it happening on *her* shift. Freshly back in town after a ten-year hiatus, she'd felt compelled to return to help her mother recover from a heart attack.

And to make a fresh start for herself.

Had she not so desperately needed any job to advance that goal—even this dead-end one for which she had neither the training nor, apparently, the aptitude—Kayanne would have laughed at the thought of being terminated.

That particular word sent another wave of panic crashing over her. A minimum-wage paycheck wasn't the only thing at stake here. An eighty-year-old woman was lost and at the mercy of fate.

Kayanne's imagination kicked into overdrive. Was Rose ambling into the path of oncoming traffic this very minute? Suffering heatstroke beneath the relentless summer sun? Or hitching a ride out of town with some sicko? If Mrs. Johansson was suffering from dementia, the possibilities were endless.

Kayanne's gut twisted into a complicated knot.

The stress of the runway was nothing compared to being responsible for another human being. Her first concern was, of course, for Rose. Her second was to keep her position—and her tenuous pride—intact without anyone else being the wiser. After all, she'd only managed to land this lousy job in the first place because the person who'd hired her was desperate to find any warm body to fill the late-afternoon/evening shift. And because he had no idea she was the town pariah. It didn't hurt any that J. R. Lemire usually let his hormones do his thinking for him. He'd been so preoccupied with her outward attributes during the interview that he'd scarcely taken the time to look over a résumé that would be far more impressive at a New York fashion house than a retirement home in Podunk, Wyoming.

Tossing a precautionary look over her shoulder, Kayanne bolted across the street and began searching the adjoining neighborhood. Yard by yard.

Half a block later, she was on the verge of hysteria when a high-pitched giggle caught her attention. The charming scene unfolding on the veranda of some stranger's home stopped Kayanne in her tracks.

And left her trembling with relief.

Were it not for the residual adrenaline playing havoc with her nerves, she might have collapsed into a boneless pile right there on the pavement. She couldn't believe that she had worked herself into such a state over a flipping *tea party!*

Suddenly in no mood for exchanging social pleasantries, she threw open the front gate and marched up a neatly groomed sidewalk with the same determination that Sherman had advanced his army to the ocean. Stopping at the bottom of the steps, she employed a voice that had on occasion intimidated some of the best photographers in the business.

"Excuse me, but just what do you think you're doing?"

Ignoring the fire flashing in her caretaker's eyes, Rose smiled sweetly and proceeded to offer up the obvious. "I'm sharing a glass of iced tea with Mr. Evans. Would you care to join us, dear?"

"No," Kayanne snapped, too frustrated to toss in so much as a perfunctory thank you for the offer.

It boggled her mind that Rose had been so close all this time. And was apparently in no mood to be rushed along. The old lady dismissed Kayanne's petulance with a wave of one hand. With the other, she held out her glass for a refill.

The look of pleasure on her weathered face touched a heart considered incorrigible by many claiming to know Kayanne. She stared into a pair of twinkling blue eyes set in a face lined by eight decades of life and caught a glimpse of a young, wild Rose. Unnerved by the image, Kayanne turned her ire on a more deserving target: her runaway's unwitting partner in crime.

The man looked to be in his early thirties. Slim but not slight, with an amiable, masculine face that stopped short of being pretty, he sat on a cushioned wicker chair, making it impossible for Kayanne to judge his height. Positioned behind a laptop computer, he gave the impression of being completely comfortable in his lightly tanned skin.

He stirred in Kayanne a sense of barely restrained fury.

"Actually, I was directing the question to your boy-friend, Ernest Hemingway."

She gestured dismissively at stacks of books piled about the porch and bit her tongue to keep from asking what kind of drivel he was in the process of writing.

The taunt only evoked a grin from him. That he appeared pleased by the comparison drawn to the hard-drinking author made Kayanne frown. That quick smile of his might well disarm someone less cynical, but she had always been more inclined to humor a bad boy sporting tattoos and an attitude than a scholar who might take the time to indulge a confused elderly woman who meandered into his yard.

"All apologies to Hemingway aside, I was just in the middle of writing the great American novel when Mrs. Johansson's unexpected visit distracted me," their impromptu host volunteered in a voice that needed no liquor to make it sound throaty and deep. It wrapped around Kayanne's nerves like a designer silk scarf.

A self-effacing smile indicated that Rose's Mr. Evans didn't take himself nearly as seriously as his words might imply. Blushing to the roots of her silver-blue hair, Rose lived up to her colorful name as she gurgled with pleasure.

"It's been a long time since any man found me a distraction."

Kayanne rolled her eyes. This guy's antiquated charm might work magic on the geriatric set, but it grated on her already frayed nerves.

"Are you sure you wouldn't like a drink?" he asked her. "I'd be happy to fix you something stronger than iced tea if that makes any difference."

Kayanne bristled.

"Why should it?" She wanted to know.

Was it possible that her reputation preceded her to

such an unlikely spot? Or did she have a scarlet *A* pinned to her chest labeling her an alcoholic? One visible to everyone but her.

"Maybe because you seem so frazzled that steam's coming out of your ears," he explained.

An open smile remained affixed to his face in spite of Kayanne's loud harrumph.

"You really are welcome to sit down and relax," he added, rising and offering her his chair.

Kayanne was sorely tempted. Rose was safe and disinclined to leave, the sun was sweltering, and Kayanne felt as rung out as a rag doll. There were certainly worse things than to unwind in the presence of someone so gracious. And good-looking.

Spying an unopened bottle of whiskey perched on the porch railing a respectable distance away from a pitcher of iced tea beading in the afternoon sun, Kayanne reminded herself that she wasn't the best judge of character when it came to men. Reigning in her edginess, she did her best to don a more professional manner. It wasn't easy considering how the receding surge of adrenaline left her feeling as contentious as a boxer.

"I'm working," she said tersely. As if that had ever stopped her from having a drink before.

"Me, too," their host said, flashing her a wicked grin before picking up his own glass and taking a long, satisfying swig.

Kayanne caught the faintest whiff of alcohol. She swallowed hard. When, if ever, would temptation loosen its stranglehold on her? She stuck a hand deep into the pocket of her standard-issue smock to connect with the touchstone that kept her grounded day by day.

And moment by moment.

Her six-month sobriety token was more precious to her than diamonds. It was a physical reminder of how far she had come. And how far she had left to go.

Humbled by her ignominious descent and working on her recovery, she cautioned herself to be on the alert for the kind of behaviors that had caused her to stumble in the first place. She had no business entertaining any thoughts whatsoever about the opposite sex when her sobriety, not to mention her job, was on such shaky ground. Certain that she simply needed to apply the same focus and drive that had launched her career as a successful model to the task at hand, Kayanne set about thwarting any troublemaker who dared to interfere with her attempt to act responsibly.

"I guess unannounced visitors saunter into your front yard wearing their pajamas every day, Mr. Evans," she said, trying not to sound shrill. "Did it ever occur to you that it might be a good idea to call the nursing home next door and report a missing person to the staff there?"

"Call me Dave," he suggested, offering her his hand by way of a belated introduction. "And, no, actually it didn't. Since I just recently moved in, I don't know one neighbor from another, which I assumed Mrs. Johansson to be."

Rose pursed her lips. "I am your neighbor, and I'm not missing. I'm exactly where I want to be."

Duly chastised, Kayanne succumbed to courtesy by

accepting the man's outstretched hand. Just under six feet tall, she seldom had the pleasure of looking people in the eyes, let alone of having to look *up* to meet such a rough and hungry gaze. Or of feeling such an alarming jolt of sexual energy from the exchange of a simple handshake. Telling herself that the absolute last thing she needed to screw up her progress was a sexual interest, she withdrew her hand and anchored it firmly to one hip.

"You can call me Kayanne."

"Like hot pepper?" he asked without any apparent malice.

"Pronounced the same as the spice but spelled with a *K*."

She supposed that the fact that Dave was unfamiliar with her name accounted for his initial lack of animosity. One of the few models prominent enough to warrant first-name recognition among New York agencies, Kayanne mentally repeated Andy Warhol's quote about fame generally lasting all of fifteen minutes. Hers had lasted somewhat longer, but the cost had almost been her life.

Dave's smile failed to hide his primal response to her, but his dark eyes seemed somehow gentler than those of most men who perused her from head to toe without bothering to hide their appreciation of her as a sex object. Other women given to tender fantasies might well fall into a pair of eyes like those and lose themselves in daydreams involving home-cooked meals, adorable children and fabulous sex.

Not Kayanne, who refused to be deterred from her

mission by anything so banal as a potential amorous interest. For someone who associated sex with hitting rock bottom, there was no such thing as a little harmless flirtation. No matter how intrigued her hormones might be, she couldn't afford to focus on anything beyond returning her client to the "Home" without drawing undue attention. As fascinating as this blond, all-American novelist may be, Kayanne wasn't about to be fired for fraternizing with the same fellow who'd nearly caused her a heart attack.

Glancing at her watch, she attempted to bribe Rose into leaving. "If we don't hurry, you'll be late for the movie showing in the rec room. I believe it's *Titanic*."

"I already know how it ends," the older woman said dryly.

Kayanne didn't appreciate Dave's booming laugh. Not only did it serve to encourage Rose, it also reached right inside Kayanne and reverberated in every cell in her body. She resented this stranger for reminding her that she was a woman with carnal needs that hadn't been satisfied for quite some time. Her muscles contracted around a tug of arousal, and she met the interest flickering in his eyes with steely resolve.

It would be nice if, for just once, a man would look past her appearance and try focusing on what she felt inside. Her temper flared to match the color of hair that once graced the covers of some of the trendiest magazines on supermarket shelves.

"Do you think there's a word in your thesaurus that might describe the peculiar relationship you have with a woman so much older than you? And maybe another one to help me get Rambling Rose here back to her room before an all-points bulletin is issued and I lose the job of my dreams?"

To Dave's credit, he only blinked twice before regaining his composure. Leaning his weight on the back of the chair that he'd offered her earlier, he said, "I believe the first word is called *friendship*. Maybe it's not one you're familiar with."

"Barely," Kayanne admitted.

Truthfully, she could think of few people who would risk an alliance with the town's most infamous heartbreaker. So far as she knew, friendship was just a weak substitute that unattractive women used in lieu of romance. And she had yet to meet a man who had so much as a clue what the word meant.

Loneliness coiled through the empty space in her chest.

"The second word that you're looking for," Dave clarified, following up on her line of questioning, "would be *please*."

It was a word that had never come easily to Kayanne. She tested it on her tongue and found it bitter. And tough to chew.

While not exactly looking to claim the title of Miss Congeniality, Kayanne did her best to curb her famous temper. She already had a long list of people to whom she needed to make amends as part of her recovery and didn't need to add yet another name to it.

"Please…" It slipped through clenched lips.

Dave's biceps relaxed as he released his grip on the

chair and rewarded her efforts by turning his pearly whites full force on Rose.

"What d'ya say you ladies drop by again some other day when your visit is sanctioned by the proper authorities so that none of us get into any trouble?"

Rose shot Kayanne a killing glance as she reached across the table to pat Dave's hand affectionately.

"All right, but you should stock up on gingersnaps. They're my favorite. Just in case I decide to stop by again. Say tomorrow. Around the same time."

After a deliberate pause, she added pointedly, "By myself."

"I'll look forward to it," Dave assured her. "But you be sure to bring Kayanne along too. Being new in town, I can use all the friends I can get. I've just signed on at the community college to teach English starting this fall, and I don't know more than a half a dozen people around here."

Ah, that explains it.... Kayanne thought to herself.

After a week of running into nothing but hostility from people who would just as soon kick her while she was down as offer her a hand up, she knew there had to be a reason why this man wasn't taking potshots at her dwindling fame and minimum-wage position.

Or propositioning her...

Kayanne didn't want to delay their departure by refusing Dave's invitation outright and causing Rose to dig in her heels again. As much as she'd love to beat the afternoon heat with a glass of tea and strike up a friendly conversation with someone who couldn't judge her by her past, duty and a pressing need to pay the bills called.

Tomorrow wouldn't be any different in that respect. Unless, of course, she could convince her supervisor to bend the rules, which was highly unlikely. J.R. struck her as the rule-conscious sort who would come to a complete stop at a burned-out red light in a deserted ghost town. At midnight.

"Until we meet again then," Rose said, holding out an arthritic hand to Dave.

Kayanne noticed how gently he took it in his own, being careful not to squeeze too hard. She almost choked when he lifted it to his lips and placed a kiss upon its leathery surface. She was tempted to ask him to kiss another part of *her* anatomy as they took their leave but didn't want to risk upsetting her genteel client with such a vulgar suggestion.

"Would you like any help in getting Rose home?" Dave asked.

"I can handle things from here by myself," Kayanne told him curtly.

The thought of anyone thinking otherwise was intolerable.

"But thank you for offering," she added as an afterthought. "And for everything else."

Such as being so sweet to Rose and so understanding of her own plight. For making her feel pretty instead of dirty for a change. And mostly for just playing along and making a difficult situation more tolerable.

"I mean it about stopping back by again sometime," Dave said. "Don't worry about interrupting my writing. The truth is that I'd be eternally grateful for the diversion."

Having been considered a *diversion* more than once in the past, Kayanne just smiled and put him off as politely as possible. "We'll see."

The likelihood of their paths ever crossing again was slight. Still, she appreciated the invitation more than he would ever know. She couldn't remember a time when a man had made her feel so welcome without expecting something in return.

"Let me see you two ladies to the gate," Dave said, coming around from behind his chair to help Rose up and make sure she didn't fall down the steps.

Delighted with the simple courtesy, she took his arm and gushed all the way to the sidewalk. It was easy to see why Rose was so enamored. In fact, they barely stepped off out of hearing distance before the older woman proved there is no age at which one is safely exempt from the green-eyed monster.

"Why don't you just mind your own business?" she hissed, yanking her elbow out of Kayanne's helping hand.

While she wasn't exactly expecting overwhelming gratitude for her efforts in locating Mrs. Johansson and returning her safely to her room, Kayanne didn't think she'd be attacked for it either. So much for harboring any fantasies about Rose becoming the kindly grandmother she'd never had.

"What are you talking about?"

"If you must know, I'm in love with Professor Evans," she said coyly. "So consider yourself warned, girlie—keep your hands off of him!"

Kayanne tried not to laugh. Rose's crush was sweet,

in a pathetic sort of way, and she saw no reason to point out the obvious difference in their ages. Any more than she needed anyone to call attention to the difference between Dave Evans's and her own background, education and standing in the community.

"Don't worry," she assured her aged companion. "He's not my type."

Rose looked surprised.

"Why the hell not?" she demanded, shattering any remaining stereotypes Kayanne might have had about doddering old ladies. "He's good-looking, smart and damned polite considering how rude you were back there."

Kayanne hoped swearing with impunity was a right one earned with age. At least that would be one thing to look forward to in the future. Why she felt the need to explain herself to a geriatric fugitive was beyond her, but she saw no need to gloss over the truth either.

"I generally go for the rebel type. Fixer-uppers, my mother likes to call them. Personally, I just feel that there's less chance of hurt feelings when the time comes to go our separate ways if both of us are irreparably flawed."

Rose shook her gray head in dismay. "What about your feelings, sweet pea? And don't try and tell me you don't have any."

"My feelings are off-limits."

Rose stopped shuffling her feet.

"Not if you want to get back to the Manor anytime soon they're not."

Kayanne forced herself to take a deep, calming breath. She could scarcely explain to herself let alone

to Rose that Dave Evans appeared to be a real gentleman and, as such, was the exact opposite of the kind of
man she used to date—before realizing that her sobriety
hinged on remaining single.

"Let's just say he scares me."

It wasn't an easy admission for a woman who worked
so very hard to appear fearless at all times.

"Or maybe it's just the stifling stability he represents
that scares me," she clarified, sorting her feelings out loud.

A stickler for honesty, Kayanne hoped she wasn't
lying to herself. For while that statement had rung true
in the past, lately dreams of domesticity crept into her
thoughts at the oddest times. She assumed it had more
to do with her self-imposed celibacy and a desire to
carve out a more normal life for herself than the ticking
of her biological clock.

"No need to be afraid of a good man," Rose informed her with an unladylike snort. "Unless, of
course, he's mine."

Kayanne bit her lip to keep from grinning. As a recovering alcoholic and a has-been model with a reputation as
long as Sheridan's Main Street, she stood as much of a
chance of hooking up with the handsome would-be Pulit-
zer prize winner as Rose herself did. Now that the crisis
of the moment was behind her, Kayanne took a minute to
consider Rose's perspective as they began their slow journey across the street. She had to admit that Dave wasn't
hard to look at. And the fact that his charm extended across
generations and beyond the bounds of barroom pickup
lines said something about his character as well.

He was exactly the sort of man her mother was attempting to pray into the life of an unruly daughter whose homecoming was as much an act of penance for past sins as it was a matter of necessity. Kayanne shuddered at the thought of being attracted to a man her mother actually approved of: stable, sober and undeniably *nice*. One could almost attach the smell of sugar cookies and wholesome goodness to him.

She imagined Professor Evans's classes would soon be overflowing with eager women far more interested in their instructor than anything he might assign them to read in the textbook. With his good looks and easy-going personality, she doubted he'd be lonely long.

Kayanne directed Rose to the back door of the retirement center, hoping to slip her in without attracting undue attention. She didn't have the heart to set the old lady straight regarding matters of propriety. What was the harm in harboring a little romantic fantasy at her age? Just because Kayanne had decided to shelve her romantic dreams didn't mean everybody else had to.

It was too bad Dave Evans was the sort of man who could make a woman regret her decision to take herself off the market.

Permanently.

Two

Dave Evans stopped typing only when it grew too dark to see the keyboard. As the sun dipped behind the Big Horn Mountains and bid him good evening, he stretched out his lean frame, put both hands behind his head and let out a satisfied sigh. He didn't know what to make of the redheaded Amazon who had strode into his yard earlier in the day, but he was grateful to her nonetheless. After weeks of wrestling with writer's block, he'd finally produced something other than tortured prose destined to fill the garbage can.

He didn't dare call this intruder by her real name. Even if their paths never crossed again, Kayanne was far too unusual a name to slip unobtrusively between the covers of a book. The woman who'd trespassed onto his property and into his novel had the same unnerving effect upon his usually aloof hero as she had upon him. Just the memory of those catlike eyes, lithe body and sassy attitude ignited a fire deep in his belly. Although no stranger to physical attraction, Dave couldn't remember ever being broadsided by such overt sensuality as hers before.

Since Kayanne's handshake alone transmitted enough voltage to electrocute a mortal man and she was already threatening to burn up the pages of his previously stalled novel, he could only imagine what she could do in real life between the sheets of his bed....

He reprimanded himself for allowing his thoughts to travel down that shameless avenue. Was this woman so intriguing simply because she was a complete enigma or just because he was feeling alone as a newcomer to the community?

From her unusual name to the defiance that had defined her grasp, Kayanne was unlike anyone else he'd ever encountered. He was fascinated by the challenge flashing in a pair of eyes the color of jade.

Jaded eyes.

Dave suspected those eyes had seen a good deal more of the world than any of the characters he'd invented with their complicated, contrived pasts. Hell, there was more vibrancy in a simple toss of Kayanne's unruly mane than in any of the words he'd so painstakingly fashioned for the cool, blond heroine of his imagination who, as of yet, had failed to dominate either his hero or his novel. His writing was seamless enough in structure to earn him a master's degree, but lately it felt as separated from the nitty-gritty of reality as the ivory towers of academia that defined both his literary style and his life.

That wasn't to say that he hadn't experienced any success as a writer. Reviews of his first novel, *Bitter Fruits,* had heralded him as the next William Faulkner. Unfortunately, he'd never been particularly fond of Faulkner. Nor had the fact that the book had won some literary awards translated into a huge advance for his next novel. Commercial success and literary success were not always one and the same. That reality lay as heavy on his chest as the impending deadline that was kicking his butt. Lately he hadn't been able to produce much of anything except writer's angst, and that didn't translate well to the page.

Dave worried that his parents were right about it being time to give up on his dream of being a full-time writer and academic. John and Eula Evans couldn't understand why their only son would choose to spend his life knocking his brains out over a keyboard in the wilds of Wyoming when he could just as easily take over the family business from the comfort of their Birmingham estate.

Frankly he couldn't understand it himself.

All he knew was that there was a monster inside him that had to be fed a certain number of words every day or it would eat him instead. He was hoping that the obscurity of this remote mountain town would allow him to prove himself on his own terms—and to break through the writer's block that had him so stymied. Simply introducing Kayanne as a minor character took his story in a fresh, new direction and breathed life into words that, up until now, had felt as dry as dust blowing across the vast Wyoming prairie. Dave dubbed his new character Spice, hoping no one would draw the connection between fact and fiction.

At the moment, he was more concerned about not letting this headstrong character take over his whole book. In the span of a couple of pages she was already making moves to push his delicate heroine all the way back to her Tara-like roots. After all the time he'd taken to develop Jasmine as a woman of substance, he wasn't about to let her go so easily into the night—even if the outspoken Spice was of the opinion that she was little more than a simpering fool. Spice might not be the nicest character he'd worked with, but the woman knew her own mind.

And took great delight in playing with his.

Later that night when Dave crawled between the sheets of his bed, he was startled by the fact that it was not his blue-eyed blond creation that played havoc behind his closed eyelids, but rather a long-legged, green-eyed beastess who left him hard and needy in his dreams.

The following morning, he took a break from his chapter to stock up on gingersnaps at the corner grocery store. Since he'd bought them expressly for Rose and her keeper, he was disappointed when they failed to show up later that day.

Or the day after that.

Or after that.

And when his writing once again turned as stale as the

cookies hardening into doorstops atop his kitchen counter, he was tempted to check into the retirement center next door to see if anything untoward had happened to the charming Mrs. Johansson—and her companion who had been acting as his unwitting writing muse.

Instead, he decided to do what Hemingway so often had done when feeling short on inspiration: he went back to the corner store and bought some whiskey to go with his fresh batch of gingersnaps.

Kayanne could feel the beginning of a migraine coming on. A mild twitching behind her right eye was working itself into a full-blown throb as she filled out yet another required piece of bureaucratic paperwork and counted the minutes until her shift would be over. Because they were so shorthanded at the center, she hadn't had a day off since her first day of working there. Between taking care of her ailing mother at home, adjusting to a new and decidedly unglamorous job, and fighting her craving for alcohol, she was feeling as brittle as a wishbone.

And just as likely to snap in two.

The last few days had been among the most trying of her life. Petulant photographers, vying divas and grueling hours under the most arduous of conditions were nothing compared to being treated like a recalcitrant teenager by her mother again.

Like a leper by old acquaintances.

And a sexual threat by a card-carrying member of AARP.

In between her mother's wheedling that she should find a good man with whom to settle down, her boss's lecherous perusal and overt disdain for their clients, and Rose's determination to get her fired, Kayanne found herself longing to wash away the indignities of life the old-fashioned way: with a bottle of tequila and shaker of salt.

It took an act of sheer willpower and commitment to the original twelve-step program to steer her past the nearest liquor store and into an AA meeting instead. Once a day she sought solace in the success stories of those who had been through it themselves—fellow drunks who neither stooped to condone excuses nor looked down upon her in judgment. Her sponsor, Bethany Moore, assured Kayanne that her present job at the Evening Star Retirement Manor was all part of a universal plan to assist in her recovery. Bethany believed that simple labor devoted to the good of others was exactly what an ex-model celebrity needed to learn proper humility. For her own part, Kayanne chalked it all up as karmic payback for her previous bad behavior.

Still, the day she'd received her six-month sobriety token, Kayanne had found the applause in that dingy, smoke-filled room warmer and far more genuine than the echoes of any star-studded event of her past.

Outside the four walls that bound her fellow AA members in blissful anonymity, life continued to present more challenges. Since her first successful break out, Rose Johansson was outdoing herself daily to repeat the feat. Tuesday she'd coerced a friend into calling the front desk with an elaborate story about scam artists targeting old-folks homes in hopes of distracting Kayanne long enough to slip out the front door unnoticed. Wednesday Rose had tried creeping unobtrusively behind a pile of laundry that had been leaving the building. When confronted, she had feigned confusion as convincingly as any legitimate Alzheimer's patient. But the next day when Kayanne had caught Rose climbing onto a chair placed strategically beneath her bedroom window, she'd dropped the innocent act and had proceeded to call her "warden" every name in the book.

It wasn't the kind of book Kayanne expected an old lady to check out of the library, either….

Claiming that an unruly five-year-old had nothing on Mrs. Johansson, J.R. had threatened to handcuff her to the bed if she kept up her shenanigans. Kayanne wasn't sure if her supervisor was joking or not. He didn't so much as bother to hide his contempt for the residents from anyone but visitors and potential clients. J.R. treated the elderly men and women who had raised families, owned businesses and fought in wars as though they were uncooperative children incapable of making even the simplest decision by themselves. His lack of people skills was partially responsible for the high turnover of staff at the Manor. The rest could be blamed on the atmosphere of impending death that permeated the place.

Despite her own reputation as a cold-hearted bitch, Kayanne couldn't bring herself to feel such detachment for the clients with whom she worked. Personally, she found them a good deal more interesting than J.R., who was apt to point out what a good catch he was whenever the opportunity presented itself. He was a man laboring under the delusion that his supervisory position more than made up for his lack of height and personality.

The way he looked at Kayanne made her skin crawl, but she did her best to shrug it off with a world-weariness that had yet to stoop her shoulders. If that little maggot thought he was going to use his influence to worm anything more than a cordial greeting from her, he would have to stand in line behind a long queue of men mistaken in their belief that they could use sex as a weapon against her.

Kayanne found herself absently wondering if Dave Evans was of the same ilk. Even though they'd only exchanged a few words in an awkward situation, he'd nonetheless made an impression on her. He'd been so sweet to Rose before Kayanne had put in an appearance that it was hard to think he'd have any ulterior motives along those lines. Of course, just because he was kind to old ladies didn't mean he was any different from J.R. in the way he treated younger ones. But as Rose was apt to point out, Dave certainly was easier on the eyes. And there was something about the man's quick smile that worked away at a girl's heart—even one as well protected as Kayanne's.

"Code ninety-nine."

A male voice over the intercom crackled with irritation. Code ninety-nine was the administration's secret way of informing workers that a resident was missing. While it didn't inspire the level of panic that such an announcement would have on Kayanne's first day at work, it was nonetheless the perfect culmination of a lousy week. She rubbed her temples. One didn't have to contact a psychic to figure out who was AWOL again.

Or where she was headed.

Dave couldn't have been more delighted when Rose dropped by looking as if she were dressed for a high tea than if the Queen of England had just announced her presence on his front stoop. Instead of the loose-fitting housedress that she'd worn the last time they'd met, today she was sporting a beige polyester pantsuit with a bright bow tied jauntily at her throat. Freshly set and colored, her hair was the same tint as the cotton candy he'd loved as a boy whenever the carnival had come to town.

"Where's your friend?" Dave asked, feigning nonchalance.

"That woman is not my friend," Rose said, taking the chair Dave offered her. "She is the bossiest, most controlling person I've ever had the displeasure to be around. You have no idea what I had to go through just to steal some time alone with you today."

Dave couldn't help but grin at the thought of Rose giving the indomitable Kayanne the slip. She didn't strike him as the sort who would enjoy playing hide-and-seek on her shift. He couldn't imagine why such a fascinating creature was hiding her beauty in, of all places, a retirement center, but he was determined to uncover the reason. As much as he wanted to believe that this budding obsession sprang only from a need to advance his own sluggish plot, he couldn't help but be enthralled with her as a person. And he wasn't fool enough to dismiss the physical attraction he felt for her as anything less than what it was.

Unmitigated lust.

He tried to look stern. "I hope this isn't another unauthorized visit, Rose."

She gave him an audacious wink that took him aback. "What Kayanne doesn't know won't hurt her."

"But it could very well hurt me," Dave replied, thinking about the many ways the redheaded drill sergeant could put him in his place. Some of which made his belly tighten.

He was in the process of looking up the number for the Evening Star Retirement Manor when Rose's keeper made a belated albeit not entirely unexpected appearance on his front porch.

"Isn't anyone going to invite me to the party?" she asked, sauntering up the walk and smiling at them both in a fashion reminiscent of the Cheshire cat from *Alice's Adventures in Wonderland.*

The way Kayanne managed to make a simple work smock look chic was worthy of at least a full page of description, Dave decided. She wasn't beautiful in the classical sense. More like Hilary Swank than the Grace Kelly type he was usually drawn to, Kayanne nevertheless had an aura about her that made a man take notice of the whole package. Tall, big boned and physically powerful, she wore sex like an exotic brand of perfume. Her hair had a windblown look that beckoned a man to run his fingers through it, looking for glints of gold among those fiery strands. There was nothing coy about the way she trained her piercing eyes on him either, tearing away his usual sense of ease and leaving him feeling exposed and guilty.

It was almost as if she knew the lascivious thoughts he'd been entertaining about her over the past few days.

Rose interrupted his runaway train of thought by snapping, "Everybody knows two's company and three's a crowd. Surely, Kayanne, you have more pressing issues back at the Manor than ruining my afternoon."

"I was just about to call," Dave interjected holding out the phone as if tendering a peace offering. "Would you care for a gingersnap and a drink?"

The flash of vulnerability he glimpsed in the depths of Kayanne's eyes was gone before she could arch a fine eyebrow into a question mark.

"Gingersnaps, huh?"

The look she gave him made him feel like the kind of scoundrel who might deliberately lure an old lady over to his place with cookies for the sole intention of getting to know her young companion better. Dave was surprised when she took a conciliatory stance and her mouth relaxed into a smile.

"I guess there's no reason for me to be a party pooper," she said, easing into the nearest chair.

Rose harrumphed. "Lordy, girl, don't you know how to take a hint?"

"Better than you apparently," Kayanne countered before turning her attention to Dave. "Houdini himself would have been easier to commandeer the last couple

of days. I was afraid she was going to break a hip climbing out a window trying to sneak over here."

Dave did his best not to embarrass Rose by laughing.
Here was the perfect opportunity to ask Kayanne for
a date to see if he couldn't get to know her better. Pref-
erably without her elderly client in tow. Figuring his
chances would be greatly enhanced if he came across
as a nice guy, he tried enlisting Rose as an ally and
working his way up incrementally.

"I have an idea," he said. "Why don't you just set up
a time every day when the two of you can come by to
visit? That way Rose doesn't put herself in danger, you
don't have to worry about her and everybody at the
Manor can breathe a sigh of relief."

Kayanne studied him so intensely that Dave had to
fight to keep from fidgeting.

"That sounds like a great idea," she said startling
him by leaning in and deliberately invading his space.
"There's just one thing I need to know before I go to my
supervisor with this proposal."

"What's that?" Dave asked, doing his best neither to
step back submissively nor to succumb to the desire to
ravage her on the spot.

Kayanne gave him the kind of hard, searching look
he suspected she reserved for men who were clearly
after one thing and one thing alone.

"Just what's your angle, buddy?"

Three

Kayanne had slapped men who looked less shocked than Dave Evans did at the moment. Taking his indignation as a positive sign that he wasn't up to anything sneaky helped take the edge off any guilt she might feel for posing the question in the first place.

"Are you always so paranoid, or do I just bring that trait out in you?" Dave asked, all former charm wiped from his countenance.

Kayanne stopped overworking a piece of gum between her jaws to scowl at him.

"It's just you."

Rose harrumphed.

A smile toyed with the edges of Kayanne's lips. On some masochistic level she enjoyed matching wits with

Rose. It beat trying to coax a simple greeting from some of her other clients who were, as far as Kayanne was concerned, overmedicated and under-stimulated. She just hoped she was as stubborn and passionate as Rose when she reached eighty.

That Dave was serving the old lady's favorite cookie thawed something that had been frozen hard inside Kayanne for a long time. Recalling the wild escapades of her past, she wondered when she, of all people, had become the world's official rule enforcer instead of its number-one breaker. God surely had a wicked sense of humor.

Her mouth watered at the thought of washing away her troubles with a shot of something other than reality for a change.

"I'll take that glass of iced tea now," she said. "That is, if you're still offering."

There. Kayanne felt proud of herself for remaining on the wagon without anyone being the wiser about how incredibly difficult it had been not to ask for the "something stronger" Dave had offered the last time she'd been here. Her crusade was strictly personal in nature. She didn't feel the need to push her newfound sobriety on anyone else. Or expect the rest of the world to stop drinking just because she'd chosen sobriety over a lifestyle that had left her empty and used.

Of course, that didn't mean that she'd forgotten all about the old gang. She often found herself wondering what they were up to. And who her hard-drinking ex was spending his time with now that she was out of the picture.

Forrester would get quite a laugh out of seeing her in a shapeless smock working with a bunch of tired, old farts—a name he bestowed on anyone over the age of forty.

Forcibly pulling herself out of the past and into the present, Kayanne dialed the number for the retirement center.

"I've located Mrs. Johansson," she said. "There's no need to worry. She's safe and sound at a neighbor's less than a block away. As soon as she finishes up visiting here, we'll both be back."

With that, she disconnected and studied Dave at length while he fixed her drink. His dusty-blond hair was cut short in a tousled, no-nonsense style favored by athletes, and there was an outdoorsy air about him that belied the sedentary nature of his writing career. If he were to offer her a tour of the house, Kayanne bet she'd find one room devoted solely to weights and exercise equipment. She found it hard to believe he maintained that physique by lifting books alone.

It was difficult aligning his nice-guy image with the latent virility he emoted. Kayanne took a moment to examine her manicured nails. If she scratched beneath his courteous veneer, would she find a hot-blooded lover? Or just another loser out to get what he could from her?

"Are you from around here originally?" Dave asked, handing her a tall glass.

The slice of lemon decorating the rim was a nice touch, she thought.

"Born and raised right here in Sheridan County."

"You've lived here all your life then?"

While not inclined to go into details about her past, Kayanne saw no reason to avoid answering questions simply designed to facilitate polite conversation.

"I didn't say that. The truth is I couldn't get out of this provincial hellhole fast enough when I was younger."

"Feeling like that, what could have possibly brought you back here?"

"My mother had a heart attack, and she needs somebody to stay with her while she recuperates."

She felt no obligation to explain that the real reason she'd taken a break from modeling was to pull herself together. Or that her mother's illness had merely been the impetus to bring Kayanne back home rather than signing herself into a private rehab center that she could scarcely afford considering some of the terrible financial decisions she'd made at the height of her drinking.

"That's commendable," Dave said. "I understand about the need to get away from, and yet still stay connected to, family."

Kayanne caught the subtle lilt of a Southern drawl in his words. She wondered if it had been deliberately schooled out of him for the same reason her agent had encouraged her to lose her own Midwestern accent. He'd found it as hokey as the apple-pie name that her parents had given her.

Dave chatted on amiably unaware of the road her thoughts had taken. Charming, gracious and funny, he was attentive to Rose without being patronizing.

Shaking her head at his lame jokes, Kayanne found

herself truly relaxing for the first time in a long time that she could remember.

Without alcohol or drugs.

If she wasn't careful, she realized that she just might let her guard down. She forced herself to remember just how dangerous that could be to her sobriety. Holding Dave's gaze, she wondered how she might feel if it ever came down to breaking his heart. Undoubtedly a whole lot worse than in previous relationships with men like Forrester who didn't have hearts to break.

She glanced curiously at the laptop sitting open on the coffee table next to her.

"What are you writing, by the way?"

Dave feigned nonchalance as he reached across her to activate the screen saver. When his hand accidentally brushed across her arm, a frisson of awareness caused her to draw back as if she'd been scalded. Kayanne wondered if the unexpected tingles affecting her nerves were wreaking havoc with his as well.

"I already told you," Dave replied glibly, "the great American novel."

Having been around artistic types a good deal, Kayanne understood that novelists were territorial, but she couldn't imagine what—or who—this man thought he was protecting. Finding his response cliché and evasive, she didn't bother hiding her irritation.

"Surely you don't think either Rose or I are out to steal your ideas?"

Dave's smile wobbled at the corners. "Of course not.

It's just considered bad luck for a writer to show his work to anyone before he's had a chance to polish it."

Past experience led Kayanne to believe men would just as soon lie to your face as trust you with the truth on even the most inconsequential of matters. Not that she cared one way or the other. As long as it didn't involve her, she didn't give a damn what he wrote about. She suspected that, like so many of the *artistes* who'd frequented the same parties that she'd attended in New York, Dave hadn't produced much of anything other than empty bottles of booze. He was probably just embarrassed to be put on the spot.

"What do you like to read?" he asked, abruptly changing the subject.

Kayanne took a moment to respond. It wasn't the type of question often posed to her, she supposed because most people assumed she didn't read much. Actually, her tastes were quite eclectic. As a girl, she'd devoured just about anything she could get her hands on, and in high school, she'd discovered a fondness for the classics that her English teachers had forced upon their captive audiences. When her modeling career had been in full swing, she'd barely had time to skim the current fashion magazines. And since returning home, she hadn't picked up much because her mother's preference tended toward overtly religious themes that Kayanne found heavy-handed and oppressive.

"It depends," she answered. "If you've got anything on the shelf, I'd like to give you a read. What exactly is it you write?"

"It's been categorized as a combination between literary and dark fiction."

Once again she was irritated by the vagueness of his response. Dave Evans sounded very much like a professor. She imagined him wowing a classroom full of women with fabulous reviews of his work.

Feeling suddenly stupid, she ventured a question. "Just what kind of book isn't considered literary?"

Apparently one needed a college education to make such distinctions. Kayanne assumed that Dave would look down his nose at the popular fiction she enjoyed reading. She didn't have a lot of patience with snobs, having encountered her fair share of them who had associated her looks with a lack of intelligence. Especially when she'd been starting out as a green kid from the sticks.

"Kay Anne!" scoffed the first agent she'd approached. "If you're lucky, a sweet, little old name like that will get you about as far as the back door in this business. Sorry, kid, but I don't have the time to invest in trying to turn a desperate hick into a silk purse."

Even now the memory stung. Less than two years later she'd sent a copy of her first major magazine cover to the same fellow signed with her real name. After a painful trial-and-error period, Kayanne had discovered she could trick people into thinking she was chic by eliminating the space between her first and middle names, and adding a little *spice* to her country packaging.

"By literary," Dave explained, "I mean the kind of

books that usually generate great reviews but lousy royalties."

Kayanne smiled at his unexpected candor. That could explain why he needed to supplement his writing income by teaching.

Ever the capitalist, she ventured to ask, "Wouldn't it make sense to combine the two?"

"Good sense and inspiration don't always go together," Dave explained.

Belatedly remembering to include Rose in the conversation, Kayanne glanced over at the comfortable recliner the older woman had claimed as her throne. She was sound asleep. Dave and Kayanne shared a look akin to that of doting parents studying a sleeping infant. Granted, Rose didn't have the same cherubic face as a baby, but in repose she managed to pull off a look of innocence.

When a deep snore erupted from her lips, they laughed out loud.

Never had Kayanne felt so comfortable in the presence of such a drool-worthy man. Studying her surroundings, she decided his home reflected equal parts of industry and gentility. Books clearly held a place of importance in this house. They were neatly stacked from floor to ceiling in built-in bookcases, arranged artfully on the living room coffee table and littered in no apparent order about the recliner. A photograph of a handsome couple that Kayanne assumed were his parents rested on the mantel next to several of him in a variety of outdoor activities such as white-water rafting and skiing. It appeared that the American dream that had always been just out of reach for her when she'd been growing up poor and scared was this man's birthright.

She couldn't imagine him writing anything particularly dark. Maybe he was afraid of exploring the sinister aspects of his own personality and was thus drawn to such things in his imagination.

Or maybe, as in the fashion industry, dark themes were simply in vogue. More photographers than she cared to remember had tried making her into an angry, cruel beauty. Kayanne's athletic body and country-fresh face were contrary to the heroin addict's look so popular on Fifth Avenue. Even with a hangover, she'd had trouble pulling off Gothic. Her meteoric rise to the top of the industry had surprised almost everyone.

Her career was the last thing, however, she wanted to discuss with Dave. One of the nicest things about him was that he knew nothing about her past—neither the glamour that had set her apart nor the despair that had brought her back home.

"So how did you end up living at the brink of civilization as we know it?" she wanted to know.

"Unlike you, I deliberately picked it. I prefer Sheridan's sleepy streets and rugged mountains to Birmingham's botanical gardens and congestion."

"Does your family still live in Alabama?"

Dave's brow furrowed in consternation. "They're so entrenched in that generational soil that just getting them to visit is a terrible imposition. Like you, they don't understand what it is about the area that's such a magnet for me. They're hoping your bitter Wyoming winters will bring me to my senses."

He sounded suddenly sad, and Kayanne noticed how quickly he tried to change the subject away from himself.

"How long have you been working with the elderly?"

"About a week," she said with a trace of chagrin. "And if Rose doesn't start being a little more cooperative about staying put, I may not make it till my first payday."

Dave gave her a funny look. "Would that be so bad?"

He wasn't the only one who wondered if she was wasting her talents working at the Manor. Nevertheless, Kayanne was under no obligation to explain her reasons to anyone.

"Do you find something about my job to be beneath you?" she asked defensively.

Dave's response was immediate.

"The real question is whether it's beneath you. Forgive me for pointing out the obvious, but it seems strange that a woman as beautiful and intelligent as you would want to hide herself in a nursing home."

Kayanne was impressed by the fact that he somehow managed to flatter and insult her at the same time. As tempting as it might be to parade her accolades before him, it was even more refreshing to be taken at face value for a change. The truth of the matter was that it would suit her just fine if Dave Evans didn't find out about her past until well after she'd moved on with her future.

Kayanne was saved from having to come up with a clever response by another loud snore, one that actually shook Rose awake. Looking embarrassed, she wiped a spot of drool off her chin.

"I hope you enjoyed your little catnap," Dave said with a reassuring smile meant to ease her mind.

"I did, thank you. Now, if you don't mind, Kayanne dear, I'm ready to go home."

Kayanne assumed that the endearment was more for Dave's benefit than generated from any genuine fondness toward her, but she was happy to oblige nonetheless. Sitting in this sunny little nook drinking iced tea was making her sappy. She saw little point in wishing for the kind of life that had been denied her. God knows her widowed mother had done the best she could to provide, and if their home lacked the warmth of this man's at least she'd never gone hungry.

At least not physically.

"You'll be sure to come back, won't you?" Dave asked as he escorted them to the front door.

Rose didn't hesitate. "Of course."

"I'll see what the boss has to say about it." That was all Kayanne would commit to. She had all she could manage trying to survive day by day without a drink without cluttering up her life with social obligations.

She helped Rose slowly down the porch steps and stopped to let her rest at the bottom. There Kayanne studied Dave as if considering whether to divulge a state secret of the gravest importance.

"Romantica," she blurted out.

When he looked at her quizzically, she gave him a grin that completely undermined the tough-girl image she'd worked so hard to perfect. It delighted her to know a little something about the publishing industry that he didn't.

"That's what I like to read."

Four

Dave had to look up *romantica* on the Internet to find out exactly what it was. A cross between romance and erotica, the description alone whetted his interest—in the enigmatic woman who'd claimed to read it as well as the genre itself. He'd never met anyone more intriguing. It hadn't escaped his notice that Kayanne didn't like talking about herself and her past. As mysterious as the waxing and waning moon, she was lighting his way through a book that was miraculously getting easier to write every day. Although Dave couldn't honestly say that he found her altogether up to the standards of gentility and charm that he usually applied to his heroines, he couldn't deny that he wanted her, either.

Just the word *romantica* conjured up images of Kayanne lying naked in bed beneath him. Ashamed that he didn't have better control over his thoughts, Dave reminded himself that her disclosure about being a closet romantic didn't bode well for turning their relationship into something of a more passionate nature. As much as he'd like to believe the lady was into fleeting sexual gratification, her choice of reading material indicated otherwise. Whether she'd ever admit to it or not, Dave suspected Kayanne was looking for a long-term commitment—just like every other woman he knew. And the only commitment he was willing to make at the moment was to his writing.

Given Kayanne's reading preferences, he doubted if she would be much impressed with what he wrote. He imagined that she would find it as pretentious as he did on those days when he was feeling most vulnerable. How ironic that his literary awards left him feeling such a fraud. Afraid that he wouldn't be able to repeat his initial literary success, he'd wrestled with self-doubt that had manifested itself in a full-blown case of writer's block.

Dave had no idea how Kayanne's unexpected presence allowed him to sidestep that block. He simply knew that she was able to blast through it with those piercing green eyes of hers as if she were endowed with superhuman powers. As disconcerting as it might be to have her alter ego Spice take over the page without even bothering to let him know what she was up to, Dave preferred chasing her on a wild ride to staring at a blank screen wondering if the only way to prime his creative pump was with a stiff drink.

If he failed to meet his looming deadline and produce something at least as good if not better than his debut novel, he would ultimately have to admit that his parents were right and do what they'd wanted him to do all along: give up his dream of writing and come home to fulfill his destiny of taking over the family business. He had no desire to spend the rest of his life litigating other people's miseries as part of the firm of Evans, Evans and—soon to be—Evans. Unfortunately his feelings on the matter were beside the point. If he couldn't turn his writing into something more lucrative and less excruciating, he'd have little choice but to support himself with his teaching job. And while that might be an acceptable option for someone raised with a lower standard of living, he'd grown up with expensive tastes. Dave couldn't imagine struggling to meet the rent every month.

The only thing more untenable would be having to sponge off his parents.

Kayanne had no idea that she was responsible for postponing his career crisis a little while longer. And while it was true that he had lost control of his plot since she'd waltzed into his life, he was happy to be writing fluently again—without feeling the compulsion to edit every single word until little but soup was left. Writing had become fun again. And in spite of his critics' stuffy literary expectations, an element of mystery and romantica was seeping into his book.

Convincing J.R. to sanction Rose's expeditions to Dave's house wasn't nearly as difficult as Kayanne had first imagined. As much grief as the old lady had caused the entire staff the past few days, everybody was eager to accommodate her insomuch as it kept them from having to clamp a police-issued monitor on her ankle or hire a full-time bodyguard to watch over her. If all it took to keep Mrs. Johansson from being forcibly detained was giving her a little time to visit a willing neighbor, then J.R. was all for it.

These outings perked Rose up like a parched flower beneath a welcome rain shower. So immediate and obvious was her transformation that other residents began taking notice. Some wanted to know what kind of elixir she was taking. Others wanted directions to the fountain of youth from her.

"It's right across the street," Rose replied coyly.

The special attention she'd started paying her hair and makeup, however, did little to improve on a wardrobe she claimed was "as outdated as the Depression." As much as Kayanne hated to agree, she was of the opinion that the contents of Rose's entire closet should be donated to the nearest Goodwill store.

"Would you mind taking me shopping today?" Rose asked, feigning a sweetness that Kayanne knew she only employed when she wanted someone to do something for her—or she was trying to impress Dave.

"And don't worry about money. It's not an issue. For all intents and purposes, I'm loaded. I'd just like to buy a few things that don't make me feel ready to fall into a casket."

Delighted at the prospect of escaping the dreariness

of the retirement center, Kayanne obtained permission to take Rose shopping and was relieved to discover that she hadn't exaggerated her financial situation. Kayanne had mistakenly assumed that most of the residents at Evening Star were there under the auspices of Medicare or Medicaid. For many, health issues, not finances, were the reason they resided at the retirement center.

That made her feel a whole lot more comfortable parking a company vehicle in front of a trendy boutique rather than a discount store where the quality of garments was considerably below her high standards. Ultimately though, style ended up proving to be more a problem than price. Kayanne hadn't realized the dearth of stylish clothes available for older women. Colors ranged from beige to navy to black, and it seemed that everything, including pants, blouses and dresses, was cut in boxy, shapeless styles that even mannequins couldn't manage to make look good.

Steering Rose into a younger section didn't help either. There, the trends gravitated to extremes, the choices being between streetwalker wear and frilly outfits suitable for prom.

"May I help you find something?" the salesclerk inquired.

"How about something in between the prosti-tot section and the coroner's corner?" Kayanne suggested candidly.

If the old saying that a designer is only as good as his last collection was true, Kayanne thought whoever was responsible for the hideous clothes they waded through all afternoon deserved to be run out of the business. The problem wasn't store specific she discovered as they perused other boutiques. That the hyper-competitive business of selling clothes completely overlooked one lucrative demographic blew Kayanne away.

And planted a seed in her mind.

With her experience and knowledge of the fashion industry, it wouldn't be an insurmountable leap from modeling clothes to designing them. If she was ever into big money again, Kayanne thought designing for the mature market might be something worth pursuing.

For the moment, however, she settled for mixing and matching accent pieces from the younger section with a few core pieces from the more matronly racks.

Rose was delighted. "I feel seventy all over again!" she exclaimed.

So pleased was she in fact that she didn't even fall asleep in the middle of her next visit with Dave as she usually did.

"My, don't you look particularly pretty today," he said, opening the door to let her in.

Although Rose was the only one to blush, the compliment pleased both her and Kayanne. As trying as their little shopping trip had proven in some ways, it beat the heck out of Kayanne's tedious routine of dispensing pills and adjusting television screens at the home. Shopping without a budget had stirred in her an innate love of fashion.

"Maybe you should consider a career in the industry," Dave suggested after listening to Rose describe in detail Kayanne's genius with textures, colors and fabrics.

Kayanne gave him a hard look to see if he was making fun of her. She wouldn't be surprised if he hadn't already heard from any number of people about her ignominious fall from the heights of Manhattan to her present status. Seeing no sign of ridicule in his features, she decided to take the comment at face value.

"I've thought about it a time or two before," she said with an edge of self-reproof that went right over his head.

Rose was less obtuse. "Let me know when you decide to market those fashion skills of yours," she said. "I'm always willing to back a good idea when it's coupled with an architect to see it through completion."

Later that week, Kayanne was flattered once again when some of the other female residents approached her and asked if she would consider helping them spruce up, too. Kayanne decided that her AA sponsor might be on to something about serving others being good for the soul. Hard work and involvement in other people's lives actually did seem to be curbing her appetite for alcohol.

Rose's comment got her thinking about blending her newfound sense of service with a career for which she was more suited. Modeling hardly prepared a girl for the grind of working in an old folks' home. And a future in nursing held as much appeal to someone of her temperament as starting up her own convent—although she figured she might just as well nominate herself Sister Superior and christen the order the Sisters of Perpetual Atonement. That Dave Evans kept popping into her head on such a regular basis lately seemed sure proof that she'd been celibate far too long. Linking sobriety to a life without men, she didn't see things improving in that area of her life any time soon though.

Her mother had other ideas about her self-imposed state of chastity. Having finally recuperated enough to start bossing her daughter around again, Suzanne Aldarmann had resumed nagging where she'd left off years ago. She'd started by informing Kayanne it was time to settle down and start producing a grandchild for her. As soon as possible.

Finally, after enduring as much badgering as she could stand, Kayanne asked her point-blank, "Do you remember that part of why I left here in the first place was because of you constantly interfering in my life, Mom?"

"Now that wasn't the only reason, dear."

A deeply religious woman, Kayanne's mother had a penchant for belaboring the past. Not that anyone could blame her. Her life had been hard—she'd lost her husband prematurely to cancer, had raised a headstrong child single-handedly on waitress wages and had dealt with serious health issues herself. Still, since reliance on a man hadn't prepared her mother to live independently, it confounded Kayanne that Suzanne's solution to everything wrong in her daughter's life was marriage.

"If you're so sold on the institution, why don't you quit pestering me and find a nice man yourself?"

Her mother's long-suffering sigh spoke volumes. "You of all people should know that no one could ever replace your father."

Kayanne bit her tongue. The truth of the matter was that she could remember little about her father except the ruthlessness of the illness that had ravaged his once strong body. What she remembered most was the terrible, traumatizing pain of losing him. At eight years old, Kayanne had felt more anger than grief at being thus abandoned. Even at that tender age, she had been willful. More often than not her father had had to step forward to intervene as the mediator between his wife and daughter. Once he was gone, the battle to conquer Kayanne's spirit had begun in earnest.

It was a war Suzanne had been destined to lose. One that had prepared Kayanne for the many skirmishes to follow in a business that devoured the faint of heart.

"Is it so much to ask for grandchildren to bring some joy to my twilight years?" Suzanne asked with a martyr's wringing of the hands.

"They'd be sure to be just as much trouble as I was, Mom," Kayanne assured her. "And at your age, I'm not sure your heart could stand that much mayhem."

What with her mother's badgering, the dearth of shopping and constant reminders of a sad childhood all around, it didn't take Kayanne long to recollect why she'd been so eager to shake the dust of this town's streets off her shoes a decade ago and make a place for herself in the world beyond. Aside from its picturesque mountains and crystal-clear skies, there was little to do in this sleepy little town. Except party.

Considering that the museum listed itself as Sheridan's number-one attraction, it was a given that opportunities abounded for illicit activities. Here, teenagers explored their budding sexuality in the backseats of cars parked at the same drive-in theater that Kayanne had frequented in her youth. And the soaring price of gas hadn't deterred anyone from "hanging Main" as a primary form of entertainment, either.

It was little wonder that young people were leaving the community as fast as they could get a diploma in their hot little hands. Kayanne still felt guilty about abandoning her mother the instant she was out of high school. And she worried how Suzanne was going to manage when she left again. Even if there were some way of better utilizing her talents in this backwater setting, she wasn't sure she would want to relocate here anyway.

With so little of interest to do in her spare time Kayanne began doodling clothing designs. With her connections, it wouldn't be all that difficult to find the right fabrics and locate seamstresses who could bring her ideas to life.

"Would you mind helping me wash my hair, dear?" Suzanne asked.

Kayanne acquiesced to one of her least favorite chores without a word of complaint. Whatever her problems with her mother, she refused to let them get in the way of her duties as a daughter. She placed a chair in front of the kitchen sink and positioned Suzanne on it as comfortably as possible. Since her mother was still weak from her surgery, it was difficult to bend her head over the sink without hurting her in the process.

"Make sure the water's not too hot. Last time you scalded me."

"I'm sorry, Mom."

. Kayanne tested the temperature with her elbow, then wet her mother's hair. Lathering a dab of golden shampoo in her hands, she recalled how she'd started drinking as a way of initiating herself into the popular crowd and escaping the dreariness of living in a home where nothing she ever did was right. She pressed the trigger of the spray nozzle attached to the faucet and cleared all the cold water from it before directing the flow to Suzanne's head.

"Try to lean back a little farther," Kayanne prompted, trying to avoid drizzling water down Suzanne's collar.

After what she'd put her mother through during her turbulent adolescent years, Kayanne considered her present servitude a fair penance. She only wished she could wash away some of those painful memories as easily as the strands of hair swirling in the white enamel sink. Her mother blamed Kayanne for putting the gray in her hair with her underage drinking and high-spirited shenanigans.

Coming from a wide-open state where the miles between towns were measured by six-packs and bottles of booze, Kayanne herself had been surprised how ill-prepared she'd been for the level of substance use that she'd encountered in the city. She counted herself lucky that she'd never been drawn to putting anything up her nose or directly into her veins. All she'd needed to anesthetize herself to the stresses of her career and personal life was good old-fashioned legal alcohol.

Forrester was one of the few people Kayanne had ever met who could literally drink her under the table.

It had been while she was with him that her own drinking had spiraled out of control. Right up until the moment he crossed the line between having a good time and being downright mean, Forrester was one of the most fun people in the world to be with. But when his hard drinking had led to hard-fisted blows, Kayanne knew she had to make a choice. Showing up for a gig sporting a black eye and bruised ribs was considered in poor taste for a swimsuit edition. No masochist who needed daily beatings to figure out something was wrong, Kayanne had left after the first incident.

And had begged Forrester from a distance to make a change.

He had, in record time, by promising to transform himself into a better man—all the while sneaking around behind her back with one of her "closest" friends. Given a history of such disastrous relationships, it was little wonder Kayanne had come to associate hitting rock bottom with men in general. She'd dated so many guys who lived on the edge that it was hard to separate healthy relationships from unhealthy ones.

"Ouch!"

Her mother bolted upright in the chair, knocking her head on the back of the sink in the process.

"Pay attention to what you're doing. While you were off daydreaming somewhere, I got soap in my eyes," Suzanne complained.

She would have none of her daughter's profuse apologies. Grabbing the towel out of Kayanne's hands, Suzanne dripped water on the floor while attempting to

wipe the offending soap from her eye. After cleaning up
the mess, Kayanne offered to set her mother's hair for
her even though she hated the thought of it—working
with hair was absolutely repugnant. Especially her
mother's, which was thin and attached to what had to
be the most sensitive scalp on the planet.

She gathered up the same pink sponge curlers she remembered from high school and started rolling her
mother's hair into neat rows. Kayanne did her best to
keep her mind on the task at hand but couldn't help her
thoughts wandering to Dave Evans. For some reason,
she wondered what kind of a drunk Dave Evans was.
Was he mean? Or the sloppy, sentimental sort who liked
to toss obscure verse around in hopes of impressing the
barflies with his academic credentials? It was hard to
imagine him inebriated. Come to think of it, since the
first time they'd met, she hadn't seen any sign of the
whiskey bottle she'd spotted on his porch.

The ringing phone caused her mother to jump again
and Kayanne to pull her hair.

"Answer that, would you?" Suzanne said, rubbing
her scalp.

"I wish you'd let me buy you a caller identification
box or answering machine so you could screen your
calls," Kayanne told her. "I hate being bothered by sales-
people when I'm in the middle of something."

"Those contraptions are a waste of money," Suzanne replied.

Kayanne knew that bringing such "modern technology" into the house would only lead to an argument

about how much money she'd sent home over the years and what had become of it. So she simply did as she was told and picked up the receiver. If there had been any way to know who the caller was in advance, she definitely would have let the phone ring off the hook rather than take a call destined to suck her even deeper into the mire of the past.

Five

Jasmine was dead. Someone dashed her brains out with a blunt object and left her bleeding all over page seventy-eight. The viciousness of the crime shocked Dave—and, on some visceral level, fascinated him as well. While he couldn't prove anything, he secretly suspected Spice, who had never made any bones about her antipathy for cool, submissive blondes with nothing between their ears but outdated moral platitudes.

Poor, beautiful Jasmine. Cut down in the prime of her youth before being given the opportunity to consummate her one great love. Dave wondered why anyone would want to kill someone so perfect. His grieving process was cut short by morbid curiosity however. He believed a certain fiery redhead had all the answers, but she wasn't talking.

Unusually tight-lipped and evasive, Spice had taken to parading a stream of incongruous lovers across the pages of a novel that suddenly seemed to be writing itself. Dave suspected her scandalous behavior was designed more as a shock tactic to throw him off the trail than from any sensual pleasure derived behind closed doors. Confused and a little jealous, Dave knew the place to dig for answers was in the real world outside his imagination.

He looked forward to Rose's and Kayanne's visits insomuch as they provided the necessary creative fuel for him to keep writing at such an accelerated pace. They also were a pleasure in and of themselves. He wished there was some way to swing an actual date with Kayanne so he could delve the depths of her personality.

While not as intimidating as the character she had spawned in his book, like Spice, there was an edge to Kayanne that cut through anything that smacked of pretense. Dave found that refreshing. He also admired her wry sense of humor and a quick wit that wouldn't let him get away with a thing. Hence he made a point of shutting down his computer whenever she was around. He wasn't nearly as worried about the threat of libel for "borrowing" from real life as he was afraid that Kayanne might feel personally betrayed if she were ever to identify herself in the thickening plot.

The sound of the doorbell prompted him to close his laptop, leaving no telltale sign of the liberties he was taking with Kayanne's life. Having never seen her in anything other than her work-issued uniform, Dave wondered what she would look like in the same thing

Spice was wearing in the scene he was presently writing. That is, in nothing at all.

Although he was expecting both Rose and her keeper, he didn't think he ever could get used to the way Kayanne changed the molecular structure of the air itself whenever she entered a room. Opening the door of his home to her was like letting fresh air into a stuffy library.

"Come on in, sunshine," he said, taking Rose by the elbow and helping her to the chair from which she held forth like a queen surrounded by her loyal subjects.

Kayanne seemed particularly fidgety today and couldn't be coaxed into sitting down. While Dave and Rose discussed various issues of the day, Kayanne meandered around the room inspecting various mementos: photographs and paintings, an eclectic collection of antiques, a western bronze and a couple of framed awards for his writing. When she tested a glass paperweight in one hand, Dave couldn't help but think about how it was heavy enough to crack a person's skull if hurled with enough force....

"I looked for your novel at the local bookstore," she mentioned in a tone best described as noncommittal. "There weren't any copies available."

That came as no surprise. The typical shelf life of a book was slightly little longer than a carton of yogurt, and much of the space in typical stores was allocated to only the biggest names in the industry. Dave's dream was to someday be among them.

"If you'd like, I'll sign one for you out of my personal stash," he offered.

The conflict that played upon Kayanne's features left little doubt that she hated feeling indebted to anyone for anything. Even something as trifling as a book.

"That won't be necessary. I had them order one for me."

Dave was slightly relieved. How would he have signed such a gift anyway?

With love?

Hot for you?

Thanks for contributing without consent to my next book....

"It should be in sometime soon," Kayanne said. "I told them they should buy at least a gross once school starts and all your soon-to-be adoring students meet you in person."

Dave gave her a funny look. Could it be possible that such a stunning woman was actually exhibiting signs of jealousy?

Her usual presumptuous self, Rose didn't hesitate inserting herself into the conversation. "Personally *I'd* love one of your books."

He smiled. "I like a woman who knows what she wants," he said, leaving the room with the promise that he'd be right back. When he returned a moment later, he was carrying a book.

"Hardback," Kayanne observed. "Impressive."

Dave handed it to Rose who clutched it to her bosom as though it were the Holy Grail itself.

"I'll cherish it forever," she gurgled, opening it to the inscription and reading it out loud. "To my dear friend,

Rose. Fondly from your next-door neighbor and admirer, Dave Evans."

Rose dabbed at her eyes with a frilly handkerchief. "I hope you know how fond I am of you, too, dear."

Kayanne was impressed. It was the perfect dedication. Thoughtful and tender without being overtly sappy. While Dave and Rose carried on a friendly conversation about literature, Kayanne sauntered over to the front window and considered the world outside this pleasant sanctuary. A harbinger of change in the air, a slight breeze rustled the tops of a stand of aspen trees. Lost in reflection about the phone call that had left her feeling so utterly vulnerable, Kayanne was startled when Dave came up behind her a little while later to share the view.

He put a gentle hand on her shoulder. "I didn't mean to scare you," he said.

Despite the intent, his touch was not in the least reassuring. It had been such a long time since she'd felt a man's hands upon her that Kayanne longed to direct them over every inch of her body. Or at the very least to lean into his hard masculinity and turn that touch into something more substantial—such as a full-fledged embrace.

Kayanne wondered what it would be like to let herself lean on someone strong. Someone who wasn't out to use her. Someone around whom she could let down her guard and share the dream of a normal life. Images of creating a home of her own with someone special flashed through her mind and left her feeling conflicted.

"Rose has nodded off," Dave said.

Turning to face him directly, Kayanne saw that the

warmth of his touch matched the heat of his gaze. Seeing herself reflected in eyes the color of melted chocolate, she caught a glimpse of a woman without a past. And couldn't help but fantasize for a fleeting instant about wrapping herself around this man and pretending to be exactly what he needed. Dave was so sweet that she hesitated inviting him into a world colored by cynicism and hard experience. Having worked so hard to overcome the shortcomings of her youth, Kayanne hated the thought of losing control of the image she'd fashioned for herself, whether as a top fashion model or as a woman doing her best to get her life back together.

The words she'd practiced stuck sideways in her throat.

"I have to ask you a favor."

Amusement toyed with the corners of his sensual, masculine mouth. "It must be something terrible to make you tremble so," Dave pointed out.

That he'd even noticed said a lot about his sensitivity. When he took her hands in his, it only intensified the tremors that had taken over Kayanne's body. Once again, she was rendered helpless by the charge of pure sexual energy sizzling between them. Blood poured through her veins like hot brandy.

Kayanne reminded herself that there were always repercussions in asking a favor from any man. Although Dave didn't strike her as the sort who might expect something sexual in return, she still hated risking their tenuous friendship. However accidental in nature it might be, Dave was the only male in town she counted as a friend.

"What kind of favor?" he asked.

Her sponsor had insisted that it was time to stop dancing around the past and confront it once and for all. Bethany seemed convinced this opportunity was God Himself knocking on her front door.

Kayanne wasn't so sure.

"I know it's terribly late to ask," she said in a rush. "But my class reunion is coming up this weekend, and I was wondering if you would mind going with me?"

"That's all?"

Dave sounded incredulous. His smile alone lifted the heavy weight pressing on Kayanne's chest.

"I thought you were going to ask me for a kidney or something even more dear."

"I wouldn't take bets on which would be more painful," she told him in all honesty.

He threw back his head and laughed at her candor. "I'd love to go. But before I commit myself to a night of such impending doom, I have to ask. Why go at all if you don't want to?"

It was a fair question. And the same one she had been asking herself ever since she'd received the call from a former classmate informing her that her old mentor Mrs. Rawlins was going to be honored with special recognition Saturday night and had specifically requested that Kayanne be present.

"It has to do with being there for a lady who was there for me when I was young and confused," she said, chewing her lower lip in consternation. "And with making amends."

To an entire town...

Watching Dave's reaction closely to see what effect that admission would have upon him, she wondered if his writer's training helped him remain so stoic. Or if he simply had no idea that her reference came straight out of AA's big book.

"I'm hoping to save time and money hunting down everybody I've offended," she explained, donning a cavalier attitude. "This way I should be able to catch most of them in one place and get it over with all at once."

Her fellow alcoholics reassured Kayanne that this business of making amends was key to a successful recovery. It was hard arguing with their collective victories. Having failed miserably at white-knuckled sobriety before, she couldn't allow pride and tricky step number nine to be all that came between her and serenity.

"In that case, I'd be honored."

Kayanne let out the lungful of air that she'd been holding on to. Pertinent information regarding the date and time came out in a whoosh of exhalation. Feeling suddenly light-headed, she swayed on boneless legs.

Dave reached out to steady her. His efforts had completely the opposite effect. Falling against him, she felt the length of his hard body as he enveloped her in his arms. Like a desert nomad finding respite in the shade of an oasis, she took safe haven in the protection of a pair of strong and gentle arms.

Minute details leaped out at her. Gold flecks in his kind, dark eyes. Laugh lines around his sexy mouth. The closeness of his shave. A subtle hint of cologne almost masked by the clean scent of soap. Kayanne wondered vaguely how Dave always managed to look as if he'd just stepped out of the shower. In spite of her determination to keep their relationship on a platonic level, she found herself willing him to kiss her!

Kayanne wondered how some women could live without sex and feel blessed when others like herself considered celibacy a curse. In her own case, she saw it a necessary measure for maintaining sobriety. Passionate by nature, she didn't know which was worse: going without alcohol or going without sex for the rest of her life.

Testing the powers of her own resistance, she told herself that one little kiss was far different than one little drink.

She closed her eyes and leaned into the kiss they'd both been wanting since first laying eyes on one another. Threading her fingers into the short hair at the nape of his neck, she pulled Dave's mouth down to hers. His lips were firm, his response as hungry as her own. There was nothing tentative in his reaction as he took control, demanding everything she had to give.

Writhing with the intensity of the pleasure that rolled through her, Kayanne melted against him and marveled at the wonder of tasting a man without alcohol on his breath. It was far more intoxicating than she could have ever imagined.

Never had she experienced such a powerful reaction to a simple kiss. A simple tongue-tangling, high-voltage, soul-merging kiss that made her want to rip off his shirt and drag him to the nearest bedroom. The air around them crackled with enough sexual current to light up the entire state during a full-scale blackout.

Behind them someone cleared her throat.

They separated as quickly as a pair of teenagers caught necking in the back seat of a car by the local police.

"I'm having some palpitations. Would you mind taking me home right away?" Rose asked in a weak voice.

Her hand fluttered delicately toward her heart as she glared a hole straight through Kayanne, who was clearly the sole object of her fury. A typical clueless male, Dave seemed unaware that Rose felt anything other than the actual fondness she professed for him. As understandable as that was given the difference in their ages, Kayanne couldn't help but feel sorry for Rose.

And a tiny bit frightened for herself.

She acquiesced to "Her Majesty's" command with all the expediency demanded of an impending heart attack. Even though technically she'd done nothing wrong, Kayanne hadn't meant to hurt the old lady's feelings. Nor did she want to be responsible for causing her cardiac arrest either.

"Do you want me to call an ambulance?" she asked.

"I'll be just fine," Rose said icily.

All her life it seemed Kayanne had been destined to hurt those she cared for the most. Some people actually claimed that her love was as deadly as poison, a charge that she knew could very well be repeated at the reunion by some of her old classmates. In the past, Kayanne supposed she'd been subconsciously drawn to men whose appeal didn't go beyond the physical for fear of endangering anyone she really loved.

A shrink would have a heyday with her neuroses.

Rose suffered no such psychological preconceptions. She knew exactly who she was mad at. And why. Kayanne supposed it was a tribute to her upbringing as a lady that the octogenarian waited until they safely cleared the front gate before turning on her.

"Why, you backstabbing little bitch!"

Six

A few short weeks ago, all Kayanne would have been worried about was how to get Rose safely back to the retirement home without compromising her job in the process. Today, her heart was on the line. Decidedly uncomfortable with being the object of the old lady's ire, she tried teasing her way back into Rose's good graces.

"For someone with heart palpitations you sure are setting quite a pace today."

Anger took all the shuffle out of Rose's feet as she made a beeline to the pedestrian crossing. Kayanne had to double her stride just to keep up.

"I pity the poor Boy Scout who tries to take your arm to help you across this street," she joked.

"And I pity the Girl Scout who puts her trust in you!" Rose spat without bothering to slow down.

"I didn't mean to hurt you," Kayanne said, addressing the pain behind that statement. "It just happened. Besides, weren't you the one who encouraged me to explore all Dave's good traits and give him a chance?"

"I didn't intend for you to give him a tonsillectomy," Rose shrieked. "I can't believe that I actually thought you were my friend."

"I am," Kayanne said, wishing there was some way to prove it.

Seeing how the old lady was in no mood for a reasonable analysis of the situation, Kayanne counted herself lucky to escape the wide swing of her purple cane. What she really needed was an alternate plan to divert Rose's attention from the crisis at hand.

"What d'ya say we work on finding you a more..." Kayanne trailed off, wanting to find just the right word. "Age-appropriate suitor."

Rose brushed off the suggestion. "I have a better idea," she huffed. "Instead of trying to line me up with somebody from the mortuary, why don't you just stay the hell away from me!"

Getting Rose settled in her room after that was about as easy as directing an angry wasp into its nest. Kayanne fretted throughout the remainder of her shift, racking her brains for somebody worthy of Rose's interest. Until she could locate the lucky fellow, however, she vowed to do exactly what Rose had asked of her and keep her distance.

Rose might not be speaking to her, but Kayanne's

mother was more than happy to fill that void. She hadn't been able to stop talking since hearing that her daughter had a bona fide date with the most eligible bachelor in town—a man who wasn't going to arrive at the front door with a motorcycle helmet and matching attitude tucked in the crook of his arm. Whenever Kayanne had the opportunity to get a word in edgewise, she warned her mother not to get her hopes up about anything long-term developing with Dave.

Asking Dave to be her date had been a calculated risk on her part. Kayanne's standard approach to dating was to use men before they could use her. It was a strategy borne out of a painful string of doomed relationships intended to satisfy the libido without engaging the heart. Even now she could think of any number of men who would be glad for an excuse to help her live up to—or down—the community's expectations. There was something particularly gratifying about the thought of showing up at the reunion with the most desirable single man in town on her arm. Something comforting about having Dave at her side as she navigated the dangerous waters of her past.

Kayanne knew this event was sure to be a test of her recent sobriety. She assumed at least one *kind* soul would feel the need to take pity on Dave by helping him rectify the mistake he'd made in agreeing to be her date. Old rumors were sure to be embellished and exaggerated. Old wounds were likely to be ripped open anew. And liquor was sure to flow.

Kayanne knew that Dave was bound to hear negative

things about her sooner or later, and there wasn't a thing she could do about that. According to the precepts of AA, all she could do was to sweep her side of the walk and hope the people to whom she owed amends did the same.

It was just too bad that wasn't as easy to put into practice as it sounded in the safety of anonymity and unconditional friendship.

The day of the class reunion arrived in blistering heat, but by evening the temperature in the mountain town dropped to a cool fifty degrees. Kayanne considered the weather a precursor of the reception she could expect to receive from her old classmates. Extreme swings of climate. There was a lot of old baggage waiting for her behind those high-school doors, and the closer it came for the time for Dave to pick her up, the more she regretted her decision to go at all.

As far back as junior high school, Kayanne remembered being embarrassed by her circumstances. Sheridan, Wyoming, might be considered the boonies by cosmopolitan standards, but there was plenty of old wealth piled behind lodgepole archways of immense ranches and the doors of merchants whose families had made their fortunes generations ago. More recently, technology allowed CEOs and independently wealthy entrepreneurs from all over the country to move into the idyllic, isolated settings where businesses could be run long-distance via an Internet connection. Kayanne found it amusing to witness the clash of old and new money in ostentatious contests where polo competed with rodeo on summer weekends as the town's favored pastime.

As a girl, she hadn't had enough familiarity with prosperity to understand that all communities had snobbish elements. She simply had never felt good enough in a system that had pandered to children living with both biological parents and enough money not to have to shop at the Salvation Army for clothes. And just as she had all those years ago growing up under the shadow of the Big Horn Mountains and a pervasive sense of deprivation, Kayanne felt ashamed of being ashamed all over again.

Everything considered, the trailer where she'd grown up had been tidy and well kept. Her mother had more than met her obligation of putting a roof over her daughter's head and food on the table. Still, cruel comments about "trailer-park trash" stung to this day.

That Kayanne had been invited to the most exclusive parties in the world as an adult was somehow eclipsed by the fact that she'd been excluded from certain birthday parties as a child because she couldn't afford a nice enough present to warrant the price of admission. And as hard as Kayanne was working on overcoming the stubborn pride that proved to be an obstacle to her sobriety, she couldn't help but take some satisfaction in the fact that she would be wearing a designer original gown tonight.

Understated in its simplicity, the black Versace halter-top dress she'd chosen for the occasion hugged her figure and emphasized her curves. Slits on either side allowed a tantalizing hint of those often-photographed shapely legs, and a seethrough wrap bedecked with tiny seed pearls provided a false impression of modesty. A triad of diamonds representing the past, present and future glittered from a gold chain resting between her breasts.

Kayanne may have looked like packaged dynamite, but on the inside she felt every bit as awkward and unworthy as she had in high school. She didn't need a shrink to tell her that the obscenely expensive dress was her way of masking old insecurities. She only wished there was as easy a way to camouflage her home. There was little to be done to spruce up the trailer beyond buying a bouquet of fresh flowers to make the front room look less drab. And less like a shrine to cheap, sentimental knickknacks.

It infuriated Kayanne that her mother hadn't used the money that she'd sent when she was commanding top dollar in her field to do what she'd asked her to do: buy a beautiful home in an affluent neighborhood and fill it with all the lovely things her mother deserved.

"I've lived in this trailer for almost thirty years, and I intend to die here," was all Suzanne Aldarmann had had to say on the matter.

There was no arguing with such logic. When Kayanne had followed up with questions about living expenses, her mother had politely thanked her for providing enough to take care of the outrageous medical expenses. That had to be worth something, Kayanne supposed. Still, she wished her mother had stashed enough away to carry her ever-irresponsible daughter through the hard times she was presently going through. She suspected some slick preacher had preyed on Suzanne's conscience and bamboozled her out of most of the money Kayanne had sent her.

Grateful to count this humble abode a sanctuary while she struggled to get back on her feet, Kayanne tamped down any shame she might feel about Dave having to pick her up here. She told herself that she didn't have to impress anybody at this point in her life.

Why then, Kayanne wondered, was she so nervous hearing the knock at the front door?

"Wow!"

Although she knew that anything she wore tonight had to be an improvement over the standard uniform Dave was accustomed to seeing her in, Kayanne couldn't have scripted a more flattering reaction to her appearance. He stood on the stoop with appreciation glittering in his dark eyes. Seeing herself reflected in that admiring masculine gaze, she could almost believe herself to be Cinderella for the night.

Yet she didn't have any magic slippers to prevent Prince Charming from hearing some nasty comment about the wayward, raggedy wild child of her youth....

Suddenly sorry she'd ever asked him to accompany her tonight, Kayanne wondered how hard it would be to convince Dave to stop at the nearest bar and blow off all that nonsense she'd spouted earlier about making amends.

Before she had a chance to ask, her mother came up behind her and asked Dave in. Giving Kayanne a thumbs-up sign behind his back, Suzanne took his jacket and hung it up in the hallway closet.

"You're quite an improvement over the boys Kay usually brings home," she told him after proper introductions were made.

Kayanne winced.

"He's not a boy, Mom."

Dave didn't seem to mind. Smiling as he was directed to a well-worn chair with crocheted doilies on the arms and headrest, he appeared blissfully unaware of being led to an execution by firing squad—a barrage of questions instead of actual bullets.

Thrown by the use of her given name, Dave asked for clarification by repeating it. "Kay?"

"Kayanne is her stage name," her mother explained. "Of course, she can go by that in the big city where it's considered chic to change your name—and I suppose your principles as well—but back home, she'll always be my little girl, plain old Kay Anne Aldarmann."

Shuddering to hear her worst fears so blithely articulated, Kayanne pointed that out. "You make me sound like a stripper, Mom."

Blushing, Mrs. Aldarmann protested so vehemently that Dave took pity on her. "Not old—and definitely not plain," he interjected. "In fact, you look gorgeous tonight, Kayanne."

Relieved that he wasn't going to torment her with the name she'd deliberately abandoned, she rewarded him with a grateful smile. Her mother was right. Dave Evans wasn't at all like the men she usually dated.

He was far too nice.

Maybe Kayanne had simply been around vain male models competing with her for the limelight so long that she'd forgotten what it was like to be with someone who treated her as though she were something special. Unbidden, an image of her father flashed into her mind. It was a grainy mental picture of a big man with callused hands teaching his daughter to dance by letting her stand on the top of his worn work boots as he moved his feet in time to a country song on the radio.

"Someday my little princess will grow up to be the belle of the ball. I just hope I live long enough to see it," he'd told her over Hank Williams's lonesome lyrics.

Kayanne struggled against the lump in her throat that threatened to suffocate her.

Hoping to staunch the painful flow of memories with a quick exit, she announced, "We'd better get going."

Realizing that was typical of the way she handled her emotions, she wondered if her grown-up losses might not seem so unmanageable if she'd ever learned to truly mourn as a child instead of avoiding her feelings. Would she have ever learned to love herself if she'd been able to forgive her father for abandoning her?

As tempting as these insights were, Kayanne refused to think about that now. She grabbed her purse—a black beaded number just big enough to hold a tube of lipstick and tiny bottle of French perfume—and prepared to leave. Her ever obstinate mother, however, insisted on a modicum of polite conversation before being abandoned for the evening. She was nowhere near done grilling her prospective son-in-law on his background and future plans.

In the middle of her inquiries, Dave spied the Aldarmann Wall of Fame. Over her daughter's objections, Suzanne proceeded to point out what everyone else in town already knew.

"You mean you didn't know that Kay's famous?" she asked incredulously.

Dave gave her a funny, hurt look. "No," he replied. "That's a little something your daughter neglected to mention."

Kayanne tugged at his sleeve but couldn't budge him. With an eye to Sherlock Holmes, he examined the myriad prints lining the wall that chronicled her life from kindergarten to her first photo in a mail-order catalogue to the latest cover shot of a well-respected fashion magazine. His brown eyes widened in sudden recognition.

"I'll be damned," he exclaimed. "No wonder you look so familiar."

Having opened Pandora's box, Mrs. Aldarmann was finally content to let the two of them go on their way.

"Have fun tonight," she called from the front porch. "And don't worry about getting home at a reasonable hour on such a special night."

Kayanne rolled her eyes in the darkness as Dave escorted her to his vehicle. She was touched by his gentlemanly insistence on opening the door for her. With a thank you and a smile, she folded her long legs into his sporty Crossfire and settled into the butter-soft leather interior. Dave slid into the driver's seat and smoothly shifted into first gear.

"I had you figured for an SUV kind of guy," she told him.

"Left it home in the garage. I thought this suited you better."

A lot of things about him suited Kayanne better than she might have ever imagined. Nice car. Nice home. Nice guy. Dave Evans was definitely a change.

The expensive ring on his right hand was another indication that he was doing all right with his writing. Kayanne doubted he could afford his current standard of living on a teacher's wages alone. In the glare of a stoplight, she considered the possibility that he was just another joker up to his eyeballs in hock. In the city, she'd learned firsthand how thin the layer of glitz separating the rich from the homeless could be. Somehow Dave seemed more solid than the flashy wannabes who so often shadowed the rich and famous using any member of that elite group to advance their own status.

The truth was Kayanne wasn't sure how to act around a man—a gentleman—who wasn't out to use her. Yet one more thing destined to throw her off balance tonight.

Dave's sense of guilt compounded with every passing mile. The second Kayanne had met him at the door wearing that amazing dress, his writer's sense of objectivity had been shot all to hell. He'd agreed to accompany her not out of any saintly desire to do the right thing by her, but as a means of forwarding his novel. Of course, that wasn't to say that he didn't appreciate being seen with such a stunning woman in public.

And being alone with her later.

Just the thought of it made him grow hard. Glad that it was dark, Dave hoped he had enough time to get his hormones under control before reaching their destination.

Spice had an equally unsettling effect on him. Having supplanted the main character in his book, Kayanne's alter ego refused to come out to play when beckoned by his muse. Lately she'd been particularly obtuse, lounging around the pool naked, casually dropping the names of other lovers in an attempt to make him jealous. That the ploy was working had Dave questioning his own mental health.

He suspected that the only way he was going to find out who had murdered Jasmine was to explore the boundaries of Kayanne's real life. Her invitation to this class reunion couldn't have provided him with a more direct avenue to her past than had she offered herself up for voluntary hypnosis.

What Dave hadn't counted on was having any tender feelings toward her beyond the overwhelming sense of lust that she always evoked in him. It was far easier fantasizing about Kayanne as some kind of untouchable temptress or an incorrigible bad girl before meeting the straitlaced mother who apparently wanted nothing more than to see her daughter happy. He was touched by the fact that although she was clearly conflicted about her daughter's fame, Mrs. Aldarmann was also proud of Kayanne's accomplishments.

Who wouldn't be? Especially considering the humble upbringing.

Having seen Kayanne's face splashed all over the media for the past few years, Dave felt like a complete idiot not to have recognized her. He'd been intrigued by this mysterious woman's circumstances before, but now his curiosity spiked as high as his testosterone level—far beyond any measure of pure literary interest. The fact that "plain old Kay Anne Aldarmann" had grown up in such modest circumstances only made her that much more fascinating as a character. Dave suspected that whether she wanted to admit it or not, Kayanne had left a part of her heart in this rugged western town that she would have to reclaim before moving on with her life.

"Why didn't you tell me who you were?" he asked.

Although on one level, Dave considered himself a cad, mining this woman's life for his own creative needs, on another, he dismissed such qualms as being integral to the writing process. His job was to record his observations of real life before filtering them through a screen of fiction.

"I did," she insisted. "If you want to know why I didn't tell you about my modeling background, rest assured that it wasn't because I was afraid of intimidating you."

Dave wondered how she managed to turn this back on him and avoid any explanation in the process. He was on the verge of asking her why she was working at the Evening Star Manor, when she reached over and covered his hand on the gearshift.

"There's still plenty of time to change your mind about going to this thing."

Dave heard a note of hope in her voice and felt a tremble run through her. As silky as her voice, her touch almost sent him driving into the ditch. It was embarrassing. He hadn't felt so befuddled on a first date since he'd been a teenager. It wasn't just Kayanne's raw beauty that affected him so deeply, either.

"Are you kidding?" he replied. "What man doesn't dream of taking a supermodel to a high-school reunion? The only thing that could be better would be if it were *my* reunion."

As nerdy as he'd considered himself in high school, Dave liked to think of his old chums drooling as he sauntered into his alma mater with Kayanne on his arm. It struck him as odd that they had more in common than he'd ever imagined. Kayanne's upbringing in a trailer park might be far different from his privileged childhood in an upscale neighborhood, but the fact that she was still struggling against her mother's expectations had an all too familiar ring to it. He could no more imagine this wild creature cooped up in such an uninspired home than he could envision himself donning the heavy mantle of a family business that left him feeling tepid.

As pleasant as Mrs. Aldarmann had been to him, Dave sensed oppression in the stifling borders of her world. He could understand why Kayanne would be tempted to deny her roots and bolt the instant opportunity had presented itself. It was harder to figure out why she had returned. He suspected that whatever had brought her back was the same impulse that would someday turn his own steps home to sort out who he'd once been—and who he wanted to become.

Worried that Kayanne might make a run for it at the next stoplight, Dave forced his meandering thoughts back to her original query about whether he would rather be someplace else.

"Have you changed *your* mind about going to this thing?" he asked.

There were lots of places they could go instead, and it didn't have to be to a bar. Kayanne's previous references to making amends hadn't been lost on him. He wanted no part of pushing someone who might be struggling with addiction off the wagon.

"No," she said with all the enthusiasm of someone about to undergo a pelvic exam. "This is something I need to do. Probably should have done a long time ago. But I have to warn you. You might hear some ugly things about me tonight. And most of them are probably true...."

Seven

Kayanne used a minimum of words to guide Dave to the high school. As tempted as she was to ask him to avoid driving by Pete Nargas's old house, it was along the most direct route, and there was little point in postponing the onslaught of feelings that the reunion itself was sure to evoke. Unable to avert her gaze, she felt a stab of guilt as they passed by the Nargas home. The place seemed downcast, as though the vitality had seeped out. The old porch swing needed a fresh coat of paint.

The sight stirred memories of holding hands, wishing upon falling stars and stealing kisses under Pete's little brothers' and sisters' ever-vigilant surveillance. Kayanne smiled at the thought of his father flipping the porch light off and on three times in quick succession to let them know it was time to call it a night before their innocent kisses could get out of hand. Through the open car window she caught a whiff of fragrant honeysuckle. In her absence, the bush had almost taken over Pete's bedroom window. As sweet as those blossoms, Kayanne had yet to find anything as redolent as her first love.

She missed the stability of Pete's loving family almost as much as she missed him. Kayanne wished there was some way of opening the lines of communication between them. But she couldn't. Not without hurting them in the process. Even Beth cautioned her about making amends if it caused the other person undue pain.

As Kayanne and Dave pulled into the parking lot, she felt her heartbeat race. It went into warp speed when Dave opened the double doors of the gymnasium and she stepped back into the past in which she'd been another person. A professional who'd endured the perils of a career that spanned both coasts, Kayanne managed a dazzling smile as she swept into the room. The distinctive odor of that gym instantly took her to her sophomore year when she'd failed to make the cheerleading squad. All arms and legs with a mouthful of braces, she'd lacked the self-confidence, not to mention the coordination, to pull off a winning routine.

Who could have predicted gawky Kay Anne Aldarmann would emerge from the painfully awkward cocoon of adolescence as such a beautiful butterfly? Certainly not her. She still found it ironic that women all over the world attempted to duplicate the auburn mane that had once been the bane of her childhood.

Even now she wondered why she felt compelled to prove herself to this particular group of peers after she'd already proven herself to the entire world.

Drawing on her runway experience, she calmed the butterflies in her stomach as she filled out her name tag with an artistic flourish.

Kayanne

Just one word. The name she'd picked for herself when she'd turned away from this town. Her last name was as unnecessary as the required tag she dutifully pinned on her chest. Recognition caused a stir as everybody paused to stare. Operating as if that stir didn't exist at all, Kayanne took Dave's hand and allowed him to escort her across the gym floor. His hand felt strong, sinewy, hairy and every bit as masculine and reassuring as its owner. Suddenly there was warmth deep inside Kayanne where before only a cold, stinging wind had howled.

The two of them made a striking pair. Kayanne looked as though she'd stepped off the cover of a fashion magazine, and Dave was a dream in a pair of dark slacks and a silk dress shirt. A diamond tie tack glinted in the dim lights. His all-American good looks rivaled those of any of the pretty boys who'd accompanied her on prestigious shoots around the world. As the most eligible bachelor in town, his presence by her side proved far more shocking than any rebel Kayanne's old classmates might have expected to accompany her. She gave him her best superstar smile.

"Lots of eligible single women here," she pointed

out. "Here's your chance to introduce yourself to the local lovelies."

"Why bother when I'm with the most beautiful woman in the room?"

It was such a sweet thing to say that Kayanne almost stopped in mid-stride to kiss him. Covertly scanning the crowd, she thought the better of it though. Why reward him by risking his sterling reputation? Not when he was doing her a huge favor just by being here.

Looking around, Kayanne was surprised by her old classmates' appearances. Prepared to be shocked by the passage of time, she discovered it wasn't going to be as hard as she'd imagined matching the adolescent faces she remembered with the countenances that were regarding her so cautiously. The head cheerleader was just as cute as Kayanne remembered, and though the quarterback was sporting a little gray at the temples, he still looked hot. A few schoolmates had widening girths and balding pates, but overall everybody looked pretty good.

The fact that people were already gravitating to the same old cliques they'd hung with then only intensified Kayanne's growing sense of panic. It seemed little had changed in the ten years she'd been gone. Before the night was over she worried that the same old people would be saying the same old things about her.

Banners hanging from the ceiling attested to the mighty Broncs' state and regional championships. Faded felt had stood the test of time better than the athletes who'd earned those titles, many of whom had long ago passed from this world. As Dave steered her across the gym floor toward the punch bowl, Kayanne felt the whispers at her back as keenly as pinpricks. She hadn't felt this self-conscious since the fateful night of her senior prom when she'd broken up with Pete Nargas and had changed the course of both their lives forever. That was the last time she remembered dating a genuinely nice guy—until letting Dave into her life.

Was it Pete's ghost murmuring his name in her ear? Or merely another classmate, with a long memory and the need to blame her for Pete's decision, who was reviving old, hurtful rumors?

Kayanne asked Dave to get her a glass of punch from the nonalcoholic bowl. She appreciated the fact that he did so without comment. Having been the girl who'd spiked the punch at more than one school dance, she knew the irony would be lost on many of her classmates. She couldn't count the number of people she knew who had literally spent a fortune on some expensive treatment center only to fall back into deadly habits the minute they rejoined their usual crowd of friends. So it was that sobriety was a salty dish that Kayanne dared not ask anyone to share with her.

Glad to have something to occupy her hands, she sipped slowly, hoping to make this drink last a good long while. Suddenly a tiny woman with steel-gray hair cut into the shape of a helmet zeroed in on them from across the floor. Kayanne's face broke into a wide smile. She asked Dave to hold her cup before opening her arms to her former mentor.

"Mrs. Rawlins!"

"I'm so glad you could make it," the woman said, wrapping herself around Kayanne's waist and giving it a good squeeze.

Kayanne couldn't remember being so glad to see a familiar, welcoming face.

"I heard they're giving you an award tonight," she said. "I wouldn't miss that for the world."

"The award is inconsequential to your being here," Mrs. Rawlins assured her. "I'm retiring this year, and I suspect this is the administration's way of making sure I follow through on that promise."

Kayanne laughed. "I can't imagine SHS without you. The school just won't be the same," she said, meaning it.

Had it not been for the likes of the indomitable Gertrude Rawlins, Kayanne probably would have dropped out of school altogether.

"You look wonderful," Mrs. Rawlins said, stepping back to take a good look. "Even better than in print."

"I hope you don't subscribe to any of those awful tabloids that go out of their way to make people look their worst," Kayanne said with chagrin. "I have to admit that I'm feeling somewhat ancient tonight. You, on the other hand, don't look a day older than when I left."

Mrs. Rawlins clucked in disbelief. She turned to Dave. "If you wouldn't begrudge an old lady a few minutes, I'd like to show Kayanne off to my colleagues, some of whom were so foolish as to actually question whether she'd make it big."

"Or even graduate," Kayanne admitted in all honesty. Recalling the unpleasantness associated with her senior year, she added, "I suspect you're the only teacher who remembers me fondly."

"Don't be ridiculous," Mrs. Rawlins said brusquely. "I distinctly remember you having the intelligence and courage to match your looks. I hope you're not still blaming yourself for what happened to Pete Nargas."

Dave's ears perked up. In truth his curiosity had little to do with developing the characters in his novel. He wondered if this Pete fellow was someone Kayanne had once loved. Someone she'd never gotten over? Did he have something to do with her fear of intimacy? Or the reason she'd left town so long ago?

"I'll wait for you here," Dave said, taking an observer's position against the nearest wall and making mental notes.

Festooned in the school colors of blue and gold, the scene took him back to his own high-school days. Crepe paper and handmade signs harkened to a less complicated time in his life. His adolescence hadn't been marked by the obvious hardships of Kayanne's; there had always been plenty of money in the Evans household. But growing up is never without pain. His family's expectations of him appeared to be the polar opposite of those with which Kayanne had been raised. If people seemed to expect failure from her, success was presumed for him. It wore the same starched and stiff shirt his father and grandfather had passed from one generation to the next. As tacky as Mrs. Aldarmann's Wall of Fame might seem, Dave wished that his parents were as supportive of his literary and academic successes as

Kayanne's mother was of her daughter's accomplishments, no matter how far removed they might be from
her own pedantic life.

"You're an unusual specimen of wallflower," a sultry
voice informed him.

It belonged to a blonde whose name tag identified her
as Valerie Davis-Mills. Dave wondered whether her
reed-thin figure could be attributed to excessive dieting
and compulsive exercising or just good genes. And he
noticed that she wasn't wearing a wedding ring.

"Didn't I see you walk in with Kay Anne?" she asked.

"I don't know. Did you?"

Her laugh was a throaty gurgle. The next thing Dave
knew, she'd stepped closer and proceeded to launch
into a line of questioning that made him feel decidedly
uncomfortable.

"You're not from around here, are you?" Valerie
guessed with a knowing smile.

Since the question was rhetorical, she didn't wait for
his response before asking another. "How long have
you known our little homegrown celebrity?"

"Not long."

"I don't suppose Kay's ever mentioned Pete Nargas to you?"

"No, but I can't say this is the first time I've heard
the name."

Torn between his curiosity and loyalty to Kayanne,
Dave tried to remain polite while keeping his answers
short and noncommittal.

"I wouldn't think so." Valerie nodded meaningfully.

She looked disappointed when Dave didn't follow up by asking her to share any of her secrets.

"What about a Jason DeWinter?"

Assuming Jason and Pete were old boyfriends, Dave felt a sudden need to put an end to a conversation that led him to believe Valerie was the type of person who relied on innuendo to make herself feel better. It had the opposite effect on him. There were better ways to re-search a fictional character than by engaging in shame-less gossip. He shook his head.

"I'm afraid not. The truth is I'm a whole lot more in-terested in the woman Kayanne is now than the girl she was back in high school."

Although Valerie's voice remained saccharine, her smile turned brittle.

"How very sweet of you," she crooned, reaching up to pat his shoulder. Her eyebrows shot up when she dis-covered the muscles beneath that shirt. "By the way, what is it that *you* do, Mr…?"

"Evans. Dave Evans. I'm presently unemployed but will be teaching English at the college this fall. With an emphasis on creative writing."

Valerie looked positively enthralled. "Right here? In little old Sheridan? You know, I've thought about taking a writing class myself. I have a stack of poems that I'd just love to have you help me dust off…."

When she finally left him to join a nearby group of old friends, Dave didn't have to strain to hear what she had to report over the patter of a DJ who was cranking out nostalgic tunes of the 1990s. Dave tapped his foot in time to the music. Everyone in his parents' social circle enrolled their children in formal as well as popular dance lessons. As much as he'd hated it at the time, as an adult he was glad not to have to worry about crushing his date's instep with his size-twelve shoes.

"You don't think she's actually got the nerve to approach Jason DeWinter in public, do you?" he heard a shocked voice ask Valerie.

Dave felt disgusted. If he'd come here looking for dirt, those *ladies* were unloading it by the dump load in the middle of the floor. It was hard to believe that anything so petty could stir a sense of jealousy in him, but it did. He didn't even know the much maligned Mr. DeWinter, but suddenly Dave wanted to punch his lights out.

He'd always assumed that high school was hell for homely girls. It had never occurred to him that it might be less than heavenly for beautiful girls as well. No wonder Kayanne hadn't wanted to come to this reunion alone. No wonder she'd thought about having a drink to steady her nerves. He could use one himself.

He pushed off from the wall and sauntered over to where Mrs. Rawlins was reintroducing Kayanne to her colleagues. Slipping an arm possessively around her waist, he felt her tremble. It was the only hint of nervousness to be discerned from a woman who carried herself as coolly as a queen. Dave's chest grew tight as unfamiliar feelings swelled up inside of him.

The writer's objectivity he'd always clung to dissipated beneath the warmth of the look Kayanne gave him. Until now he had never seen the slightest glimmer of weakness in those mystical eyes of hers. It utterly destroyed all of the signs he'd posted around his heart to keep trespassers out.

Dave wasn't quite sure exactly what he was protecting this woman from. He only knew that it was imperative that he be by her side for the rest of the evening and that he treat her like a precious object in the face of mudslinging and outright envy. That wasn't particularly difficult to do. None of the men in the room could take their eyes off her, and Dave was no exception. On one hand, he felt like the luckiest guy in the world to have earned this woman's trust. And on the other, like the biggest schmuck on the face of the earth for secretly betraying her.

As Mrs. Rawlins left them to take a place of honor at the table set up in the front of the room, Dave wondered if it would ever occur to Kayanne that she had far less to fear from the specters of her past than she did from him. If she ever were to read his manuscript and put two and two together, she would undoubtedly be hurt by some of the jagged descriptions he'd written. Likely she would be offended by the lustful turn his plot had taken.

Kayanne dragged him into the present moment by squeezing his hand hard.

"Whatever happens in the next few minutes," she whispered, "promise that you won't leave me."

Dave's muscles tensed as he followed her gaze to a man in his late forties. Somewhat short and slight of stature, he still retained a handsome visage with his bright blue eyes. The fact that he wasn't wearing a name tag on his brown tweed jacket indicated to Dave that he was probably a member of the faculty. The man suddenly grew red in the face as he recognized Kayanne. Had she not stuck out her hand and forced him to acknowledge her, Dave suspected the fellow would have bolted for the door.

"Mr. DeWinter," she said. "What a surprise to see you again."

Eight

Kayanne studied the man quivering in front of her with something akin to shock. In high school, through the eyes of innocence, she'd viewed Jason DeWinter as the wisest and handsomest man alive—almost a kind of god. Later, in drunken contemplation of the wrongs done to her, she'd convinced herself that he was nothing short of a monster—a married adult who had deliberately manipulated a young girl's grief for his own gain. A sexual predator of the worst sort.

A wolf in trusted counselor's clothing.

She was having trouble getting her mind around the fact that this man with the limp, sweaty handshake wasn't an imposter. Neither deity nor devil, Jason was as mortal as she herself was. And it occurred to her for the first time in her life that he might even be more vulnerable.

It would be a lie to say that Kayanne hadn't wavered between wanting to make amends for any part she may have played in causing him to stray from the path of marital fidelity and dressing him down in front of the entire throng for a fraud and a sexual deviant. Out of the corner of her eye, she noticed Dave's hands curled into fists where they hung at his sides. She took comfort in the fact that he was willing to rush to her defense without even knowing the history leading to this confrontation. It was tempting simply to turn tail before he could hear the sordid details of her misspent youth, but Kayanne felt it important that Dave know her for who she was—and what the community saw her as. If he wanted to deepen their relationship after that, Kayanne would know she'd found something special.

Something worth sticking around for.

"Kay? Kay Anne Aldarmann?" Jason asked, looking as if he were unable to believe his eyes.

His ability to speak appeared as impaired as his vision.

"I didn't...realize you'd be here.... You look...terrific...."

Kayanne bit down on her tongue to keep from commenting on *his* appearance.

And you look so very small and old and frightened that it's hard not to feel sorry for you.

Jason cleared his throat. "I understand that you've done...quite well for yourself.... I'm happy for you, Kay. Really...I am."

She had to fight the urge to look away from the man who had caused her such heartache. Having come this far, however, she saw no reason to dance around the issue any longer.

"I don't know exactly how well I'm doing," she replied. "I'm back living at home, working at a menial job and trying to get my head screwed on straight after all these years."

Her old high-school counselor swallowed hard. Looking around to see how many pairs of eyes were watching him, he moved closer, presumably so it would be harder to eavesdrop. When Dave took a menacing step in his direction, he retreated accordingly.

"I'm sorry," Jason said.

His voice cracked. His eyes watered. And Kayanne realized with a start that he truly meant it. His unexpected remorse was balm to old wounds that had never properly healed. She wondered if he had been carrying around his own fair share of guilt for the past decade. In all the times she'd run through this particular scenario in her head, she had never once imagined feeling pity for the man who had abused his position and taken advantage of a confused teenage girl.

Tonight, however, time, distance and sobriety altered her perspective. Instead of humiliating him by slapping him across the face or curling up in a fetal ball and letting him hurt her for another decade, Kayanne felt an amazing change come over her. It was as if she were watching herself from a distance and wondering why she had ever given such a scared little pip-squeak so much power. How much of her life had she wasted holding the past against the future? Weary of carrying around the heavy burden of resentment, she asked herself what good could possibly come of nursing her bitterness any longer.

"I forgive you," she said, feeling surprised to hear those words come out of her mouth.

Suddenly a strange, tingling sensation shot from her fingertips throughout her whole body as a brilliant light enveloped her. She felt warm all over—weightless and free. Jason continued talking as if completely unaware of the light surrounding them. Looking to Dave for support, Kayanne found him equally unaffected by what she'd once heard called a white-light experience. Dave was glowering at Jason as if considering the pleasure of tearing him limb from limb as the other man tried ineffectually to explain himself in a rush of words.

Kayanne wondered if she was going crazy.

"That was such an unhappy time for both of us," Jason was saying. "You were dealing with Pete's tragic decision and you came to my office shortly afterwards blaming yourself. You were so beautiful, my wife and I were having marital trouble, and I was young and stupid. I was also worried that you might try something like Pete did."

So you slept with me, a high-school senior who wasn't nearly as sexually experienced as she would have everyone believe?

Kayanne cut him off. The power of forgiveness was too extraordinary to risk under the weight of misspoken words.

"There's no reason to go into it all over again. People make mistakes," she said simply.

Standing here all these years later, she was able finally to grasp the truth. The man she had trusted above all others hadn't intentionally hurt her. In her hour of need, she'd turned to an egotistical, inexperienced counselor for help and mistaken what he'd had to offer for love. Embroiled in his own problems and caught up in trying to comfort her, Jason had discovered an attraction over which he'd had little control. That didn't mean he hadn't exercised poor judgment and that his decisions hadn't hurt her deeply when the community had rallied behind him to cast her as the Jezebel who'd killed their favorite son and had made a married man forsake his vows. It just meant that Kayanne was ready to let go of that painful part of her past and move on. At long last.

"I wish my wife had been able to see things that way. She filed for divorce shortly after you left," Jason said, blinking back tears.

"I'm sorry."

Kayanne really was. More for his wife than for him. It couldn't have been easy for her living under a cloud of doubt and rumor. And it must have also been hard competing with all the needy young girls who put her husband on a pedestal far above the geeky adolescent boys their own age.

Jason wet his lips. "I don't suppose there's any chance that you and I could possibly get together for some—"

This time it was Dave who cut him off.

"No," he said, leaning in so far that the other man had

to take a step backward or risk falling over. "She most certainly can't. Not ever. Not with you."

As much as Kayanne resented having anybody speak for her in such a manner, she couldn't help but be touched by such a gallant, protective move. The fact that Dave had been privy to one of the most revealing and unflattering conversations of her life should by all rights have sent him scurrying for the door. That he was still there by her side ready to do battle for the sake of her tattered reputation was incredibly moving.

If she wasn't careful, she might just fall in love with such a hopelessly romantic fool. And that could only spell *Disaster* with a capital *D* for them both.

Dave raised his closed fist from where he had it cocked at his side to emphasize his point. Kayanne put a hand gently on his arm to restrain him.

"That's not such a good idea."

Although neither man was sure if she was addressing him or the other, Kayanne defused the situation with a soft look.

"Would you mind dancing with me now?" she asked Dave.

Without so much as another word, he took her in his arms and swung her onto the dance floor, casting a final dark look over his shoulder at the infamous Mr. DeWinter.

That sorry son of a bitch!

Dave didn't claim to understand all of what had just happened. Only enough to be enraged at the idea of a grown man abusing the trust of his position with a minor.

Why Kayanne had taken the brunt of this town's ill will as a teenager while DeWinter was still a school counselor was beyond Dave. At the very least, the creep should have been fired. Running him out of town on a rail would have been more to Dave's liking. The man's audacity sickened him. You would think the little pervert would have been worried about Kayanne's father killing him.

Then he remembered. Kayanne had had no father or burly brothers to protect her. The thought of her fending for herself at such a young age caused him to pull her even tighter against his chest. He was glad that the slow song the DJ played lent itself to intimacy. Kayanne felt so good in his arms that it seemed as if she had been special ordered to fit against the hard planes of his body. Strong both physically and emotionally, she didn't fit the stereotypical anorexic, self-absorbed waif so often associated with supermodels. Yet it was her unexpected vulnerability that caused Dave to wrap himself around her in an effort to protect her from those who seemed to take delight in her troubles.

He couldn't believe she'd actually been able to forgive that little slimeball. It wasn't something Spice would do—and yet another indication that he had sorely misjudged her real-life inspiration. Beneath Kayanne's initial brashness was a woman of greater depth and character than he'd ever imagined.

And beneath the fabric of her slinky dress was a body he couldn't get out of his mind no matter how hard he tried. During waking or sleeping hours.

Dave's desire to make the lecherous Mr. DeWinter

swallow his teeth like a handful of Chiclets gave way to the overwhelming desire for something more carnal. Beneath a twirling mirrored ball, he fell headlong into Kayanne's warm gaze. As green as the first blades of a springtime meadow, her eyes had the power to melt all his defenses.

"I can't believe how good you are to me," she whispered into his ear.

Smelling like heaven, Kayanne leaned in even closer to make sure Dave heard that ridiculous assertion. With the evidence of his arousal pressed hot against her, he dared not allow her to pull away for fear that everyone else in the room would be aware of his lack of self-control as well. Holding her against him, he swore softly in response to her assessment of his character. The way Kayanne was looking at him as though he were some kind of knight in shining armor made him feel a sham.

How could he possibly tell her that his armor was tarnished by the fact that he'd agreed to escort her tonight for the sake of getting into her head? And that he was similarly motivated to get into her pants? When she laid her head trustingly against his shoulder, Dave resolved to keep her safe from all men—himself included.

"I think you're amazing," he told her.

"Thank you," she said, tilting her head up to look straight into his eyes and hold his soul up to examination. "For being there for me."

Something hard stuck sideways in Dave's throat. He couldn't imagine that Kayanne could have ever brought herself to confide any of the details of her involvement with Mr. DeWinter in her morally upright mother. Nor could he imagine her being able to keep her mother from hearing embellished versions from interested friends and neighbors. In a community that prided itself on everyone knowing everything about everybody, it would have been impossible to keep such a secret.

Dave wondered if Kayanne had run off to the big city to avoid facing her mother's disappointment. Or just to make life easier for Jason DeWinter.

The unshed tears glistening in her eyes made Dave want to rise above his own selfish desires and become what she foolishly believed him to be. A white-hatted hero. What did it matter that they were as ill-suited as Don Quixote and his beloved Dulcinea?

Never had Dave had such intense feelings for a woman. Stroking her hair, he reveled in its texture and felt Kayanne soften in his arms. He wondered how long he could continue holding her up with his own boneless limbs.

Her breath was as sweet against his skin as the fragrance she wore. Dave had been dreaming of Kayanne's kisses ever since Rose had so rudely interrupted their first one.

Brushing his lips gently across hers, he heard a murmur of protest die in her throat. His fingers tangled in her hair.

He touched her lower lip with the tip of his tongue, inviting her full participation. Warm and soft and inviting, her mouth opened expectantly. He felt her tremble in his arms. And heard a moan that echoed his own.

The music, the people, the surrounding scenery all faded into nothingness. Blinded to everything but the feel and taste and perfection of this woman, he sealed them together in a fusion of heat and longing.

To embrace fire without self-immolating was something new to a man who, if he were honest with himself, was more than a little intimidated by Kayanne's wild side—and notorious past. Like many of his colleagues, he sometimes found it difficult to live beyond the pages of his books. And this desire was nothing like he'd ever written before.

He kissed her long and deep and hard. She kissed him back, holding onto his shoulders, digging in with her nails in a way that brought more pleasure than pain.

"What do you say we get out of here," Kayanne suggested in a whisper that was full of promise.

As chance would have it, at that exact moment, a drunk collided with them, bringing the rest of the world back into sharp focus. In spite of the fact that he'd spilled his drink all over Kayanne's designer dress, the bleary-eyed man stepped back and assumed the posture of someone *expecting* an apology.

"Hey," he slurred, concentrating on Kayanne's name badge as if it were fading in and out of focus.

He took a hiccup step in her direction and squinted at her. When recognition finally dawned on him, he blew enough alcohol in her face to make her draw back in disgust.

"Hey, buddy," he said, poking a finger in Dave's chest. "You'd better be careful. The black widow kills her prey after she mates."

Gentle by nature, Dave didn't know what exactly came

over him as he stood looking down on the man's prone body less than a minute later. His hand hurt where it had scraped against the man's belt buckle. He couldn't quite believe that he'd actually hit that jackass, but the evidence lay irrefutably whimpering on the floor in front of him. Usually drunks didn't have this kind of an effect on him. Tired of all the innuendos, snide remarks and flat-out maliciousness directed at Kayanne over the evening, Dave had struck back the only way he knew how.

The hurt expression on her face had unleashed a beast in him. As much as Dave hated to admit it, he felt little remorse about driving his fist into the bum's soft belly and leaving him crumpled in a heap. When the screams around them died down, he donned his best Cary Grant imitation of a good-natured man pushed past his limit. Regarding the assembled crowd staring at him in appalled curiosity, he put forth a question to all of them.

"Does anyone else have anything nasty to say about my date?"

Nine

Seeing how it was a rhetorical question, Kayanne didn't wait around for an answer to Dave's inquiry. They remained only long enough to see the drunk on the floor get dragged away by some of his friends and to listen to Mrs. Rawlins's short speech before making a quiet getaway.

Once outside and safely tucked into Dave's car, Kayanne wasn't sure how she was supposed to feel. Angry that he felt the need to protect her when she was perfectly capable of doing that for herself—as she had been doing for the past ten years? Embarrassed to have been made a spectacle of in front of her old mentor and classmates? Or grateful that a knight in shining armor had stepped forward to defend her questionable honor?

Mostly Kayanne was confused. Forgiving the man whom she'd been blaming her troubles on for the past decade left a hole in her life she needed to fill with something other than contempt. With the exception of a few notable jerks and one mouthy lush, most of her old classmates had actually been quite warm and complimentary. And the man whom she'd initially seen as the most unlikely romantic interest in her future—her date for the evening—was melting the polar ice field of her heart faster than a Popsicle in a microwave.

Life was proving far more unpredictable than Kayanne could have ever imagined. Her world was spinning out of control. It felt rather like being drunk. Alcohol chipped away at inhibitions, letting her take chances that she would never make when sober then providing her with a handy excuse for her behavior the next day. Tonight Kayanne was on the verge of taking the biggest risk in her life with her eyes wide open and her senses unimpaired.

Could there be anything more frightening than falling in love stone-cold sober?

Her standard approach to dating was to use men before they could use her first. It was a strategy borne out of a painful string of doomed relationships intended to satisfy the libido without engaging the heart. Experience whispered in her ear to take things slowly. She refused to listen.

Dave and she were both grown-ups who understood the score. They were consenting adults who, for whatever reason, needed to carry this relationship to the next level. What difference did it make that such a step might be their final one? After becoming intimate, Kayanne couldn't imagine resuming their friendship as it had once been and waving cordially to one another on the street as if nothing had passed between them.

Dave pulled up in front of his house. He leaned forward and put one hand on the side of her headrest. With the other, he tucked a lock of hair behind her ear. The gentleness of that small gesture sucked the breath out of her lungs.

"Would you like to come inside?" he asked her.

Finding her throat too tight to allow words out, Kayanne simply answered with a nod. No shy virgin, she felt out of sorts with herself for being so nervous. She had been with men before. Innumerable men had sought her out as an elixir for eternal youth. Or a status symbol that put them in an exclusive club of men who had slept with a supermodel. Kayanne herself had considered sex as a weapon ever since Pete Nargas had taught her the foolishness of love in its purest form.

What she was feeling for Dave was different from anything she'd ever felt before. Neither innocent nor manipulative, it was lust refined with genuine affection. And it was every bit as risky as that first sip of whiskey. Kayanne's sobriety was based on control, and since what she was feeling at the moment was far out of her control, she had to ask herself if it was possible to date casually and stay sober.

There was certainly nothing casual about the way her heart beat so wildly against her chest. Nor the roar in her ears caused by the blood thrumming through her veins. Later, she wouldn't be able to recall Dave opening the car door for her. Or the front door to his house. Or the door to his bedroom for that matter. He didn't carry her like some naive bride up the walk and over the threshold, but Kayanne couldn't remember her feet ever touching the ground either.

The rest of the evening, however, was indelibly etched into her memory.

Dave didn't wait to reach the bedroom before making his intentions crystal clear. He didn't bother asking her if she wanted a cup of coffee or needed to recap the events of the evening. Instead, he simply put his hands around her waist and pulled her to him. It was an act that could have easily been designed to show her just how much bigger and stronger he was than her. Instead it made Kayanne feel incredibly safe. There was no way this man would hurt her. Not physically.

Not intentionally.

Wrapping one arm around her waist, Dave stroked the bare skin of her exposed back with the other, deliberately grazing the sides of her breasts along the way. He was driving her crazy. Involuntarily, Kayanne arched like a cat and heard herself purr. She felt him reach for the delicate clasp at her neck, which he undid with an expert flick of his finger.

The silky fabric slipped away to reveal her bare breasts, and Kayanne fought the urge to cover herself. Her nipples tightened into perfect tight rosebuds as Dave stepped back to admire his handiwork.

"Wow," was all he could manage to say before following his gaze with greedy fingers. He touched her gently, cupping her in his big masculine hands, fondling her and brushing his palms across her taut nipples. Then he kneeled in front of her to take her in his mouth. He sucked with all of his mouth, teeth, lips and tongue all working together to render her powerless.

When her knees almost buckled and Kayanne could handle no more, she said in a raspy whisper, "Stand up."

When he complied, she rewarded him by grabbing both sides of his shirt and yanking it open. Buttons plinked as they hit the hardwood floor. She reached around to undo her own zipper. Her dress pooled on the floor. Dave pulled his shirt out of his pants, tore it off and draped it on the banister. Socks and shoes were abandoned on the way up the stairs. His briefs hung on the doorknob of his bedroom door.

Kayanne didn't take the time to appreciate the simple masculinity of Dave's bedroom with its sparsely decorated walls and big, comfy bed. One minute she was standing wearing nothing but lacy panties with a matching garter belt holding up her nylons, and the next she was lying naked on her back atop the fluffy comforter. They didn't bother turning the sheets back.

They were two people coming apart at the seams, desperate to find out whether kisses that melted bodies could do the same to their souls. Under the circumstances, it was a wonder that Dave had the wherewithal to remember the condoms he kept in the top drawer of his dresser. A tangle of limbs, they clawed at one another in a frenzy. Naked flesh was hot upon naked flesh.

Searing, slick, demanding, the feelings simmering between them since the first time they'd exchanged curious glances came to the surface as immediate and scalding as lava pumping over the edge of a volcano.

Entwining her hands at the nape of Dave's neck, Kayanne riffled through his hair and found it soft to the touch. She breathed in the musky fragrance that was only part cologne and all him. It stimulated her need to taste him. She licked the salt from his neck and found it good upon her tongue.

His hands clasped the back of her head and drew her away so that she had no choice but to look straight into the eyes of the man who was about to make love to her.

"Hurry," she commanded.

Willing and wanting, she had never been so ready for a man.

Happy to comply, Dave positioned himself strategically over her. Women could say what they would about size not mattering, but Kayanne begged to differ. When Dave showed himself to her in all his masculine splendor, she gasped. Then ran a painted fingernail down the length of his hard sex. And up again.

His skin stretched even tighter. She took him in one hand and squeezed gently, lingering when he moaned. Holding him thus, she felt the full extent of her feminine power.

"You like holding me in the palm of your hand, don't you?" he asked, and she knew he meant it as much symbolically as literally. The hard edge to his voice told Kayanne that she was playing with fire.

"I do," she admitted, succumbing to her need to have him inside her.

Dave paused only long enough to reach for the ripe globes of her breasts. He held them in his hands as if they were matching chalices of pure gold, then dipped his head to suck greedily at their swollen nipples. Kayanne fought the urge to beg him to take her immediately. He sheathed himself with protection before pressing himself against her engorged entrance and kissing her deeply. Unable to stand the sheer bliss of his lips and hands and manhood upon her at once, she tore her mouth away from his and screamed when he entered her.

Slick and hard, he filled her in ways that no other man ever had. Her scream echoed his moans of ecstasy. Grasping her buttocks in both hands, he plunged into her with an unnecessary apology on his lips.

"I don't want to hurt you," he murmured.

"You won't," she assured him, alternately mewling and purring.

I'll never let anybody hurt me again. Not even you....

Releasing his hold on her thick mane of hair, Dave pillaged her body with his hands. As a starving man savoring the rarest delicacy, he devoured her as if fearing nothing would ever taste as sweet again.

Kayanne couldn't make out the words he muttered. Were they words of love? Or oaths protesting her power over him?

Straining for release, he climaxed in an act that was poetry to behold. Usually Kayanne held herself back and watched with a certain amount of disinterest men's foolish attempts to dominate her either physically or emotionally. This time was different.

This time, Dave took her along with him for the ride, cresting only when he was certain she was ready to climax. It happened so fast that she had no chance to restrain herself, to pull back emotionally, let alone to analyze the situation. Never had Kayanne made love with such abandon. Never had she felt so free. So wild. So completely beautiful inside and out.

When Dave exploded in her arms, it was all she could do to keep from crying.

Holding on to her last shard of dignity, she dug her nails into his broad back and smothered any endearments that might make her sound needy. It was a long trip back to the reality of her own skin. If there was such a thing as heaven on earth, Kayanne was convinced that this had to be it. It was as close to perfection as she had ever known.

And just as she'd feared, it was more addictive than any spirits she'd ever tried.

Slick and wet and spent, they clung to one another in the darkness as orphans tossed upon tumultuous emotional seas. The rare man who understood the value of after-play, Dave held her tenderly, stroking the length of her arm with his fingertips. His deep breath warmed her bare skin. Placing her head against his chest, Kayanne was reassured by the steady thumping of his heart. She feathered kisses on his chest and contemplated the pull between the ordinary and the sublime. It was so powerful, it rivaled the miracle of the white light that had appeared out of nowhere to mend her tattered heart.

Was it possible that God was not stingy with His miracles as to grant but one a customer?

For a brief, shining moment, Kayanne let herself imagine someone as good and decent as Dave loving someone as tarnished and world-weary as herself. Images flashed into her mind's eye, imprinting themselves upon her soul. Wholesome images that were far from glamorous. And far more appealing. Images of Dave lifting her hair off her neck to nibble playfully while she did the dishes. Slapping his hand in jest as he sneaked a bite from the meal she had simmering on the stove. Waking him in the morning with a hot cup of coffee and a smattering of kisses. Cheerful morning glories entwined in the front picket fence. A baby curled up in a crib.

Of course, planting emotional roots meant taking risks, and Kayanne wasn't sure she could ever commit to that. Still, the possibility of starting life over with a man whose love went more than skin deep took hold of her imagination. And refused to let go.

Out of the darkness came a startling question that shattered their companionable silence along with any illusions Kayanne might have had about finding protection from the past in the sanctuary of Dave's strong arms.

"Would you mind telling me who Pete Nargas is?"

Kayanne wondered if he was asking because of that stupid "black widow" remark made at the reunion. As idiotic and irrational as the man who'd made it, the comment still had the power to wound her deeply.

"He was my first real boyfriend," she said, keeping her voice deliberately flat.

Dave drew a heart on her shoulder with his index finger. Kayanne had no idea why that tender gesture opened a door that had been nailed shut for so long, but suddenly she felt the need to share with him everything that she'd kept bottled up inside her.

"He was the hometown darling. Captain of the basketball team. Honor student. A genuinely nice boy."

The problem, she went on to explain, was that he fell madly in love with her.

"I, on the other hand, was more in love with the idea of being in love," she admitted. "But I did care for him a great deal. It was just that I had my own dreams at the time, and they didn't include enrolling in the local community college and being pregnant at seventeen."

She wondered why she should expect Dave to understand when no one else had. Did she sound as selfish to him as she sounded to herself?

And as guilty?

"Pete was obsessed with me. He couldn't handle it when I wanted to break up with him. Eventually, to spare his feelings, I accepted a promise ring that I shouldn't have and tried to make something work that wasn't meant to be. I finally broke up with him officially after the prom. It was an ugly scene. He threatened to kill me. When that failed to change my mind, he said he'd maim me so that no other man would ever want me. The thought of me being with anyone else drove him crazy, I guess."

The terror of his threats remained with her to this day. And were part of the reason she was afraid to let anyone get close to her.

It was hard not to interpret the silence that followed her disclosure as a personal indictment. Jagged blades of regret filled the space between them. Kayanne had never been able to forgive herself for what had happened next. She wished there was some way to make the re-telling easier.

There wasn't.

Kayanne hadn't spoken of the incident indepth to anyone except Jason DeWinter. Considering where that had gotten her, she was understandably hesitant to un-lock that door again. Sighing, she wiped imaginary blood from her hands onto the sheet.

"He killed himself shortly after I broke up with him. Left a suicide note that everyone in town saw as a con-demnation of me personally."

She took a moment to compose herself before con-tinuing.

"Aside from the craziness at the end, Pete was basi-cally a good boy. He wasn't the type to pressure me into having sex. Said he wanted to marry a virgin."

"Ah, honey," Dave mumbled into the cascade of au-burn hair spread upon his pillow. Though he tightened his grip around her shoulders, his embrace remained in-finitely tender.

"Does that mean Jason DeWinter was your first?"

Kayanne nodded against his shoulder. Suddenly she was sobbing for all the times she hadn't been able to shed a single tear. Like a dam giving way to years of neglect and building pressure, she crumbled and was swept away by the force of those memories.

"I should have decked that son of a bitch when I had the chance," Dave told her.

Kayanne was surprised by the vehemence of his reaction. She'd been waiting for him to do what everyone else in town had done at the time—blame her for Pete's death and call her a home wrecker. A slut without any morals whatsoever.

"Jason was young, too," she reminded him.

Dave's voice grew hard. "You might be willing to forgive that cretin, but I'm not. Downplay it all you want, but what he did was wrong. On many levels."

He leaned up on his elbow to look into her tear-streaked face. Kayanne did her best to focus on what he had to say and not the effect he had on her physically.

"None of it was your fault. You were a high-school student, and he was a counselor. He took advantage of you when you most needed adult guidance. The man should be in prison."

Kayanne put a hand on the hard plane of Dave's chest. "It was all such a long time ago," she said with a long-suffering sigh.

The last thing she needed in her life was more scandal. She remembered her mother sitting her down shortly after Pete's death and asking if she'd done anything to lead Mr. DeWinter on. Hearing that question spoken aloud by the one person who shouldn't have had to ask had sent Kayanne lurching out of the nest on wobbly, wet wings.

Looking back on her youth from the safety of Dave's cozy bed, she could analyze things more clearly than when her world had been caving in around her. Associating her lack of intimacy with Pete at least in part for why he killed himself, she had given herself to Jason as a form of penance. One that had sent her ricocheting from one bad relationship to another ever since.

Kayanne had trusted her father and Pete, both of whom had betrayed her by dying. Then she'd put her trust in Jason, who had used her and thrown her to the wolves. Was it any wonder she was commitment-phobic? In her mind, love was inexorably mixed up with death, deception and atonement, thus making her recent yearning for domesticity all the more confusing.

Moved by the fact that Dave, now knowing what he did, still felt the need to defend her, she considered the possibility that he might be different enough from other men to risk taking a chance on. The biggest problem was that all the romantic relationships she'd been in since high school had revolved around alcohol. Kayanne might be willing to put her battered heart on a platter one more time, but she could not afford to risk her hard-fought sobriety.

No matter how promising the relationship might be.

Or how wonderful the man might be.

It wasn't right to let Dave go on thinking that she'd played the part of the poor victim for the past decade. The night seemed made for confessions.

"Listen," she said, laying her history before Dave like a stained rug. "I don't want to mislead you. I'm no fair maiden who needs to be rescued from an ivory tower. I've been with lots of men since Jason DeWinter, and I don't think it's a good idea for you to run around trying to beat all of them up."

Kayanne held her breath waiting for him to explode. It wouldn't be the first time she'd left a man's bed with an oath on his lips. Forrester probably would have slapped her for such an antagonistic remark, but once again Dave proved to be cut from a finer cloth.

"You're right," he admitted, leaning down to kiss her on the lips. And cheeks. And earlobes. And on closed eyelids where, despite every attempt to push him away, Kayanne could not erase flickering images of spending the rest of her life with such a good and gentle man.

"First of all," he said, attempting to set the record straight, "I'm the one who needs to be rescued from an ivory tower. And secondly, now that you're with me, you can forget about those other men because they don't matter anymore."

Ten

Kayanne's heart soared like a kite far above the tedious fields where mere mortals played. Never could she have imagined Dave reacting to her candor in such a generous, high-minded fashion. Perhaps a second chance at love wasn't entirely out of the question for her after all. For one glittering moment, she walked up to the home of her dreams and peered right in the window. Tender images of living with this man, having his babies and sharing the rest of her life with him provided a glimpse of heaven on earth.

Then she spied that same bottle of whiskey that had been sitting half-empty on Dave's front porch the first time they'd met. Kayanne knew that just because she didn't want to drink anymore didn't mean Dave shouldn't be able to imbibe. History confirmed the fact that most of her favorite writers did their best work while under the influence, and she had no reason to believe that Dave was any different.

As much as Kayanne wanted to believe that she could be around other people who were drinking without slipping into dangerous old habits, she simply couldn't afford to trust herself so early in her recovery. The urge to drink was still strong in her, and she doubted it would ever completely go away. It had taken all of her willpower tonight just to resist temptation. Had Dave not been by her side at the reunion, she might have fallen off the wagon and landed face first in the spiked punch. It didn't take much of an imagination for her to envision a night that could have ended far differently.

Alcohol abuse was the reason she'd left Forrester, and Kayanne was convinced that if she wanted to maintain her sobriety, she would have to die an old maid. She wanted to believe that a woman could have a full and meaningful life without a man. Seeing Mrs. Rawlins again reassured her that being alone wasn't necessarily a bad thing. Satiated from mind-boggling sex and enjoying the warmth of Dave's strong body, however, Kayanne wasn't sure she wanted to live such a life.

It was important to weigh her present sense of euphoria against waking up clearheaded every morning. Nor could she dismiss the mysterious white light that had enveloped her when she'd forgiven Mr. DeWinter. Kayanne believed it to be a sign from God. Counting herself lucky not to have accidentally killed somebody before coming to her senses, she didn't want to risk stumbling back into her old life of missed appointments, meaningless relationships, drunk driving and fuzzy thinking.

As tempting as it might be to wrap herself in a lovely cotton-candy fantasy, Kayanne couldn't quite bring herself to believe in happily-ever-afters for people like her. Flesh-and-blood people who made awful mistakes that no amount of penitence could fix. Should she ever fall back into her old ways, the possibility of dragging Dave down with her was untenable. She never wanted him to regard her as she'd ultimately come to see Forrester— as a mean, hopeless drunk.

Dave lay in the dark with Kayanne in his arms and tears in his eyes. Long after her breath had ebbed to a steady rhythm, he continued stroking her hair. He couldn't have fashioned a more tragic history for her had he written it himself. Having crossed the line between fact and fiction, he could no more return to looking at her life objectively through a writer's microscope than he could turn his feelings on and off. He literally ached for her.

Kayanne made him want to be the man that she thought he was. A better man. The kind who could slay dragons and make her laugh at the same time.

If such expectations weren't reason enough to make him think twice about becoming more permanently involved with her, he also needed to remember that Kayanne came with a complete set of emotional baggage. Being a normal man however, that didn't seem to matter nearly as much to him as the fact that she also came like no one he'd ever known before. Fantasies of her in bed paled next to the real thing. A pure sexual being, Kayanne exuded passion with every breath she took, making it impossible for a naked man such as himself to think straight. It had been all he could do to keep from proposing to her when he'd climaxed.

The intensity of his emotions confounded him. It was unlike anything he'd ever felt before.

Why he felt the compulsion to protect this woman when it was clear to the entire world that he was the one who needed protection from her was beyond him. Of course, that didn't change the way he felt about her. Smart enough not to fight something as elemental as his body, Dave accepted that he had to have her. It was as simple as that.

His innate sense of optimism dawned as brightly as the sun the following day. Disheveled from a night of great sex and hard sleep, Kayanne looked beautiful in the early light. Dave bid her good morning over the plate of scrambled eggs and toast that he carried into the bedroom on a tray.

Sitting up and stretching, she asked, "What did I do to deserve such special treatment?"

Dave gave her a hungry look that had nothing to do with food. "You should know."

Taking a bite, she moaned with pleasure. "A girl could get used to this kind of treatment."

"That's the plan," he told her, wiggling his eyebrows maniacally.

Sitting beside her on the bed, he took her hand in his

and looked deeply in her eyes. "I have a question for you, sweetheart. And it's an important one."

Kayanne leaned back into her pillow as if preparing herself for the worst. She put down her fork and said, "You have my full attention."

Dave took a deep breath and speared her with a sizzling gaze.

"Would you consider moving in with me?"

Kayanne nearly choked on her toast.

When she'd been a little girl, her mother had drilled into her that disgusting old analogy about a man not buying the cow if the milk were free. Even now, as a grown liberated woman, she associated premarital sex with a subsequent breakup. Even though she wasn't exactly looking to get married any time soon, the thought of cohabitating with such a sexy roommate held a whole lot more appeal than spending nights watching game shows with her mother. Her newfound closeness with Suzanne was wearing thin under the constant proximity of living in a fifteen-by-seventy-foot trailer. If last night proved anything at all, it was that Kayanne was tired of sleeping alone.

Totally ignoring the emotional costs, she ran the logistics through her mind. If she moved in with Dave, she'd still be close enough to check in on her mother while allowing her the opportunity to adjust gradually to independent living. Regardless of where her relationship with Dave led, Kayanne wasn't planning on living with her mother forever. Eventually, she intended to pick up her modeling career where it had left off. Full throttle.

Getting hooked up with a hopeless romantic wasn't any way to advance her career goals, but something inside Kayanne assured her that was the right thing to do.

"This is sudden," she pointed out, not wanting to ruin something so perfect by rushing things.

"The heart knows what it wants," was Dave's sage reply. "And I want you."

"I want you, too," Kayanne admitted.

More than anyone else she'd ever met. She wondered if it would surprise Dave to know she'd never lived with another man. For her, sex was one thing. And commitment was quite another.

"I'll take the day off from work tomorrow, and we'll start moving your stuff in right away," Dave said, taking charge of the situation.

Kayanne held up both hands. Heat rushed to her face. As much as she hated to, it was time to put a pin in this hot-air balloon before it set sail for Destination Heartache.

"Hold on. Before you go getting the cart before the horse, there's one more thing I should tell you."

In spite of the fact that she'd had lots of practice admitting her problem to other alcoholics at AA meetings, she found the words extremely difficult to get out. Once Dave heard her out, she expected him to rescind the offer. She toyed with the edge of her sheet, wishing there were some way of softening the ugly truth.

"I'm a lush," she said, averting her eyes from his.

The fact that Dave didn't act all that surprised set Kayanne back some.

"That might be a bit harsh, considering that I've

never seen you take a drink—even though last night you had to be tempted," he pointed out.

She started to argue, but Dave cut off any further protests by covering her mouth with his and proceeding to convince her without words why she'd be a fool to turn him down. Once she felt as limber as a rag doll in his arms, he did his best to reassure her.

"We'll work it out. Between the two of us, there isn't any obstacle we can't conquer. You just have to be willing to ask for my help. And accept it when it's offered."

That he neither dismissed her illness nor turned away in disgust was nothing short of miraculous. A rush of gratitude filled Kayanne's heart and spilled over in the breaking light of day as she contemplated the power of hope. Physically and emotionally spent, she thought she had no more passion to give.

She was wrong.

Dave caressed her cheek with the knuckles of one hand. The other sought the cleft between her legs where the glow of awareness rekindled the blaze that he'd started earlier. Intimacy arched between them.

He tested her willpower with the tip of his tongue against the seam of her lips. Reaching behind herself, Kayanne grabbed the brass bars of the headboard with both hands and gave herself over to the pure pleasure of being dominated by a man who knew exactly what he was doing.

He rolled on top of her, nudging her legs apart with his own. His mouth grew more demanding. His kisses more intense as he plied her with his tongue and plunged the depth of her mouth at will. Trailing his fingertips along her rib cage, his hands settled at last upon her waist, lifting her up so that she had no choice but to feel the extent of his arousal against her belly.

Moaning, she kneaded her fingertips into his muscles growing slicker by the minute with beads of sweat. Dave ran his hands down her buttocks and drew her possessively against himself. Staring deeply into her eyes, he entered her in a sudden thrust that gave voice to her pleasure in guttural, nonsensical syllables. She threw back her head and gave herself fully to him.

He filled her completely. Physically, emotionally, spiritually. Kayanne knew that she'd never find a more satisfying fit if she searched the world over. She clung to him in both desperation and faith.

Dave took a labored breath.

"Say yes," he commanded through gritted teeth. "Say that you'll move in with me."

Kayanne flexed her hips against his, urging him to succumb to the need to climax quickly. Unable to wait a second longer herself, she gave him the answer he longed to hear before exploding into a million shining shards of bliss. "Yes, oh, yes!"

Only then did Dave pour himself into her, sealing their bodies tight and calling out her name as if flinging a plea heavenward.

Spiraling back to her senses an eternity later, Kayanne came to the conclusion that nothing had ever felt as right as her decision to be with this man for as long as he wanted to be with her. It was pointless to doubt his goodness. After everything she'd told him, after all that he'd heard by way of nasty innuendo and gossip, he was still willing to take a chance on her. Only a saint could resist such stubborn determination. And everyone in town knew that Kayanne was no saint.

Nor was she a coward.

A woman who would rather live with mistakes than regrets, she was bound to her word—even if it was given in the throes of orgasm. Savoring the feeling of closeness that being in this man's arms brought her, she snuggled up against him and let a sense of contentment wash over her. If it were in her power, she'd never move again.

"There's just one more thing," she mumbled against the strong column of his neck.

"What now?"

Dave sounded incredulous that there could possibly be anything else to disclose before committing to their new living arrangements.

Kayanne's voice was only half-teasing when she posed a final question. "How are we going to break the news to Rose?"

Having things all worked out in his mind, Dave was feeling good about life as he moved Kayanne's meager belongings from her mother's trailer into his spacious home. During the day, Kayanne would be away at work, unconsciously providing the impetus to move his plot along. And during the night, they could pleasure one another like there was no tomorrow.

Loading the last of her boxes into the back of his

SUV, he refused to dwell on the possibility that Kayanne may very well grow tired of playing the penitent and go back to her glamorous lifestyle. If that happened, Dave supposed he could always resume his boring old life with stuffy colleagues and dusty manuscripts. Worse yet, if he couldn't make his writing pay off on a more regular and substantial basis, he imagined himself working for the family firm receiving transfusions of ink to replace the blood that Kayanne made boil with a simple look.

In spite of his previous glib response, Dave took very seriously the acknowledgment that she was an alcoholic. Kayanne hadn't been particularly coy about dropping hints about making amends early on in their relationship, and he'd noticed that she never drank in his presence. Having simply assumed she was a teetotaler, he'd been taken aback when she'd hinted at stopping by a bar rather than going to the reunion.

Dave couldn't help but wonder what effect her condition would have on his own life. While he didn't consider himself a problem drinker, he did occasionally oil the creative pump with a cocktail or a beer, and the thought of going cold turkey didn't much appeal to him.

Would it be all right if he had a drink in her presence?

Would she think he was trying to sabotage her efforts?

The last thing Dave wanted to do was jeopardize Kayanne's sobriety. He'd always taken for granted his ability to drink without fully realizing what a blessing it was to be able to stop at one or two. He hated the thought of sneaking a highball behind her back.

He wondered what his parents would make of someone as complex as Kayanne. His normally reserved
mother maintained that familiarity bred contempt. If
that was truly the case, the living arrangements he'd
proposed might well prove a fairly painless tonic to the
romantic inclinations that were interfering with any pre-
sumption of logical thought. Every minute of the day
and night he could think of little else but Kayanne. She
was an obsession that threatened to take over not just
his storyline, but his whole life.

If Dave wasn't careful, he suspected he might not
fare any better than poor Jasmine, who'd paid the ultimate price shortly after Kayanne had stepped onto his
porch. However unrealistic it was to think he could survive living in close quarters with nothing more than a
nick or two to his big old compassionate heart, it was a
risk he felt he had to take.

Life with Dave was filled not only with passion, but
also lots of fun. Having grown up in a home seeped in the
odor of perpetual grief, Kayanne's early existence had
been marked by a frugality of both the pocketbook and
the heart. Tender words were as rare in the Aldarmann
house as disposable cash. Thus she had fallen in more
easily with men like Forrester, who were prone to melo-
dramatic bursts of angst and wild spending, than men
like Dave, who smiled easily and often at simple things.

His generosity of spirit even extended to his closet.
He acted surprised that she'd actually brought so little
along in terms of personal effects.

"Over the years I've learned to travel light," Kayanne said, subtly warning him in advance that he might very well come home someday to find her gone.

But Dave wasn't an easy man to pick a fight with. In response, he simply squirted a whiff of her expensive perfume in the air and took a deep breath.

"I like the fact that you've made a conscious decision to acquire only the very best rather than fill your life with junk," he said.

Kayanne wondered if he was referring to past lovers rather than things as inconsequential as jewelry and fragrances. Recalling all the cheap relationships she'd thrown into junk drawers in the past, Kayanne thought this fresh-faced, smiling Adonis deserved someone less jaded to share the sunshine of his optimism. She didn't want to leave Dave feeling as depleted as men such as Forrester had left her.

When she attempted to underscore the fact that their living arrangements were only temporary, Dave refused to listen. Instead, he turned up the stereo and danced her to the bedroom, where he kissed such foreboding thoughts away, reminding her with each loving caress to enjoy the here and now rather than dwell on future miseries. Accustomed to using sex as a weapon, Kayanne found herself befuddled when it was used so masterfully against her.

Generally speaking, life with Dave proved to be a picnic. Weekends and evenings were spent hiking, biking, bowling and playing tennis. Every so often he even coaxed her down to the basement to lift some light weights in his makeshift gym. Nights were spent exhausting one another in pleasures of the flesh far after all the late, late shows signed off. Not that Kayanne kept track of such things. Unlike her mother's trailer where the blare of the television filtered into every room twenty-four hours a day, the TV was seldom turned on in her new home.

One promising Saturday morning after staying in bed until the sun could no longer be restrained by the blinds, Dave suggested a camping trip. Picturing herself as some dark, Gothic maiden imprinted implausibly upon a Currier and Ives scene, Kayanne laughed at the absurdity of it before agreeing to go.

On their way out of town, they stopped by the grocery store to pick up a six-pack of cold pop. Dave promised a mess of fish for dinner, and Kayanne had made dessert herself—chunky chocolate-chip cookies the size of his fist. She enjoyed filling the house with the aroma of comfort foods that had been off-limits for so long in her line of work. Participation in Dave's active lifestyle allowed her to consume all the calories she wanted without worrying about weight gain. The unexpected freedom was a slice of heaven.

"Delicious," Dave told her as she fed him cookies on the way up the mountain.

Kayanne was gratified when he raved how good they were. Grabbing her by the wrist, he ignored her protests and sucked melted chocolate from her fingertips.

"Just a precursor of things to come," he promised.

A flame licked between her thighs. Generated from

a white heat, the fire burned hotter and cleaner than any ignited from the desperate desire that had been extinguished so easily in past relationships.

They thoroughly enjoyed each other's company and the scenery as they drove to the picturesque Cloud Peak Wilderness. There, Dave wasted no time assembling his new fly rod. Kayanne whistled in appreciation when he stripped off his sweatshirt to exchange it for a cooler T-shirt. Grinning, he gave her his best beefcake-calendar pose.

"You're pretty buff for an academic," she told him, resting her chin in her hands and admiring the view from the blanket she'd spread on the ground.

Rolling onto her back, she studied an ideal Wyoming summer sky. Ribbons of wispy clouds floated across a blue so bright it warranted sunglasses. Squinting, Kayanne tried to remember the last time she'd been so happy. The answer came to her in a single word. *Never.*

Dave asked her to spray him with a fine mist of mosquito repellent, which she did before handing him a bottle of sunscreen.

"Mind returning the favor?" she asked.

Kayanne was wearing cutoffs and a flowered-print halter top that brought out a softer shade of green in a pair of eyes that Dave said reminded him of aspen leaves in the springtime. Kayanne held her long mane of hair out of the way as his hands rubbed liquid sunshine into her skin. He lingered along the swell of her breasts where they peeked out from the sides of her top.

"There's not a soul around," he murmured into her

ear before slipping his hands under the halter to fondle their ripe fullness.

Kayanne neither chastised nor pushed him away. Instead, she arched her spine and let her head fall back, catching strands of her hair in the sticky lotion not yet absorbed into her skin. The next thing she knew, Dave was untying the knot at the nape of her neck and nuzzling the hollow between her neck and shoulder blade. Reveling in the sensation of being so thoroughly fondled, she wondered if this wasn't what it must have been like for Adam and Eve before they were tossed out of paradise. Isolated from the rest of the world, Kayanne felt no shame being half-undressed in the warm sunshine.

Sighing, Dave regretfully retied her top. "I'd better get fishing before the sun goes down."

Kayanne donned an artful little pout. "Are you sure I can't tempt you to stay a little longer?"

"If I don't catch dinner, I won't have any energy left to do to you later what I promised I would."

He emphasized his point by covering his hard-on with an old fishing hat decorated with an assortment of flies and lures.

"Looks like you already caught a whopper," Kayanne teased.

She declined his offer to accompany him to the stream, saying she'd rather read a steamy novel to get her in the mood for what was to come later—that was, if he could be counted on to keep his promises. Beaming, he took off. Kayanne surveyed him through heavy eyelids. Wearing a pair of khaki shorts and an old, battered hat, he looked better than any airbrushed boy toy of her past.

The scent of pine filled her with a rare sense of belonging. Home at last in these sacred mountains, her spirit sang with the rushing river. She dozed in the midst of a meadow so thick with wild sunflowers that it looked as though it had been painted with butter. When she opened her eyes an hour or so later, Dave was standing over her with a stringer of trout. He couldn't have looked any prouder presenting her with a world-record trophy sailfish.

"Dinner," he announced, puffing his chest out in his best caveman imitation. "Breakfast, too, for that matter."

Drops of water slid off the fish's tail onto Kayanne's bare ankle. She bolted upright with a girlish squeal.

"I didn't know you were such a sissy," Dave said with a disapproving shake of his head.

"If you want to see real panic, just wait until a bear wanders into camp."

The revelation that he kept a .44 Magnum stashed away in the glove box for just such emergencies helped allay her concerns. That evening, they roasted s'mores over an open campfire and fed them to one another as if sampling the finest aphrodisiacs. And perhaps they were—if what followed shortly thereafter in the confines of a down sleeping bag was any indication.

Falling asleep beneath a canopy of stars twinkling overhead was a dizzying experience. It was like falling into the universe's mixing bowl. Kayanne felt something hard inside her chest crack open as the healing that had begun with an act of forgiveness and an amazing white light continued to work its magic into the farthest reaches of her soul.

Eleven

Unlike her more religious mother, Kayanne didn't believe in signs from God in the form of stray pennies found on the ground or randomly turning to just the right bible verse for whatever ailed a person in times of need. She didn't prescribe to the notion that AIDS was a sign of God's displeasure with the world. Or in any of the splashy headlines about the fulfillment of Nostradamus's end-of-the-world predictions with every natural disaster.

Nevertheless, on the way home from her first camping trip, giddy with a newfound sense of joy, it was hard to dismiss the possibility that God just might be trying to tell her something. Coming out of the foothills of the Big Horn Mountains, a lone antelope stepped into the middle of the road and forced their vehicle to come to a

complete stop. The buck deliberately turned his head to
look straight at Kayanne, making it impossible to miss
the black lacquered heart that his horns formed above
his head. Squeezing Dave's hand, she hoped she wasn't
the only one to read the magic into the incident.

Of course, she told herself that if she bought into that
kind of superstitious nonsense, she'd also have to as-
sume the storm sweeping across the skyline in an omi-
nous curtain of dark, swollen clouds was a portent of
things to come as well. When the lowest lying of those
clouds caught on the ragged tips of mountaintops and
spilled their fury upon a panorama virtually untouched
by human hands since the inception of time, Kayanne
couldn't help but shiver with a chilling sense of foreboding.

If Dave shared her sense of apprehension, he didn't
show it. Ever since she'd burst into his life like a storm
on the horizon, he'd felt happier than ever before. Life was
suddenly wonderful. The colors of the sunrise made their
way onto his pages and into his heart. As did the splash
of raindrops against the window. And the smell of fresh
cut grass. He heard himself whistling at odd times, glad
to be carving out the life he wanted on his own terms. The
smothering job awaiting him in the steamy South receded
to a distant possibility instead of the crushing likelihood
it had seemed just a few short weeks ago.

Kayanne was present in everything he did. Not satisfied with killing off Jasmine to supplant her as the leading
lady in his book, she took over his thoughts as well.

Every heroine in every book Dave read became her. It didn't matter whether the author was describing a short blonde or a delicate brunette; in his mind's eye, she was a feisty redhead with cat-green eyes and a heart of gold.

His own book was coming along fine, and he didn't even miss liquor as he'd first thought he might. It had felt strange pouring himself a plain soda when it came time for a break from writing, but as the words began to flow onto the page almost effortlessly, without the aid of alcohol, he accepted the fact that Kayanne was all the inspiration he needed. Day after day, his fingers flew over the keyboard as he struck a rhythm that didn't allow time for the painstaking revision that had marked his past efforts.

His prose took on a more sensual, expansive tone as she taught him to look at the world differently. The wanton character who had so shamelessly taunted his hero at the start of his book became softer and more complex with each new chapter. Perhaps because of her faults and mysterious past, Dave knew his readers could no more resist falling in love with her than he could himself.

A meticulous author who tended to labor over every word, Dave was frankly uncomfortable with where this raging torrent of prose was taking him. But after weeks of struggling to get so much as a single paragraph down to his satisfaction, he simply buckled himself in as Spice took the driver's seat and headed for an unknown destination. That wasn't to say that Dave considered every word golden, only that he accepted there would be time enough for revision after his first draft was completed.

His project was coming along so well in fact that he felt no remorse in turning off his computer every day the minute Kayanne came home from her shift. Rather than admit to hiding anything from her, he considered spending the rest of his day playing with her a reward for a day's hard work. He supposed that was what had been missing from his writing all along: a sense of balance that only such a woman could bring to his life. It would be too easy for someone of his nature to bury himself in his work, cut himself off from life with other academics and offset his growing loneliness with a strenuous physical lifestyle. Perhaps that was why he'd chosen the least populous of the fifty states to settle down and write his next novel in virtual obscurity. Maybe he secretly subscribed to the notion that only tortured, lonely lives could spawn great literature.

Possibly that was why he kept a lone bottle of whiskey secreted away in the back of his cupboard just in case his newfound inspiration failed him. All the rest he'd poured down the drain—over Kayanne's protests.

"You don't have to do that on my account," she'd told him. "I'm the one with the problem, not you."

Dave had lightly brushed off her concern. "It won't hurt me any to clean up my life right along with you. I like feeling less tied to the bottle myself."

The indulgent smile Kayanne had given him had made him feel naive. His idea of being addicted was clearly much different than hers. A heavy weight that he vaguely recognized as jealousy had slowly begun to crush his spirit. It was an emotion he credited only to the pettiest characters in both the books that he read and wrote. He did his best not to think about Kayanne's past, pushing aside any nagging doubts he might have. Though he avoided prying into her past beyond what she'd already told him, it bothered him to think about the men that she had been with before him. The thought of Kayanne leaving him for some glamorous playboy who knew his way around a camera played havoc with his guts.

Forget it, you'll make yourself crazy. What's in the past doesn't matter as much as what's in the here and now.

He freely admitted that Kayanne wasn't like anyone he'd ever brought home to meet his parents. Fiery and passionate, there was also a delicate side to her that few people saw. Laughter didn't come easily to her, but when she tossed back her magnificent mane of hair and let go of her inhibitions, the sound was pure music. And the fact that she was starting to trust him allowed that wondrous sound to fill his home more and more often.

Although Kayanne believed that she would never ever completely conquer her desire for alcohol, she was down to attending an AA meeting once a week. She always returned home calmer and more grounded than when she'd left. And she never failed to thank him for his part in her continued sobriety.

Dave was both touched and frightened by that. He was equally moved by the way she fretted over her clients, especially Rose, who still made an occasional appearance on his front porch. She hadn't quite forgiven Kayanne for stealing her man. That bothered Kayanne more than anyone might imagine. Only Dave knew how hard she was trying to find Rose a more age-appropriate companion. And to liven up the stifling atmosphere over at the Evening Star Manor for all the residents for whom she was coming to care so deeply.

In her spare time, Kayanne devoted herself to designing a new line of clothing geared to older buyers. Dave was duly impressed with her plans. She didn't want to jinx things by being overconfident, but all it had taken to get the ball rolling was a few well-placed calls to her fashion contacts in Manhattan.

"I wish you'd quit your job and focus on your designs full-time," Dave told her. "There are lots of ways to help your friends and make better use of your talents in the process."

Kayanne gave him a tired smile. "As much as I appreciate your support, I really can't resign until I have the backers to turn my designs into something more than a pipe dream."

Dave suspected it was more than that. Kayanne's current paycheck might not be much, but it kept her from feeling completely dependent on him. Even though she trusted him more and more each day, he committed himself to a gradual process of winning her over completely. So when he offered her money in support of her dream, he tried not to take her refusal personally.

She was more open to other kinds of help.

"Good news," he announced one evening after she'd just hung up the phone with a local seamstress who'd volunteered to sew samples of her designs. Kayanne was hoping to take them to the center and do an informal market analysis herself. "I think I met somebody today who just might be perfect for Rose."

Kayanne looked at him hopefully. She was so frustrated with the local pool of eligible men that she had even considered hooking Rose up via an Internet dating service.

"Does he have a pulse?" was all she wanted to know.

"His name is Joe Hansen. He works at Wallyworld as the greeter. Been retired for years and went back to work to keep busy. Says he'd rather wear out than rust out. Heck of a nice guy."

Kayanne was so encouraged by this news flash that she proceeded to show her gratitude by scattering kisses on Dave's neck and slowly working her way down his chest. She undid his top shirt button with her teeth before allowing him to do the rest.

"You're awfully tough on my shirts," he told her in a voice that let her know he didn't mind at all.

After divesting him of his shirt, Kayanne opened her own blouse and gently directed his head down to the hollow between her breasts where he greedily indulged. She didn't have to stroke him to make him as hard as a rock, but she did anyway, and in the fading light of day proceeded to satisfy him completely right in the middle of the living-room floor. Spilling into her, Dave gave every ounce of his entire being to her: marrow, bone, flesh, blood, memories, hopes and dreams. Their lovemaking transcended the physical to reach a higher plane where soul met soul beneath slick, hot flesh.

Dave knew that there would probably always be places inside Kayanne that he'd never be able to touch.

But when she curled up beside him naked on the rug in front of a cold fireplace and smiled at him, he rejoiced to see the wounded look in her eyes was gone. He never wanted to be responsible for putting that look back on her face again.

Luckily, Kayanne didn't have to wait for the bookstore to call with information on her ordered copy of Dave's first book. One day while cleaning, she found a copy unobtrusively stuck on his bookshelf. She read it all in one sitting but didn't bother to mention it to him later because it had left her feeling so sad. His words were like poetry on the page, but the scenes he painted of the South—dripping magnolia blossoms, gracious living and the rich loam of dirt stained by the blood of a civil war—made her feel separate from the man whose bed she shared. His beautiful words divided their two worlds as neatly as a math problem and reminded Kayanne that they were from as different backgrounds and experiences as one could imagine.

Wondering if she was having any impact on his writing at all, she hoped that his latest work in progress lacked the elegant aloofness that marked that first novel. Kayanne wanted his next hero to be characterized more by genuine love and less by longing for the kind of woman who existed only in the fantasy world of the male ego. And she wanted a heroine to relate to as well. Someone of flesh and bone with an interesting past and enough flaws to make her worth cheering for. Someone she didn't resent for perfectly coifed blond hair, neatly manicured nails and impeccable manners. In short, Kayanne wanted somebody real to read and care about.

And she wanted a happy ending, too. Not the kind of depressing conclusion that pandered more to literary critics than avid readers like herself. She wasn't looking for some gossamer ending that implied there would be no bumps on the road beyond the last page, but if Kayanne was going to invest her time reading a book, she wanted a satisfying conclusion that gave her hope of finding lasting love herself.

A closet romantic, she didn't want to discuss Dave's first book with him for fear of appearing jealous of a fictional woman that she detested. Besides, whenever she asked to see his latest project, he always found some way to put her off. She noticed that he never worked on his book when she was around, always taking care to shut down his laptop completely whenever she was in the room.

Kayanne supposed he was entitled to be protective of his work, but that didn't do a thing to lessen her curiosity. In fact, it only heightened her desire to see what he was writing so diligently while she was off at her job. She didn't know his password and would never have violated his privacy by trying to break into his files, but when the day came that she stumbled upon a printed draft of the first few chapters, she didn't talk herself out of reading them, either.

Dave was at the college setting up his office, so there was no reason to rush through the stack of papers while looking over her shoulder. If the chapters were good, she would casually mention it to him before kissing him senseless and making him forget all about any little breach of privacy on her part. If they weren't, she'd keep her disappointment to herself and kiss him senseless anyway.

They were good.

Good enough to make her long for the smooth bite of liquor to erase his cruel, poignant words from her mind forever.

Kayanne felt blindsided. All this time, she'd been under the impression that Dave actually had tender feelings for her beyond what they shared physically. Having fallen hopelessly in love with him, she was embarrassed that in weak moments she'd actually allowed herself to consider the ultimate fantasy of marrying him and having his children.

All the while he'd been playing her for a fool.

She'd never met a more calculating person in her whole life than this man with his lying, generous smile and magical hands. The whole time she had been falling for Dave like some stupid schoolgirl, he had been standing back, observing, and putting every unflattering, minute detail of her so-called life down on paper.

Laughing at her.

One didn't have to be a genius to see how he had connected her to his trampy female protagonist. It didn't take a great leap of the imagination to link their names together, either. Or the fact that they shared the same red hair, green eyes and questionable pasts. Dave captured perfectly on the page the way Kayanne walked and talked and mistreated his poor, suffering hero—some stupid SOB who kept mooning over a Barbie doll by the name of Jasmine.

Kayanne read only to the end of the scene where she found herself implicated in Jasmine's death before putting the manuscript down in disgust. She didn't think she could suffer through the love scenes, seeing her heart and her legs splayed for the entire world to gawk at. Having been taught to guard her heart by some of the best con men in the business, Kayanne chastised herself for not seeing this treachery coming long ago.

Hurt, embarrassed and angry, she baptized the next *New York Times* bestseller with the flow of hot tears. Then promised herself it would be the last time she cried over a man. This particular one would damn well never see her tears. Forrester might have scared and humiliated her with his fist, but the emotional blow Dave delivered was far more crippling. For Kayanne, trusting him at all had been a tremendous leap of faith.

Out there in the big old cold world, she'd encountered many men like Jason DeWinter and Forrester who all wanted something from her. Prestige, money, contacts, sex. Those were things Kayanne could understand, if not accept. But this? How was she to deal with a literary rape that left her feeling more violated than any physical act of violence? How was she supposed to compete with another woman who was made of nothing but words? It wounded her to think that all the while she'd been making love to Dave, he had been dissecting her performance right along with her motives. And judging her.

Never had Kayanne been more insulted and hurt in her entire life. And she'd had more than her fair share of humiliating experiences from which to draw a comparison.

A literary whore, she felt dirty. She kicked the coffee table and screamed. She tore at her hair. And when she was done, she felt gutted. But no closer to knowing how to proceed than before venting all her emotions on an empty room.

Should she confront Dave when he walked through the front door by waving the evidence in his face?

Should she burn it? Light up the old fireplace, toast marshmallows over his laptop, and let him try to reconstruct his precious masterpiece by memory?

Perhaps sue him for libel?

Knowing it wouldn't be wise to rush into any decision feeling the way she did right now, Kayanne reached for an old friend as she headed for the cupboard where Dave had a bottle of whiskey with her name on it stashed away.

"Anybody home?"

Dave's voice echoed through the house. Although he'd done it for years, he hated coming home to an empty house. He'd easily gotten used to being welcomed home by a woman whose eyes lit up the instant he hit the front door. Breathing in the scent of homemade minestrone soup simmering in a Crock-Pot, he marveled anew at the fact that Kayanne took such pleasure from cooking for him. Nothing could have pleased him more than seeing his supermodel lover immersed in domestic bliss. Just watching her bend over his long-neglected flower garden was enough to send him into erotic fantasies.

"Honey, I'm home," he said, acknowledging how that old chestnut characterized every man's need to make his presence known in his own home.

The silence that met this announcement was unnerving. Usually Kayanne came running to give him a big hug and make him feel like the king of his humble castle. Today the only sound that greeted him was the clock on the mantel chiming out the hours. Three o'clock on a Saturday and no sign of Kayanne.

Something was terribly wrong.

Loneliness blew through Dave like a cold blast of wind. Where was she? He wondered how he could have grown so accustomed to her presence that even a short absence filled him with such a horrible sense of emptiness. He looked around for a note informing him of her whereabouts.

Nothing.

Just an open cupboard door.

A trickle of sweat ran down his neck at the realization that that was where he kept the only bottle of booze in the house.

"Please no."

Swallowing hard, Dave called out her name. His imagination raced faster than his feet as he searched the house room to room starting with the bedroom.

Maybe she'd taken ill and was just resting.

Maybe she was pregnant and didn't even know it

yet. Maybe he'd have to be the one to point out the signs of morning sickness to her. He'd been careful about using condoms, but Dave knew there were worse things than fathering children with the most beautiful woman on earth. The very thought puffed him up with sudden pride. He wondered how Kayanne felt about children. Surely she wouldn't do away with an unborn child without his knowledge.

Taking the steps by twos, Dave considered what kind of father he would be. Hopefully not one who would force his child into a profession he didn't love. Nor one whose judgment might cause his children to hesitate about marrying the love of their life simply because of differences in social backgrounds.

Get a grip on yourself, he told himself. *You're making yourself crazy for no reason.*

He'd never given much thought to marriage before. Just committing to living together had been a gigantic step for a man who placed a high value on his privacy and independence.

Dave threw the bedroom door open. The room was empty. Completely empty of any sign that Kayanne had ever been there at all.

Her things were gone. Her clothes and jewelry and fascinating, feminine fragrances.

All gone.

Dave hadn't thought it possible to miss the sight of cosmetics taking up space on his bathroom counter, but at that moment there wasn't anything he owned that he wouldn't have traded for such a comforting nuisance.

He sat down on the edge of the bed and faced the awful truth. Kayanne had left him.

Just like that.

Without so much as an explanation.

She'd warned him that she traveled light in case the urge to move on ever struck, but it had never occurred to Dave that she'd vanish without even saying goodbye. Telling himself that something must have happened, that she must have been called away unexpectedly, he imagined the worst. Her mother had taken ill again and she was at the hospital. Giving blood. Or Rose was on her deathbed demanding to see Kayanne so she could make peace with her before crossing over.

Dave knew that it must be a sin to wish for a catastrophe just to provide a legitimate reason for Kayanne's disappearance, but he didn't care. He'd take any thread of hope offered. Swamped by panic, he played the events of the day over and over again in his head. Had he said something to upset her? Done something insensitive? Not done something that he should have done?

Had Forrester returned to carry her away on a magnificent black Harley-Davidson motorcycle with the promise of more wild, exciting times? Dave pictured Kayanne's long hair blowing in the wind as she snuggled up against Forrester's leather-clad back, both of them laughing at the idea of her ever settling down with anyone as ordinary as a college English professor. Acid poured into Dave's stomach, eating him up from the inside out.

There's got to be a logical explanation. She wouldn't do this to me. She just wouldn't.

But all Dave knew for sure was that Kayanne was gone. And he couldn't imagine life without her. Determined to track her to the ends of the earth if he had to, he went in search of clues. It didn't take him long to find one in his office: an open bottle of Jack Daniel's whiskey with an empty glass and an AA token next to it.

A sinking feeling caught him off guard, causing him to stumble. Looking down, he recognized a page from his manuscript at his feet. He bent down and examined it. It was from the chapter in which he'd first introduced Spice. Swearing, Dave crushed his own words into a ball and launched it across the room. Remedying this terrible mistake wouldn't be nearly as easy as pressing the delete key.

Twelve

When Kayanne showed up on her mother's doorstep unexpectedly, she discovered an unlikely ally in Suzanne Aldarmann. She took one look at her daughter's face, enfolded her in a hug and welcomed her back home. What surprised Kayanne even more than the rare display of physical affection was the fact that her mother didn't press for any details. She simply put on a pot of coffee and helped her move back into her old room. It was a process that didn't take long.

"Do you want to talk about it?"

"I don't think I can, Mom. Not yet." Kayanne swallowed hard. "Maybe never."

Suzanne patted her hand. "It's never easy watching

your child suffer heartache, and you've certainly had your fair share, honey."

It was funny how much that simple acknowledgment meant to Kayanne. Her throat closed around a solid lump.

"I'd hoped this one was different," Suzanne said, taking care to avoid mentioning Dave's name specifically.

"That's the trouble," Kayanne explained. "He was."

Her mother handed her an entire box of tissues, stared straight into her daughter's eyes and cut to the heart of the matter. "You've got it bad, don't you?"

If AA had taught Kayanne anything, it was that she had to be honest with herself. After a lifetime of keeping secrets from her mother, she admitted with a sigh, "I love him, Mom."

Suzanne put an arm around her daughter's shoulders and commiserated. "You poor thing."

Kayanne supposed she hadn't shared much about her romantic relationships with her mother for fear of shocking her. Mostly because in the past those relationships had been more about sex than love. Suzanne was far more qualified to discuss the latter, having considerable personal experience in dealing with the loss of her one true love and none in filling the void her husband's death left with meaningless relationships.

"Have you told him that you love him?" Suzanne asked gently.

"No, thank God."

Not in words anyway.

That, at least, was something for which to be grateful. Kayanne couldn't bear the thought of those three little words making it onto the pages of Dave's manuscript in some mocking manner. Especially considering that she'd never said them to another man except her father.

Since there was nothing more that could be said that wouldn't belabor her broken heart, the two women worked together in silence for the remainder of the afternoon, each tending their separate memories. Kayanne was making room for her suitcase in the back of her closet when she came across an old box of memorabilia.

"It's some of your old awards, report cards and diaries that I've been saving for you," her mother said. She held up her hands to ward off an attack. "Don't worry, I didn't read any of them."

Kayanne was glad. What good could come from rummaging through the hurts of the past—unless it was to put the pain of the present into perspective? She'd survived her father's death, her first sweetheart's suicide, a disastrous relationship with a married man and countless ill-fated flings, including an ongoing one with alcohol. None of them matched the intensity of the anguish she felt over Dave using her.

When a sharp rap on the door made her jump, she told her mother in no uncertain terms, "If it's Dave, tell him that I'm not here."

Suzanne didn't argue. She just quietly went to answer the door, leaving her daughter alone to sort out her things and her thoughts. Five minutes later, Dave filled the doorway with his broad shoulders. Kayanne couldn't imagine what he'd said to smooth talk his way past her mother, but she wasn't pleased to see him. That in spite of the way her heart leaped to her throat threatening to divulge her body's treachery.

"Well, if it isn't 'Enry 'Iggins come to make a respectable lady out of a poor flower girl. You'd best set the good china, Mum, for me gentleman caller," she hollered in her best Eliza Doolittle imitation before her voice turned sharply bitter. "And I do use that term loosely."

"She's not here," Dave said. "Your mother was gracious enough to give us some privacy to work through our problems ourselves."

Afraid of falling back into his tender gaze and never being able to find her way back home, she deflected her gaze. Abandoned by the one woman in the world whose support she should have been able to count on, Kayanne dropped all pretense of good manners.

"What is it you want?"

Her bedroom was so small that Dave could touch both walls at the same time if he chose to. Knowing how dangerous it was being confined in such a small place with him, she considered rushing the door to escape. The likelihood was that such foolish action would simply land her on her back upon the old twin bed. And if the bed didn't break beneath their combined weight, Kayanne feared that her willpower would. She couldn't bear the thought of the humble little room that had nurtured her childhood dreams finding its way onto the pages of Dave's next novel.

"First and foremost I came to see if you're okay."

Kayanne rolled her eyes. "By okay do you mean if I'm out 'indiscriminately cavorting with a string of second-rate lovers'?" she asked, quoting a line directly from his work in progress.

Dave winced to hear his own words thrown in his face. "I mean okay as in sober."

Kayanne was blunt. "What do you care? Don't let the fact that you haven't found me drinking myself to death in the gutter keep you from using it in your book."

Dave's face darkened. He reached out to place the pad of his thumb under her chin and tipped her head, forcing her to look at him.

"Whatever you think of me right now, don't ever doubt that I care a great deal about you."

Kayanne jerked her head away. How could he possibly manage to sound so sincere all the while twisting the knife deeper into her back?

"If you ever get tired of writing, you've got a great career ahead of you as an actor," she told him. "It sure as hell takes a flair for the dramatic to waltz in here pretending concern when all you're really doing is scoping out more sordid details for your next chapter."

She grabbed a diary out of the box she'd been sorting through and launched it at him. It bounced off his head.

"Maybe you can find some dirt in there from my junior-high days that might be useful in developing a misbegotten gutter snipe as a foil for your perfect heroine."

Dave rubbed his forehead. "Now listen—"

"No, you listen," she said, taking as careful aim with her words as with the diary she'd fired at him. "I'm just fine. A little hurt and worse for wear. And, yes, to address your concerns, I did have to think long and hard about having a drink after reading your true opinion of me. But after careful consideration, I decided you weren't worth it."

Kayanne read the relief in Dave's face. And the hurt. Pouring that glass of whiskey down the drain had been one of the hardest things she'd ever done. The smell alone had almost been enough to push her over the edge. Her white-light revelation hadn't taken away her desire for alcohol, but it had given her the strength to defy her demons. Given the circumstances, that was as close to a miracle as she could hope for.

"I've decided it's time to get rid of all the poison in my life—starting with you," she stated flatly. "So now that you've relieved your conscience as to the state of my sobriety, why don't you just run on back to your life and finish your masterpiece without any more *inspiration* from your trailer-trash muse?"

Dave struggled to keep his voice level. "I know you're hurt. And I want you to know how proud I am of you for resisting temptation, but you're walking a thin line here so be careful not to say anything today that can't be taken back tomorrow."

That said, he risked life and limb by taking another step toward her. One more and he'd be right on top of her. Kayanne jumped up off the bed to face him toe-to-toe.

"Why shouldn't I? You have no compunction in how you use your words. You can change anything I say with a few lousy keystrokes. You can twist my words to fit your purpose or put your own words in my mouth for that matter. I can't believe you have the gall to tell *me* to be careful what *I* say. How about you being careful what you put down on the page for posterity? For everybody and his dog to read."

"I didn't mean to hurt you," he told her.

Even if that was true, Kayanne wasn't sure that was reason enough to forgive him.

"Maybe not," she said. "But the bottom line is that you weren't even as honest with me as the paparazzi scum who sell their garbage to the tabloids. Even they have more integrity than to literally screw somebody before doing the same to them in print. As far as I'm concerned you can go right on living the rest of your life vicariously through me if that's what you really want to do. But don't ever make the mistake of thinking you can control me off the page."

Kayanne took some satisfaction in seeing his eyes cloud with pain as her words hit their mark. He was lucky. If she'd been a man, she likely would have backed up those words with her fists.

Dave shook his head adamantly. "Sweetheart, I don't want to control you. I just want to be with you."

Kayanne hated herself for secretly thrilling to the endearment he tossed her way. Dave looked so convincingly sorry that she was almost tempted to buy the cheap remorse he was peddling. Almost.

When he reached for her hand, she drew back as if to slap him. To his credit, he didn't so much as flinch.

"Go ahead," he told her. "Hit me if it'll make you feel better. Looking at it from your perspective, I suppose I deserve it."

"You suppose so?"

Kayanne despised the pettiness that marked her tone. As tempting as it might be to leave a red mark across his handsome face, she didn't want to give him the satisfaction—especially since it would just lead to a wrestling match in her bedroom. Not a good idea given the fact that anger and passion were so closely linked. She didn't dare risk the objectivity needed to maintain her present level of fury. Nor could she afford to squander her remaining shred of dignity on one last roll in the hay—one that might very well deposit her back into the bottle and put a cork in it for good.

"I'd like you to read the rest of the book. It's almost finished," Dave said, tentatively broaching the subject. "Spice isn't at all what she seemed to be in the first few chapters, the ones that you read. In fact, I'm hoping that you and the rest of the world will fall in love with her—just like I did."

Kayanne's heart did a slow flip inside her chest. Was he actually admitting that he loved her? Or simply referring to the woman of his imagination, the one he'd christened Spice as a play on her own name? How could she trust anything this man said? He could simply be trying to pacify her so that she didn't sue him to stop publication of his book.

Did he really believe he could make things better just by writing a new ending to his story? Dave may not be vain about his good looks or his privileged background, but Kayanne had never met a writer worth his salt who didn't lay his ego on the line with every word he wrote. Striking out in anger, she landed a hit below the literary belt.

"Better yet, why don't you just kill off Spice, resurrect the impeccable Jasmine, and put her back in your bed where she belongs? You obviously prefer making love to a fantasy over a real woman who is less than perfect. One who actually might have had an interesting life before meeting you."

All the air left Dave's lungs in a single whoosh.

"And while we're on the subject of Jasmine," Kayanne continued, not heeding his advice about watching what came out of her mouth in a fit of rage. "I'm glad I killed her. She was a simpering fool. And as fake as half the boobs on a Los Angeles beach. As far as I'm concerned, she deserved to die, along with all the rest of the one-dimensional characters that men dream up to flatter their big old egos."

Kayanne was surprised to see a tiny smile toy with the edges of Dave's lips.

"You're right," he admitted. "About everything. Right about me using you to advance my story. Right about Jasmine. And most of all, right about me living vicariously through you. The question now is whether or not you'll ever be able to forgive me."

Like a light switch being flipped off, all the fight went out of Kayanne. She understood that part of her struggle with substance abuse was a driving need to be right. Suddenly, being right didn't seem nearly as important as being happy. Especially since that long-term rancor was only going to lead her straight back to the bottle.

Kayanne dropped onto the bed in a posture of defeat. She sat on the edge holding her head in her hands, trying to come to terms with the person she wanted to be. That most definitely wasn't the world-weary cynic that Dave described in his book. There was no white light involved in this acceptance—just an understanding that she, of all people, was obligated to grant forgiveness when it was asked of her.

Especially when she so deeply loved the person asking.

"Don't worry," she said, looking deeply into his eyes and trying to memorize the golden flakes floating in those dark irises. "I won't do anything to stand in the way of getting your book published. Whether or not I took exception to what I read, it was good. Really good. A great improvement over your first book."

Dropping to one knee, Dave did his best to assure her. "The book's insignificant. I'll destroy it if that's what you want. Your feelings are what matter the most to me."

Kayanne shook her head. That wasn't what she wanted. The words he'd written were already burned into her memory never to be erased. Emotionally spent, she saw no reason to punish Dave beyond the hateful things she'd already said to him. She managed a wobbly smile.

"I think you've got a bestseller on your hands. One that should guarantee you'll never have to go home to run the family business unless you decide that you want to. For what it's worth, I really do wish you well."

The furrows in Dave's forehead deepened as he took both of Kayanne's hands in his. "It sounds like you're giving me the brush-off."

"I'm letting you go as a friend."

Dave looked shocked when the enormity of that statement hit him. "You can't possibly mean that we're through."

Kayanne's smile slipped. "It's for the best."

"I'm on my knees," Dave pointed out. "Begging you to give me another chance."

She studied the face that she loved: eyes the color of aged wood, dusty hair soft to the touch, a mouth that smiled generously and often, and tanned skin pulled over angular handsome features. The thought of this man loving anyone else killed her. And yet, she couldn't deny him the opportunity to move on with his life. He had every right to take some fresh-faced coed to the family plantation. Someone his parents would welcome into their family with open arms. Someone like Jasmine.

A note of desperation stole into his voice. "Since I'm down here on my knees already, why don't I go ahead and make it official by proposing?"

It was the last thing Kayanne expected. She didn't know how to react. She didn't even know how much she'd wanted to hear those words until they were actually spoken aloud. All the glamour and glitz of modeling faded into nothingness compared to a lifetime spent with the man she loved. Sharing not only his bed but also his dreams. It was more than she'd ever allowed herself to hope for. Certainly more than anything waiting for her in the big city.

Unfortunately, Dave's proposal felt like an afterthought, something intended to make things right by temporarily smoothing hurt feelings. Not something on which to base a lifetime decision. Kayanne brushed her lips lightly against his. Determined to remain strong, she fought the sob struggling to rise to the surface.

"You shouldn't propose to me because it just wouldn't work."

Her voice was gentled by a truth too painful to be spoken above a whisper.

"Because whatever Spice becomes by the end of your book, *I* can never become anything other than me. Reading those first few chapters made me realize that on some level you'll always be ashamed of me."

Dave hotly protested the ridiculousness of that assertion, but she put a finger to his lips and asked him to let her finish.

"Given our differences in background, education and experiences, your family would never accept a wild child like me. And I can't say that I blame them. My life hasn't exactly been low-profile."

The stricken expression on Dave's face told Kayanne that he'd given this some thought himself before reaching a similar conclusion. While he might conveniently forget to mention to his parents that he was living with her, marriage required family knowledge, involvement and, ultimately, approval. Kayanne didn't want to put that kind of burden on him when it was obvious that he was struggling to separate his needs from theirs as it was.

"It's okay," she assured him, doing her best to sound cavalier. "Can you imagine me at some stuffy academic banquet making small talk with fellow professors about the Shakespearean authorship debate? And their reaction when they discover the only degree I have is a high-school diploma?"

"Who gives a damn about what anybody else thinks?" Dave yelled.

"Believe it or not, I do."

No matter how far she'd come, Kayanne could never outrun her past. Beneath all those slick magazine spreads was a little girl who wouldn't ask friends over to play for fear they would make fun of where she lived.

"Knowing you're ashamed of me would be worse than not having you at all. You have my blessing to end your book however you want, but I'm going to put an end to this real-life relationship right now. I've made up my mind. As soon as I'm sure Mom can get along all right without me, I'll be leaving for New York."

Thirteen

Dave had no doubt Suzanne Aldarmann would manage just fine without her daughter. *He* was the one who couldn't imagine life without Kayanne. Glancing at the nearly finished manuscript that he'd deposited on the kitchen table when he'd first arrived, he cursed it under his breath as he closed the front door of the trailer behind himself.

What a mess he'd made of things.

An eternal optimist, he still held out hope that Kayanne would relent and read the remainder of his book; the best-case scenario being that she would see how Spice's amazing transformation over the course of the novel mirrored his perception of her. And see how much he loved her through prose that truly elevated this book to another level.

She would be moved to give him another chance.

Aside from hoping that this book held the key to repairing their relationship, Kayanne's opinion mattered to him. More than she knew. Though she had a tendency to put herself down for her lack of formal education, Dave valued her judgment as much if not more than the opinions of his colleagues. For one thing, she was brutally honest. And intuitive. Despite popular opinion, one didn't reach the top of the fashion industry by being a bubble head. The few times he'd asked her for help either in plotting or with something more personal, her insight had proven invaluable. It hurt him deeply to hear her refer to herself as his "trailer-park muse."

Of course, Dave knew he could sugarcoat the truth all he wanted, but it wouldn't change the fact that he had used her. Shamelessly.

Never mind that it had been innocent at the start. Writers draw their inspiration from any number of incidents and people who spark their imagination. Life in all its complexities is fair game to them. The point where Dave had crossed the line was in failing to talk to Kayanne about the liberties he'd taken with her life when she'd moved from being a fictional character to his lover.

Furthermore, while it was true that he hadn't portrayed her in the most flattering light after their first contentious meeting, from that moment on she had taken over his life as well as his book. And both were better for it. She breathed fresh air into prose and a life too

laden with concerns about what other people thought—
Dave's parents included.

It would be a lie to say that he hadn't considered the
possibility that they might look down their noses at
Kayanne. Then again, he may have misjudged them—
just as he had her. For all the emphasis they placed on
status, John and Eula Evans's marriage was based on
mutual respect. It was a respect they'd extended to their
only son as well. As much as they hated seeing him
"waste" his talents frittering away his expensive education only to move as far away as he could from the
family business, they ultimately supported his decision
to become whatever he wanted to be. In addition, they
offered him a safety net. One that he'd been less than
gracious in accepting.

The more Dave thought about it, the more he wondered if Kayanne might not fit into his family better than
he himself did. She certainly knew how to appreciate
what was missing in her own life: the stability of a two-
parent family and a love that wasn't based on lies. It was
the kind of life he wanted.

And the kind of life Kayanne deserved.

Dave saw the fact that she'd turned down his proposal
of marriage as simply another obstacle to overcome, not
a reason to give up hope altogether. Time had amazing
healing properties and he prided himself on being a
patient man. He went home to wait for Kayanne to read
the chapters that he'd left for her and fall in love with
them. And with him all over again.

All that was missing was the last couple of chapters.

And a ring.

A great, big, beautiful diamond that proclaimed to the whole world that this amazing woman was his till the end of time. Wanting to shout the news from the rooftops, Dave started by placing a very important, belated long-distance call.

"Mom," he said when she picked up the receiver, "I've met someone...."

A day passed. Then another. Time moved as slowly as brackish water. When Kayanne failed to contact him after the third day, Dave began to worry. She wouldn't take his phone calls. She returned unopened the letter over which he'd agonized. And one morning, he found his manuscript on his doorstep with no indication that she'd read a single word of it.

As his deadline loomed, Dave threw himself into his work, hoping to use his angst as the necessary fuel to finish his book. He prayed that Kayanne would recognize her own wild perfection in the character that she'd spawned. She occupied his every thought and rendered him completely unable to function in any capacity. She was his obsession. Without her in his bed, he couldn't sleep. He couldn't eat. And he damned sure couldn't write.

How much easier it was to write about love from a safe distance than feel it burn in his veins like a lethal injection. He could no more finish his book than he could plug the hole in his chest where his heart used to be. Loneliness filled every nook, cranny and corner of his life. Work lost all meaning for him.

As did life.

Not the type ever to consider suicide, Dave came to a better understanding of how a young boy like Pete Nargas could become so desperate as to actually pull the trigger on himself. Dave developed empathy for every lovesick, besotted character that he'd ever minimized before. In short, he joined the brotherhood of the brokenhearted and was forced to reevaluate his view of the frail human race.

So it was that Rose found him sitting unshaven on his front porch considering a bottle of Jack Daniel's whiskey at ten o'clock one morning. He could hear her tsk-tsking all the way up the sidewalk. And he didn't score any gentleman points by jumping up to help her to her seat, either. She looked around in displeasure at his once-tidy workplace.

"You're looking well," he said, clearing off a place for her.

She really did. There was something different about her. She looked less dowdy. Younger. A paisley silk scarf held artfully with a dragonfly brooch accentuated a new spring-green jacket. And she had artfully applied makeup to a face that wore a more determined look than Dave had ever seen before.

"Wish I could say the same for you," Rose told him, not bothering with social pleasantries. "You're a mess."

She shook her head in disgust and sniffed as if smelling something particularly distasteful. Like a rat foraging in its own filth.

"Nice to see you again, too."

The sarcasm was lost on her. "No wonder Kayanne left you. I would've, too," Rose pointed out, making it apparent that she wasn't in the market for a drunken boyfriend. Clearly she had all her wits about her today.

Being rejected by an octogenarian didn't improve Dave's mood any. He responded in an equally candid manner. "If you don't have anything constructive to say, I'd appreciate you letting me drink in peace."

"Fine. If you don't want to know how Kayanne's doing, I'll just be on my way then," Rose snapped, struggling to get to her feet.

Dave's pulse quickened at the sound of that lyrical name. Hope was resurrected in the rapid beating of his heart. Had she sent a message for him? Anything at all was better than the silence that presently held him imprisoned. He jumped to his feet and did his best to appease the old lady.

"Just sit tight," he told her, "I'll go get the gingersnaps."

He'd deal later with the fact that the only cookies in his pantry were as hard as hockey pucks. Right now, he had to do whatever it took to keep Rose placated until he gleaned every sliver of information about Kayanne that he could. Rose harrumphed, settled into her chair and smoothed out the wrinkles in her skirt.

"Don't bother," she said. "I'm here for one thing, and it's not your lousy cookies. It's to get two people who I care very much about to admit to being fools. After fifty years of marriage to the same man, God rest his soul, I believe I'm qualified to offer a little unsolicited advice in matters of the heart."

Dave leaned forward anxiously. "I'll take any advice you have to offer, Rose."

She nodded sagely. "The truth is I can't stand seeing either one of you two kids let pride stand in the way of your happiness. Trust me. True love is a gift that isn't offered often in this life so you'd better hold tight to it when it comes around."

Having been duly chastised, Dave proceeded to shoot a barrage of questions at her.

"How is she? Has she said anything about me? Did she read anything I sent over? Has she changed her mind about leaving?"

Shaking her head, Rose clucked in disapproval. "The poor thing's terrible. Ever since she quit, all she does is mope around. Nobody wants to see her go back to New York. That girl's the best thing to happen to the Manor since they opened their doors. She's organized socials, gotten the ladies feeling pretty again, and done more for the old fellas' libidos than Viagra. She's even got a beau lined up for me. A nice fellow by the name of Joe Hansen."

Blushing, she stopped to shake a bony finger at Dave. "Then you had to go and ruin everything by breaking her heart."

A selfish part of him was glad to hear that Kayanne was having trouble functioning without him. That meant she still had feelings for him. Such encouraging news was overshadowed by the prospect of her leaving. For good.

"I proposed to her," he said in his defense.

It wasn't easy admitting that she'd flatly turned him down, but Dave didn't much appreciate the entire senior citizenry holding him solely responsible for depriving them of their one bright spot of the day, either.

"How?" Rose asked bluntly. "Did you have a big, old expensive ring in a black velvet box with you at the time? Did you plan out what you were going to say and pop the question in some romantic place and in some heartfelt way? Or did you just sort of casually mention that since you were already down on your knees begging forgiveness for being a jackass that you might as well propose in some offhanded way that any proud woman might interpret as an afterthought? Or worse yet as a way to ease your own conscience about hurting her so badly?"

Adrift in his own pain, Dave hadn't ever looked at it like that. The fact that Rose knew the details of his failed proposal told him that she was in Kayanne's confidence. While that bothered him on some level, it also held out a glimmer of hope.

"At least I've got her to stop talking about leaving until after the fashion show," Rose continued. "That means you've got until the end of the month to pull your head out of your heinie and set things right. Make her see how much you really love her. And need her. And want her."

Visions of caveman techniques came to mind, but as Rose had already pointed out, a gentle touch was called for. Kayanne had been muscled by too many men in her life already, and none of them had been able to force her to do anything she didn't want to.

"Fashion show?"

Rose opened her purse and drew out an invitation, which she handed him.

"I'm counting on you to be there," she said before stiffly getting to her feet and leaving him to figure the rest out for himself.

There was a commotion in the dressing room that demanded Kayanne's immediate attention. She was all too familiar with the nerves, squabbling and power struggles that went with putting on a fashion show. But the smiles, laughter and camaraderie that met her as she stepped into the crowded room was something altogether new. All around her, stunning women were having the time of their lives.

The fact that they were senior citizens didn't lessen the satisfaction Kayanne felt as she surveyed their glowing faces. If Rose had taught her anything, it was that a woman was entitled to feel beautiful all the days of her life. The seed for this fashion extravaganza had been planted the first time Kayanne had accompanied Rose to a boutique and had found nothing appropriate in stock. It had occurred to her then that this was an age group the industry had all but forgotten. In a business that generated over a hundred and seventy billion dollars a year, it was virtually an untapped market.

Her mistake had been in mentioning it to Rose, who had been pushing her ever since to undertake a new venture. Rose had promised to act as a silent partner and put up the capital to launch a new line designed especially for older women. Kayanne's mother had wanted in as well. It seemed she hadn't squandered all the money her daughter had sent her on missionaries and con men after all. She had a healthy portion stashed safely away making steady if not spectacular interest. Added to the local support were big-name backers who'd already expressed an interest in marketing Kayanne's name and designs.

"When have you ever been able to remain silent on anything?" Kayanne had asked Rose, a fact underscored when the older lady had wheedled from her the details of her break-up with Dave. Rose could no more remain quiet on that issue than on matters of politics or religion. Ever since meeting Joe Hansen, she had been feeling particularly generous and wanted everyone to share in the joy of her budding romance. She seemed to feel personally obligated to set things right between Kayanne and Dave.

"You deserve to be happy," Rose had told her.

"What we deserve and what we get are often two different things," had been Kayanne's wry reply.

Nonetheless, the idea of marketing her own brand of specialty clothing was intriguing. As was Rose's suggestion that they hold a fashion show to launch the idea and get a grassroots feel for whether it was truly worth pursuing. There was something appealing about designing clothes for women who could never grow too old for the runway. Something about designing for women who'd seen enough of the world to value comfort and style equally. The only thing keeping Kayanne in town right now was her mother's health, which was improving every day, and the fashion show that Rose had inveigled her into putting on.

They'd arranged to use the community hall for the evening, and Kayanne was astonished to see a packed house when she peeked out from behind the curtain. People of all ages crowded in to see their grandmothers, mothers, wives and sweethearts strut their stuff. If tonight's reception was any indication, she might actually have a chance of selling her new line of clothing when she got back to Manhattan, a place whose glitter had lost much of its shine for her.

Suddenly Kayanne found herself desperately missing Dave. She wished he was there to share this moment with her. To hold her hand and settle her nerves with his steady humor—and his mind-blowing kisses. Her throat tightened around the object stuck there. It could well have been her heart. She cursed Dave soundly for intruding on her thoughts at the most inopportune times. Like every other minute of the day. That only made it all the more difficult to focus on the crisis at hand.

"What's the problem?"

Kayanne assumed a light tone with the assembled crowd in the dressing room. She was afraid some of the ladies might be getting cold feet and didn't want to have to confiscate any alcohol being used to steady anyone's nerves. The way she was feeling at the moment, Kayanne wasn't sure she'd be strong enough to resist taking a swig herself.

"Why did you call me in here anyway? It looks to me like everything's under control."

Rose stepped forward to a round of polite applause and presented Kayanne with a huge bouquet of fresh flowers.

"Whatever happens out there tonight, we just want to thank you for what you've done for us. For making us feel desirable again."

Kayanne looked around the room and saw nothing but smiling, grateful faces. All of the women gathered about were gray and wrinkled. Some were still grieving missing breasts from mastectomies and until now hadn't ever been able to find clothes that didn't make them feel freakishly self-conscious. A few would need walkers to help them down the makeshift runway. Swathed in a rainbow's array of colors and textures, they were all incredibly beautiful.

And brave.

"I'm so proud of you," Kayanne said, giving each one a flower from the bouquet to carry during her debut. More nervous for her elderly friends than she'd ever been for herself, she checked her watch and announced, "It's almost time to get this show on the road."

Five minutes later, she was sitting in the front row directly in front of the runway watching the curtain go up. Butterflies danced in her stomach and doubts toyed with her mind.

What if one of the models falls and breaks a hip?

What if the audience doesn't like my designs?

What if they laugh?

Or boo?

Who in the world do I think I am trying to launch a new line in Podunk, Wyoming, when there are over five thousand designer showrooms in New York alone?

Sitting next to her, Kayanne's mother squeezed her

hand and gave her a reassuring smile. "Everything's going to be just fine."

It seemed only fitting that Rose was the first model of the evening. She shimmered down the runway in a mid-length dress of pale blue that was appropriate for attending a formal affair or simply dining out at an elegant restaurant. With all the aplomb of a seasoned veteran, she smiled at Kayanne, blew a kiss to Joe Hansen who was sitting behind her, and tossed a lily over her shoulder to a young lady sitting with her grandfather. The audience was utterly enchanted.

Kayanne heaved a sigh of relief and settled in her seat to enjoy the rest of a very special evening. She didn't know exactly how special it was going to prove to be until Rose stepped out from behind the curtain after the last model had completed her turn.

"As a finale to tonight's festivities, we have a special guest who is going to model his own version of humble pie for us," she announced with a sly wink.

Then she reached through the curtain and exchanged places with Dave in a move that proved she could have been a magician's assistant as well as a fashion model. Kayanne's palms grew sweaty at the sight of the man she loved dressed in a white tuxedo with tails, holding a dozen red roses and looking better than any airbrushed model she'd ever seen. He looked terribly nervous. That this clearly was beyond his comfort level only endeared him to Kayanne all the more. She couldn't imagine what Rose had done to get him to agree to such a public exhibition, but the instant that he stepped out onto that stage, she knew she didn't want to live another minute without him.

He cleared his throat, stared into the lights, and deliberately sought her out. He began his long journey down the runway to the hoots and hollers of an audience delighted to be getting far more than they had paid for. Dave stopped at the end of the runway and looked directly at Kayanne. Bending down on one knee, he cleared his throat.

"It was brought to my attention that my earlier proposal lacked a certain romantic appeal. This is my clumsy attempt to remedy that. I want everybody in this room and the entire world to know how much I love you, Kayanne. If I promise to never, ever hurt you again, would you please consider making me the happiest man alive by agreeing to be my wife?"

As moved by the trickle of sweat running down the side of his face as by the elegantly wrapped box that he pulled out of his jacket pocket, Kayanne knew how hard it was for him to so publicly put himself on the line. Any nagging doubts that he might have proposed before only to assuage her hurt feelings dissolved, along with her fear that he was secretly ashamed of her. A man didn't risk this level of embarrassment unless he felt anything other than the most convincing love.

Rose was right. She was a fool.

Kayanne stood on wobbly legs to take the roses from him.

"Say yes!" called out one overly involved onlooker, setting off a chain of such cheers.

"Go on, honey," her mother urged, dabbing her eyes with a tissue.

Dave helped her up onto the runway by way of a strategically placed stepladder. Juggling his flowers, she accepted a ring box from him and held it up so that the audience could take a peek.

"It's perfect," she said over their oohs and aahs.

Then she wrapped her arms around his neck and kissed him fully on the lips. Any resistance to the idea of spending the rest of her life with this man melted beneath the heat of a flame destined to burn throughout eternity.

The crowd roared.

"Yes!" Kayanne told him through a blur of tears. "Yes, I'll marry you."

Dave refused to let go of her. His arms remained anchored solidly around her waist as he whispered in her ear. "I'll burn the manuscript if you want me to."

"Over my dead body," she whispered back. "I love what you've done with my character. And more importantly what you've done to me. To us."

Dave's eyes lit up with the realization that she'd actually read the chapters he'd given her. And liked them. With Kayanne by his side, he couldn't imagine anything keeping him from achieving all of his dreams. He beamed.

"Just be careful not to make Spice too good in the final chapters," she warned, fearing his tendency to swing from one extreme to the other. "And remember. You're marrying a real woman, mister. One with real emotions, a checkered past and immediate needs…."

Only more than happy to oblige on that last count,

Dave was forced to settle for what was audience appropriate at the moment, promising to meet those needs more completely once he got her where he wanted her in his bed. Bending her deeply at the back, he gave the crowd the finale they wanted—a real old-fashioned Hollywood kiss.

Basking in the thunderous applause as a cast of sexy senior citizens joined them on stage, Kayanne felt she'd finally come home. Home to a man who loved her for who she was. A man who understood that love alone had the power to change a beast into a beauty—from the inside out. Home to a life that made her feel productive and happy. Home to the belief that she deserved a happy ending just the same as any character her husband chose to put in his next bestseller.

Real life just didn't get any better than that.

When business is pleasure…

Turn the page for a sneak preview of

The CEO's Scandalous Affair
by
Roxanne St Claire,

the thrilling start of THE GARRISONS *series,*
available from Mills & Boon® Desire™
in September 2008.

The CEO's Scandalous Affair

by

Roxanne St Claire

"We've reached our cruising altitude, Mr. Garrison. Would you care for the usual?" The lone flight attendant on the G5 that the Garrison family routinely rented for business travel smiled benevolently at him. Her prematurely gray hair was, as always, pulled back into an elegant bun, her simple dark suit unmarred by even a fleck of lint.

"Thank you, Christine, I would. Anna?"

Across the small expanse that separated the two widest leather recliners on the plane, Anna had already lined a granite-topped table with a sea of manila folders and papers, and she had a laptop open and fired up for work.

"It depends," she said. "What is the usual?"

"Tomato juice and Tabasco."

She made a face. "Coffee, please."

"Come on, Anna," he urged. "Live dangerously."

He hoped for a clever quip, an easy smile, but got only a shake of her head.

"Just coffee, thank you." When the attendant nodded and moved toward the galley, Anna lifted a paper and held it toward him. "I've compiled a list of pending open items for your attention, Mr. Garrison."

He didn't remind her to call him Parker. Anna Cross was back to business in a big way. It was as though she'd been wearing a sign that said This Is Work, Not Fun ever since she'd arrived at the executive airport and climbed out of her little Saturn wearing her most staid suit selected from a wardrobe that couldn't be called anything but *ultraconservative*. Navy jacket, shapeless trousers, flat shoes.

Where was the girl who felt pretty in pink underwear?

Parker took the list, and reminded himself that he was the one who'd suggested she accompany him to *work*. He'd made that clear. At least, that was how he rationalized what was, at the moment, an impulsive idea brought on by the not-so-semi state of arousal the bathroom encounter had left him in.

He knew why he'd suggested Anna accompany him to London.

But did she? Sure, she was a terrific, grade-A, indispensable administrative assistant. Sure, she was attractive, classy and intelligent enough to make small talk with the high rollers at the hotel gala. And best of all, he trusted her. She had no gold digger's interest in his money, ready to translate one weekend in Europe into a lifetime of luxury like so many of the women he knew.

But, to be honest, not one of those was the real reason he'd made the unorthodox suggestion. The real reason was simple: he liked what he'd seen in that bathroom. And he wanted to see more. And seeing, he knew as sure as he breathed, wouldn't be enough.

Under any other circumstances, he'd make his move and he'd make it in about five minutes, launching a romantic, sex-charged weekend with champagne and hot kisses at thirty thousand feet. Seducing a woman was an art and a pleasure he took seriously. And often.

But something indefinable held him back. Something oddly unfamiliar had him waiting for a clear invitation, a straightforward cue from her.

Maybe she'd take off her jacket, playfully taste his spicy tomato juice, unclip her barrette and give her hair a sensual shake. That was what other women would do. They'd throw in a head-tilting giggle; slide their bare, pedicured feet on his lap and let the games begin.

But not Anna.

She pulled a pair of butt-ugly reading glasses out of her purse and slipped them up her pert nose. She tightened the clip that held her hair severely off a face devoid of anything but lip gloss and maybe mascara. Then she took her copy of his agenda, pointed to item number one, cleared her throat and said, "You mentioned the Nassau property. I have the files."

Not only did she refuse to send a single cue of feminine interest, she doused his low simmer by mentioning the biggest headache in his life.

He took the file and flipped it open.

"Is there something in particular you're looking for?" she asked.

There sure was. Dirt. Problems. Issues. Anything that could get rid of the half sister who'd just been named his equal partner at Garrison, Inc. "Just want to see how the business is doing."

"Last quarter's financials are on the left side, including occupancy rates and banquet revenue," she told him. "On the right, you'll see information about new resort programs and key employee files. The manager of the resort, Cassie Sinclair, seems to be running things quite smoothly."

At the mention of her name, Parker sucked in a slow and disgusted breath. He flipped through the pages, immaculately ordered and filed, frowning at the excellent revenue stream and the strong outlook for the next season based on advance reservations.

"Is something wrong?"

Yes, something was very, very wrong. He wanted the property to be a disaster. Wanted something he could hang on Cassie Sinclair to prove she couldn't be a Garrison.

"No," he assured her.

"Oh, I thought I might have misfiled something."

"Have you ever misfiled anything, Anna?" he asked with a teasing smile.

A soft blush rose in her cheeks. "If you're asking if I ever make mistakes, I think you, of all people, know that I do."

Mistakes like lingering in his shower a little too long? He held her gaze, still hoping for a spark of connection, but she looked away—as she always did—just as Christine returned with the drinks, some fruit and freshly baked muffins.

Parker returned his attention to the file. "The place is turning a nice profit," he said, half to himself.

"You make it sound like that's a problem."

Should he confide in his assistant? Maybe a little shared confidence would loosen her up. At least get her to slide out of that straitjacket she wore. Plus, he needed someone to talk to. Someone he trusted.

He lifted his tomato juice and took a long drink before he dove in. "Cassie Sinclair, it seems, is more than just the manager of the Garrison Grand-Bahamas."

"She is?"

"She's my half sister."

Anna's jaw dropped an inch. "No way."

He gave her a bittersweet smile. "Evidently there is a way. It's called an affair and my father had one for a long time, resulting in the birth of a woman who is now, according to his will, my equal partner in Garrison, Inc. and—" he held the file up "—the owner of this hotel."

"I don't believe it," she said, dropping back into her seat.

"Neither do I. But that's why God invented lawyers," he said with a shrug. "And why I have to make an appearance in London this weekend."

"Will she be there?"

"Oh, I doubt it. But it's only a matter of time until this gets out to the very small and incestuous hospitality industry. It can't help my business. I'm attending this event for visibility and positioning. More of a PR move than one that will impact the bottom line."

"So that's why you were talking about DNA testing and contesting the will," she said. "Oh, and why…your mother…" Her voice drifted off.

So the rumor mill had already started churning.

"My mother has her way of coping." He picked up the drink again. "And I'm afraid it's not Tabasco in her tomato juice."

She gave him a sympathetic look. "Your family is strong. You'll weather this storm."

"I hope you're right."

"You just have to stay focused and keep running everything the way you have. You can't let this distract you."

The unsolicited—and amazingly accurate—advice took him by surprise. "You're right, Anna. Very astute." He smiled and leaned forward, inexplicably drawn to her. "Thank you for being so understanding."

She held his gaze just long enough to give him hope that the cue he wanted was right around the corner. But she just handed him another file.

"When you're ready to go over the agenda for the marketing-firm meeting, it's all in here. And I'm able to take any e-mail dictation now," she added, tapping the open laptop. "I'll download it and send it when we arrive in London."

Oh, yeah. Anna Cross was all business today, and being a smart CEO, he ignored the urge to reach across the space that separated them and unclip her hair just to see what she'd do. She was way too valuable an asset to him to let hormones screw it up.

* * * *

Don't forget to look for
The CEO's Scandalous Affair
next month.

MILLS & BOON
Desire 2-in-1
On sale 15th August 2008

Scorned by the Boss by *Maureen Child*

This millionaire thinks he can win his assistant back with seduction.
Then she discovers his ploy and shows him two can play his game!

The Texan's Secret Past by *Peggy Moreland*

Mandy knew that *working* for charming rancher Jase Calhoun
would lead to heartache, so why'd she gone and *slept* with him?

❧

The CEO's Scandalous Affair by *Roxanne St Claire*

This Miami millionaire had dated his way through almost every
eligible woman in the city… Could his unpretentious assistant
make him rethink his policy on romance?

Seduced by the Wealthy Playboy by *Sara Orwig*

Brittany Garrison needed his help to rescue her sinking business…
but didn't know millionaire Emilio Jefferies' price would
be her seduction.

Series – The Garrisons

❧

The Kyriakos Virgin Bride by *Tessa Radley*

Zac Kyriakos was the definitive alpha male – bold, powerful
and passionate… So how could innocent Pandora resist the
wealthy Greek's charms?

The Billionaire's Bidding by *Barbara Dunlop*

Hotel magnate Alex Garrison wants her family's business, and
he's prepared to do anything for it…even propose!

FREE

2 BOOKS AND A SURPRISE GIFT!

We would like to take this opportunity to thank you for reading this Mills & Boon® book by offering you the chance to take TWO more specially selected 2-in-1 volumes from the Desire™ series absolutely FREE! We're also making this offer to introduce you to the benefits of the Mills & Boon® Book Club™—

- ★ **FREE home delivery**
- ★ **FREE gifts and competitions**
- ★ **FREE monthly Newsletter**
- ★ **Books available before they're in the shops**
- ★ **Exclusive Mills & Boon Book Club offers**

Accepting these FREE books and gift places you under no obligation to buy; you may cancel at any time, even after receiving your free shipment. Simply complete your details below and return the entire page to the address below. You don't even need a stamp!

YES! Please send me 2 free Desire volumes and a surprise gift. I understand that unless you hear from me, I will receive 3 superb new volumes every month for just £4.99 each, postage and packing free. I am under no obligation to purchase any books and may cancel my subscription at any time. The free books and gift will be mine to keep in any case.

D8ZEE

Ms/Mrs/Miss/Mr..Initials ....
BLOCK CAPITALS PLEASE

Surname ....

Address ....

....

....Postcode ....

Send this whole page to:
The Mills & Boon Book Club, FREEPOST CN81, Croydon, CR9 3WZ